Copyright © 2024 by Amanda M. Lee

All rights reserved.

No part of this book may be reproduced in any form or by any electronic or mechanical means, including information storage and retrieval systems, without written permission from the author, except for the use of brief quotations in a book review.

❀ Created with Vellum

ALL QUIET ON THE WITCHY FRONT

A WICKED WITCHES OF THE MIDWEST MYSTERY BOOK 24

AMANDA M. LEE

WINCHESTERSHAW PUBLICATIONS

PROLOGUE
16 YEARS AGO

"Don't you think we're a bit old for this?" I asked in my most put-upon voice.

I, Bay Winchester, was a teenager. Sure, I was something of a new teenager, but a teenager, nonetheless. Some things weren't dignified when you were a teenager. This was one of them.

"I'm, like, ten years older than you, and I'm doing it," my great-aunt Tillie responded.

"Ten years?" My cousin Thistle was dubious as she crossed her arms over her chest. She wasn't a teenager yet, something I endlessly held over her head because I was much more mature than she would ever be. Even though she wasn't as wise as me—a fact, not something I'd made up—she was the best at pushing Aunt Tillie's buttons.

"That's what I said," Aunt Tillie fired back.

"Aren't you, like, eighty?" my cousin Clove asked. Her dark hair was pulled back in a bun because she thought it made her look older. She was trying to pass for a high schooler because of her crush on Eric Gordon. He was eighteen. Clove was not. Even if she managed to pique his interest, which wasn't going to happen, our mothers—

they all lived and worked together—would put the kibosh on any relationship attempt. All of her efforts were wasted, but she didn't seem to care.

"I am not eighty." Aunt Tillie looked scandalized. "I'm in my prime. Even if I was in my seventies I would be in my prime."

"I read a study that said a woman is in her prime when she's eighteen to twenty," I volunteered.

Aunt Tillie slowly tracked her eyes to me. "And?"

"You can't be in your prime if you're not between those ages."

"Who says I'm not?"

"Our eyes," Thistle replied. "We're not stupid. Or blind."

"Are you sure?" Aunt Tillie fired back. "I've never thought of you as one of the great thinkers of our time, Thistle. In fact, if I'm rating intelligence in the house, you fall in the bottom third."

Thistle's eyes narrowed. She and Aunt Tillie had a tempestuous relationship, which was putting it mildly. "What did you just say?" she growled.

"You heard me." Aunt Tillie never backed down. "The only one you're smarter than is your mother. I guess it makes sense that you would inherit her brains. That's how it works."

The statement, however simple on the surface, had me furrowing my brow. "Does that mean you think I'm like my mother?" I demanded.

"Well, you're bossy and you think you run your little age group of girls here, when in reality I'm in charge of everyone. You do what you want even when common sense tells you otherwise. That sounds like Winnie."

I was officially offended. "I am nothing like my mother."

"Also, the common sense thing goes for all of us," Thistle said. "You're the queen of ignoring common sense."

"I'm the queen of the world," Aunt Tillie countered. "Never forget that."

"If you say so." Thistle was blasé. "What are we doing again?"

Before Aunt Tillie could answer, Clove took over the

conversation.

"What did I get from my mother?" she asked. She was doing that blinking thing she did when she was about to have a meltdown.

"You got your boobs from her," Aunt Tillie replied without hesitation. "I mean ... you're in middle school and could moonlight as a stripper. Those things will come in handy when you're an adult."

"I want to be known for more than my boobs," Clove complained.

"Then crack a book once in a while," Aunt Tillie replied. "Bay knows she won't get by on her looks, which is why she reads all the time. That's why she's smarter than you."

That didn't sound like much of a compliment, although she likely meant it as one. "Thanks. I guess."

"Oh, don't get pouty." Aunt Tillie sneered. When she'd tapped us to help with her new endeavor—she was opening her own detective agency in Walkerville—she said it would provide a means for us to learn a skill. So far, all we'd learned to do was whine, and we were already proficient at that.

"I don't want to be known for my boobs," Clove insisted. "I mean ... it's okay to be known for my stunning intellect *and* my boobs, but not just my boobs."

"Then you'd better become more diligent in your studies." Aunt Tillie was never one to lie to us about our abilities. She didn't sugarcoat anything. If she thought something, she laid it out there for us, so we had no choice but to hear her opinion. "Because your cousin is getting a reputation as the brains of this operation." She jerked her thumb at me. "And your other cousin is getting a reputation as the mouth of the group."

"I'm pretty sure I'm just as smart as Bay," Thistle groused, jutting out her lower lip.

"I'm not sure that you are," Aunt Tillie replied. "You're smart, but your smarts involve manipulating people. The good news is that you inherited that ability from me and not your mother. It shows there's still hope you'll grow into the other stuff."

I was almost afraid to ask the obvious, but curiosity was always my downfall. "What other stuff?"

"The stuff that only Thistle will be able to provide your group," Aunt Tillie replied. She gripped the staff she held tighter—why a private eye needed a staff I couldn't say—and leaned forward, as if preparing to impart some great wisdom. "Here it is, girls. Clove is going to be the looks of the group. She has her mother's dark hair, and no matter what she says, she's going to use those boobs as a weapon, because they're going to be fantastic."

Clove preened.

"Thistle will be the attitude of the group because she can't help herself," Aunt Tillie continued. "People will be drawn to her because of that attitude. They'll tell themselves she's funny when she's actually mean. She'll be a decent thinker, but she'll be lazy."

"Oh, I love you too," Thistle drawled.

Aunt Tillie pretended she hadn't spoken. "As for Bay, she'll be the leader. She won't be the prettiest."

"Thanks." I shot her a sarcastic thumbs-up.

"She won't be the one with the most street smarts," Aunt Tillie continued, "but she *will* be the one with the best overall package. She'll be pretty enough. She won't have to deal with sagging boobs when she gets older because her hips are bigger than her boobs. She's bossy and likes to take control. Do you know what that means?"

"It means you're talking out of your rear end," Thistle offered.

"It means that you all have your strengths, and if you learn to work together, you'll be an unstoppable force," Aunt Tillie said.

"That could be the nicest thing you've ever said to us," Thistle drawled.

"Don't get used to it. I'm not here to make you feel better about yourselves. I'm here to give you a test of sorts."

Now we were getting to the truth of the matter. "What test?"

"Do you know who Kent Covington is?"

I had to run the name through my head for several seconds.

"Isn't he the guy who runs the pharmacy?"

"That's right. I'm pretty sure he's a pervert."

"What does that have to do with us?" Thistle asked.

"The goal of the Tillie Winchester Agency of the Blessed is to eradicate perverts."

I had questions. "No offense, but why do you think he's a pervert?"

"I saw him following Cindy Sutton the other day. He was fondling himself. That's the true sign of a pervert. And Cindy mentioned over coffee the other day that she feels as if she's being watched. It's Kent."

I scratched my cheek. Something still felt off. "Why do you care that Cindy is being creeped on?"

"I don't like perverts."

"That's not it." I shook my head. "Last time we were in the pharmacy, Mr. Covington told you that you could get a bigger discount if you used your AARP card. You said that was for old people."

Aunt Tillie's eyes flashed, and her nostrils flared. "It is!"

"Then you complained the whole way home that he thought you were old," I continued.

"I'm only ten years older than you," Aunt Tillie replied. "I'm in my prime. How many times must I tell you?"

"I don't think you can be in your prime at eighty," Clove said reasonably.

"What did I say?" There wasn't even a hint of a smile on Aunt Tillie's face now. "I'm not eighty."

"You're not twenty," Thistle argued. "You're in your sixties. You're pushing seventy. That's pretty far from twenty."

"I'm done talking to you." Aunt Tillie raised her hand and obliterated Thistle's face from view. "We're here to take down a pervert. The rest of this isn't important."

"I'm still confused about why you believe he's a pervert," I said. "Just because he tried to help you—"

"I'm not old!"

"But you are." Thistle patted her arm. "It's okay. We still love you. Well, I don't, but they do."

Aunt Tillie's eyes were narrow slits of frustration. "You're on my list, Thistle. At this rate, you'll never get off it. We're here to do a service for the town of Walkerville. We're going to catch the pervert."

I had one problem with this scenario. Okay, more than one, but I had one big one. "Why would Mr. Covington perv on Cindy? She's, like, ten years older than him."

"I know!" Aunt Tillie threw up her hands. "He should be perving on me."

"Because you're in your prime?" I pressed.

"Exactly." Aunt Tillie looked relieved. "Girls, one thing you need to learn if you're running a detective agency—a noble profession I hope you all follow in ... except for you, Clove—is that more often than not, the enemy is someone you know. It's very rarely a stranger."

"Then why do they hold all those stranger danger school assemblies?" Thistle challenged.

"Because they're morons, and that was a thing back when your mothers were in school. Everyone thought there was a stranger on every corner ready to grab kids. While it's true strangers sometimes abduct people, more often than not, the real criminal is someone you know."

I was intrigued. "How do you know that?"

"That's just how it works." Aunt Tillie held out her hands. "The thing is, you can't really know people. You'll know some about the people you're closest to, but there are going to be hundreds of others you know only slightly, the people you wave at in town when you see them once a week.

"You'll think you know those people because they say the right things, and they smile when they're supposed to smile, and they even donate to charities. But you can't know everybody," she continued. "Sometimes the enemy you should fear most is the one next door."

"Are you talking about Mrs. Peterson?" Clove asked on a breathy whisper.

"No. Mrs. Peterson is terminally boring," Aunt Tillie replied. "Her greatest joy in life is knitting stuffed animals and putting on plays with them."

"Where does she do that?" I asked.

"Her bedroom. It's quite pathetic. You don't have to worry about Mrs. Peterson."

"But you do think we have to worry about Mr. Covington?" I prodded.

"There's obviously something wrong with a man who thinks Cindy Sutton is a better catch than me."

I was too tired to fight with her. "Can we get this over with? I would like to be home in time to watch *True Blood*. There's a new episode tonight."

"I thought you weren't supposed to watch that because of all of the nudity," Aunt Tillie argued.

"Are you going to rat us out?" Thistle challenged.

"No." Aunt Tillie shook her head. "I might watch it with you. That Eric guy is all kinds of hot. Now he would know a woman of substance."

"It's worse when we watch with you," Thistle complained. "You insist on providing demonstrations when you think their sex scenes are too elaborate."

"That is also something you should thank me for." Aunt Tillie snapped her fingers. "Now, let's head out. We need to spy on Kent, catch him being a pervert, and then expose him to the town."

"What if that doesn't work?" I asked.

"I'll hex him to wet his pants once a day for a week."

I pursed my lips, considering, and then nodded. "That sounds like fun too."

"We'll see if he ever suggests the AARP card again."

"Something tells me he won't."

1
ONE
PRESENT DAY

"I don't know why you're being so difficult." Landon Michaels, my husband and the current thorn in my side, paused with his fork halfway to his mouth. There was a huge meatball speared upon it because it was Italian night at The Overlook, the inn my mother and aunts ran in Hemlock Cove, Michigan. "Meatball is a fine name for a dog."

As if to prove it, he shoved the entire meatball into his mouth and proceeded to chew.

"We're not naming the dog Meatball." I was firm on that. The homemade meatballs were delicious, but whenever I pictured myself outside calling our new dog, I wasn't yelling the name Meatball. "It's a stupid name."

"It's *my* dog," Landon reminded me sternly. "It was *my* Christmas present."

A Christmas present I'd gotten him when I realized he desperately needed a pet. The way he cooed over Aunt Tillie's pet pig Peg had proven that Landon needed something to love—something other than me.

"Pick a different name," I gritted out.

"You've already vetoed all the names I suggested," Landon replied sourly. "I don't think you should even get a choice in the matter."

Perhaps sensing trouble, my mother cleared her throat from across the table. The look on her face was stern. It basically said, "Don't ruin my dinner with your petty arguing." She tried to play peacemaker. That was her lot in life as the oldest of her trio.

"What names has Bay vetoed?" Mom asked. Winnie Winchester was nothing if not pragmatic. "Maybe Bay will find something she likes better upon hearing the name a second time."

That wasn't going to happen. All of Landon's names had been stupid. Still, if she wanted to stick her nose in our argument, she'd earn what was about to happen.

"Well, first there was Bacon," Landon started.

Mom made a strange noise in her throat.

"I realized right away that was wrong," Landon offered hurriedly. His shoulder-length hair was swept back from his angel-kissed face, and for the first time since I'd met him, I wasn't snowed by his good looks. Bacon was a ridiculous name. "Then I thought about BLT."

"Because that's your favorite sandwich?" Aunt Marnie asked. She was the middle sister and liked to think things out ... right up to the point she got annoyed that everybody wasn't moving fast enough, and started barking out orders.

"That's not his favorite sandwich," I said. "His favorite is a Reuben."

"That might be a cute name," Aunt Twila offered.

"Bay says no food names." Landon gave me a dark sidelong look. "She's turned into a tyrant."

"She learned it from her mother," Aunt Tillie said from the head of the table. She was already three glasses deep in her special wine, and her cheeks were flushed. Her eyes were flushed with mischief, a combination that worried me.

"What do you have against food names?" Mom asked me.

"Dogs aren't food," I replied.

"You named your dog Sugar when you were a kid."

"Sugar is a confection."

"So, Flour would make a good name," Mom replied dryly.

"What about Hemingway?" I asked Landon. "That would be cute for a dog."

Since the dog in question—or rather the puppy I'd adopted from a local family who had found themselves with an unwanted litter just in time for Christmas—was under the table licking Peg to pieces, I rubbed my foot over his back to get him to yip his agreement. Whenever the dog was with Peg, however, nothing else mattered. They were mired in a love affair for the ages.

At least from the dog's point of view. I wasn't certain how Peg felt about him. She preferred Aunt Tillie's company, which didn't say much about her instincts.

"Hemingway was a drunk," Landon replied.

"What about King?" I wasn't ready to let go of my literary dreams. "You love Stephen King books."

"No." Landon shook his head. "I like Doughnut."

"Absolutely not. Get off the food names."

"Then get off the literary names."

We glared at each other. It was rare for us to argue so much. We would likely make up over cake—unless he wanted to name the dog Cake.

"What about Pippin?" I wasn't ready to let it go. "Pippin was my favorite hobbit."

"Sam was your favorite hobbit," Mom corrected. "Clove's husband is named Sam, so that doesn't really fit."

"It would be confusing," Twila agreed knowingly.

"What about Smaug?" I asked. "Our dog can be as strong as a dragon."

"Are you trying to kill me?" Landon looked betrayed. "I like Pancake."

"Get off the food."

Chief Terry Davenport, sitting to my right, cleared his throat when it became obvious the argument showed no sign of dissipating. "You're being pains," he complained. "Let's talk about something else."

I was more than ready to table the conversation, which was likely why we'd had the still unnamed puppy for three weeks. He mostly came to "here, boy" and "come on, buddy." "Let's talk about your engagement."

Chief Terry had proposed to my mother—after years of flirting and months of the sort of steady relationship I always wanted them to have. Now they were settling down to plan the wedding. I wanted to be part of it because ... well, just because. I had my own father, of course, and I loved him. He spent half my childhood living in the southern part of the state, though, and I rarely saw him. Chief Terry had always been here. He stood as a surrogate father for me and my cousins. I wanted him to officially become family.

"I think we're just going to go to city hall," Mom said.

"No." I shook my head. "You can't do that."

"Why not?" Mom wrinkled her nose. "A big wedding isn't important. We can have a reception. It's the party that's important."

The party *was* important. The wedding, too, was important to me. "You should say your vows in front of everybody," I insisted. "That makes them real. It doesn't have to be a big wedding. We can have it here. You need a ceremony."

Mom was suspicious. "Why?"

"Because you guys deserve a wedding." I looked to Chief Terry for confirmation. "Tell her you want a wedding."

Chief Terry shrugged. "I'm actually in it for the wife and the cake. Your mother gets to decide. I get to have her for the rest of my life. That's all that matters."

I frowned. "That's the most ridiculous thing I've ever heard."

"Sounds like something I'd say," Landon said as he bit into another meatball.

"That's why it's ridiculous." I shot him a dirty look. "You have sauce all over your cheek."

"I'm saving it for later," he replied.

I jabbed a finger at him before turning back to Chief Terry. "A wedding should be a big deal."

"I've already been married," Mom reminded me.

"Chief Terry hasn't. He should have the wedding of his dreams."

"Bay, I'm getting the woman of my dreams," Chief Terry countered. "That's more than enough for me. If your mother doesn't want a big wedding, I won't argue."

I flopped back in my chair, my bad mood on display. "Nothing is going my way right now, I swear."

"You still have me." Landon kissed my cheek. "I love you more than anything. Doesn't that make you happy?"

"You just got sauce on my cheek."

"And Parmesan cheese," he confirmed. It was impossible to miss the gleam in his eye as something occurred to him.

"We're not naming the dog Parmesan," I growled.

"I love cheese," Landon persisted. "If you're not a fan of Parmesan, what about Brie? That could be a dog's name."

"A female dog," Mom said.

"You can name a dog anything," Landon said. "How about Cheddar?"

"Stuff that meatball in your mouth and shut it," I ordered. My full attention was on my mother now. "It doesn't have to be a big ceremony. It can just be family. You don't even need a fancy dress. You should have something so we can all be there."

"But why?" Mom looked genuinely perplexed. "I don't understand why you're so worked up about this, Bay."

She didn't understand, and I was having trouble explaining. How could I tell her that I'd pictured the wedding so many times as a child —long before they allowed themselves to become romantically engaged? "Never mind," I said. I was being a baby. "Do what you want." I was determined to move past this conversation too. "What are you going to do about your house?" I asked Chief Terry, turning to more pragmatic matters. He spent every night in The Overlook with my mother, but still owned property in town.

"I'm going to sell it," he replied. "In fact, I have some people coming this afternoon to look around and make a list of things that need to be fixed before I put it on the market."

"It should sell pretty fast," Landon noted. "Property is at a premium in town."

"It *should* sell fast," Chief Terry agreed. "It's been a good house. This is obviously my home now." He beamed at Mom, who stared back at him with hearts in her eyes. "I'm moving in full time this week."

"Don't you basically live here already?" I asked.

"Kind of," Chief Terry hedged, "but I haven't moved any of my stuff in. I'm starting that this week."

"He packs a suitcase each week, and even does his laundry at his house," Mom explained. "He's worried about taking up too much of my space."

"You shouldn't worry about that," I said. "Landon took over half of my closet, and I still love him. Well, when he doesn't want to name the dog Pickle."

"That was a joke," Landon argued. "I was in the mood for dill pickle potato chips."

"You're a glutton," Chief Terry said. "Get off the food names."

"Maybe we'll name the dog Terry," Landon fired back.

Chief Terry chuckled. "There's no way Bay will allow that. She wants a literary name."

"No literary names." Landon emphatically shook his head. "I don't want a literary name."

"Well, I won't agree to a food name," I insisted. "It's just not going to happen."

"I can't wait until you have kids," Mom said. "Will I be calling my granddaughter 'girlie' for years until one of you wears the other down?"

"Sage," Landon said. "Her name will be Sage."

The annoyance I'd been feeling with him disappeared.

"Wasn't Sage the name of the girl you met when you went to the future?" Mom asked.

I nodded. "Yes, a future that wasn't real," I reminded Landon. He desperately wanted the girl we'd seen to be real. Even though we'd been hopping through time thanks to a spell Aunt Tillie had cast that had gone awry, Landon was convinced that parts of it were true.

"I have faith," he replied simply. "Just out of curiosity, why can we name our kid Sage but not our dog Peanut Butter?"

All of the sympathy I'd been feeling for him disappeared. "You're trying to drive me crazy, aren't you? I don't want to name any of our kids after spices. You know how I feel about that."

"Bay is a lovely name," Mom argued.

"For a leaf you throw in the crockpot to season soup."

"Oh, you're just whining to whine at this point." Mom waved her hand. "It's Landon's dog. You should let him name it whatever he wants."

Under the table, the puppy yipped excitedly.

"See." Landon leaned in and wrinkled his nose, making sure I could look nowhere but into his eyes. "As for that kid, I don't care what her name is. If you're opposed to the spice names, okay. The name doesn't matter. I just want that kid."

"What if I can't give you 'that' kid?" That kept tripping me up. "What if we have a boy?"

He opened his mouth. I knew he was about to say, "You don't have boys in your family." My cousin Clove had recently given birth to a boy, however—much to Aunt Tillie's distress—so that was no longer true.

"Then we'll live happily ever after," Landon replied. "You, me, our son, and our dog Lasagna."

I wanted to be annoyed with him. "We'll keep talking about the name. As for you moving in, I don't see how it will be that much different. There's plenty of room here," I said to Chief Terry.

The quick looks that darted between my mother and aunts told me I was missing something.

"Right?" I prodded.

"Well, we were hoping to set up an office for Terry," Mom started. "We can't really afford to give up one of the guest rooms, so we thought updating the basement and putting in an office might work."

"What's wrong with that idea?" Landon asked as he spun some spaghetti on his fork.

Mom jerked her thumb at Aunt Tillie and glared.

"That's where I make my wine," Aunt Tillie complained.

"Illegally," Chief Terry grumbled.

"That's my space," Aunt Tillie insisted.

"Then we thought about turning a corner of the greenhouse into an office," Mom continued. "That was vetoed as well."

"That's where I keep my still," Aunt Tillie complained.

"Illegal still," Chief Terry added.

I pressed my lips together. I could see where this conversation was going.

"We're still trying to figure it out," Mom said. "Terry can't move in without an office."

She looked despondent enough that I decided I needed to fix the problem. "Why not the attic?" I asked. "It's been empty since Belinda and Annie moved. I haven't seen them in a few weeks, by the way. Is everything okay with them?"

"They seem fine," Mom replied. "Belinda is dating someone. She's making new friends. They haven't been driving here as often now that they've found a good rental house in Hawthorne Hollow. Annie is in the school play, and I told Belinda that we would visit them. I plan to invite them to dinner next week."

I liked Belinda and Annie. Annie was magical. It was always good to check in when a child had magic the mother couldn't even fathom. "You haven't said if anything is wrong with the attic. Can we set up an office there?"

I didn't think Mom's expression could get any darker, but I was wrong. She pointed at Aunt Tillie again. "Tell her what you're doing up there."

"That's where my clown collection is," Aunt Tillie said.

Landon choked on his spaghetti. "Your what?"

"My clown collection," Aunt Tillie replied primly. "You might not realize this, but I'm a clown connoisseur."

"Apparently, she's been ordering clown dolls and hiding them in the attic. She has fifty," Mom said stiffly. "I had quite the fright when I went to check out the space."

Landon asked, "What fresh hell is this?"

"Clowns are misunderstood," Aunt Tillie insisted. "They're whimsical."

"What are you really doing with them?" I asked as Chief Terry's phone dinged with an incoming message.

"Who says I'm doing anything with them?" Aunt Tillie demanded. "Maybe I just like clowns."

"Nobody likes clowns," Landon said. "You're up to something evil."

"You're on my list," Aunt Tillie warned.

Still suspicious, I flicked my eyes to Chief Terry, who was getting to his feet.

"I apologize," he said as he gave Mom a "what are you going to do" shrug. "It seems the Blue Moon Inn is on fire."

I jolted at the news. "Really?"

He nodded.

"I'll go with you." I abandoned my spaghetti. "I'll get photos for the newspaper."

"I'll go too." Landon's plate was so clean I had to wonder if he'd licked it when I wasn't looking.

"You just don't want to be in the inn now that you know we have clowns," I said.

"We all do what we have to, Bay." Landon looked to my mother.

"Will you keep Chowder safe while we're gone? Don't let the clowns get him."

"He'll be fine," Mom assured us. "I can't believe the Blue Moon Inn is on fire. That's just terrible."

"I'll let you know when I have more information," Chief Terry promised her. "Those going with me, we're leaving now."

"Because you're scared of the clowns too," I said.

"Terrified," Chief Terry agreed. "A fire is better than a clown."

I agreed. "Chowder is a 'no,' by the way," I said to Landon as we headed for the door.

"I figured."

2
TWO

The Blue Moon Inn had opened several years ago. The owners, Frank and Alice Milligan, had grown up in Walkerville, before it had been rebranded to Hemlock Cove, and were older than me. I didn't know them well. When they returned to town about five years ago, they worked various jobs until they decided to buy the old Dobkins house. It was big enough to convert into a small inn and was always full during tourist season. They lived there with their daughters, Hope and Grace, and from all outward appearances seemed to be living a happy life.

I was sad for them. All their hard work was going up in flames.

Landon muttered about clowns under his breath, and when we turned on the road that led to the inn, I stopped thinking about how I was going to use that to torture him later—perhaps dressing the puppy as a clown would frighten him into giving in and naming the dog Aragorn. Instead, I focused on the flames shooting into the sky.

"It's still going?" I asked.

"Apparently so." Chief Terry parked on the road because the parking lot was full of firefighters and emergency personnel. He met one of his men on the driveway. "Report," he barked.

The officer was Clyde Hanson, who was nearing retirement. He wasn't exactly known for his diligence, which was why he'd never received a promotion. I'd once asked Chief Terry why he kept him on the payroll; he said some people found a spot they were comfortable in and stayed in it most of their lives. I'd always found that odd, but Clyde didn't aspire to be anything he wasn't. That had to be peaceful.

"We got a call from a motorist," Clyde replied. "He saw the inn on fire. We have no idea if the Milligans or guests are inside. There are multiple vehicles in the lot." He pointed, as if we'd somehow missed the fact that there were five vehicles in front of the inn. "By the time we got here, it was fully engulfed and ... well ... we can't seem to get close enough to check the back of the inn."

My antenna went up. "Meaning what?"

"Meaning that whenever we try to get to the rear of the property, where the fire doesn't look as bad, the heat gets too bad. We've had two firefighters pass out."

Landon slid his gaze to me, his question obvious. *Magic?*

I could only shrug in response.

"We'll go through the woods." Landon tugged my sleeve. "We won't get close unless we think it's safe. Maybe we'll be able to see something from a different angle."

Chief Terry nodded. "Don't do anything reckless."

Landon kept a firm grip on my arm as we skirted around the inn. I felt Clyde's gaze on my back, but I didn't look over my shoulder.

Landon led me into the woods. I was relieved once I knew we were out of sight. "What do you think?" he asked when we got to the east side of the property. "Can we get in there?"

"You want to run into a burning building?" I asked.

"There are five cars in the parking lot," Landon replied. "A family lives there, but apparently nobody has come out of the building, Bay."

"Maybe they're in the woods or something."

He made a big show of fanning out his arms. "Do you see them in the woods?"

"They have kids, Landon. Two girls about thirteen. They could be in there."

"The guests could have kids too," Landon said. "We have to try to get in."

Our first approach was at the rear. As we neared the building, the heat ratcheted up.

"It's almost as if the flames are getting bigger," Landon complained as he swiped at his face. "What about you? Can you sense anything?"

"I'm not sure." I reached out with my senses. I didn't exactly run into a wall, but the way to the inn wasn't clear. Something felt off. "We need help." I raised my hands and ignited my magic. "*Come*," I intoned.

Within a split-second three ghosts—including Viola from the newspaper office—appeared between the trees.

"Seriously?" Viola demanded. Despite how irritating I found her, she was still better than the last ghost I'd had at The Whistler. "I was just bingeing *Bones*. David Boreanaz is hot. I'd like to see his bone. I'm already on the third season."

"Yeah, I'm pretty sure that's not what the show is about," I said. "We have something more important to worry about." I pointed to the fire. "I need you to go in and look for survivors."

Viola balked. "The building is on fire."

"You're already dead," I reminded her. "Go!"

"Fine." Viola started through the trees. "You're kind of a pain, Bay. Has anybody ever told you that?"

"You're not the first. Hurry. There must be kids in there."

"A really big pain." She disappeared, along with the other ghosts, and Landon and I kept pushing toward the inn.

The heat was unbearable, and after a few minutes, I grew concerned I might pass out.

"I think this is your show, Sweetie." All traces of our earlier argument were gone.

"Make sure nobody is watching," I ordered.

He nodded. "Do what you have to do."

I wasn't gifted when it came to controlling the weather like Aunt Tillie. She could've brought down a tempest to douse the flames. We did, however, have something going for us. I magically lifted the blanket of snow that had settled between the trees and sent it flying toward the inn. There was a sizzling and more smoke, but the temperature dropped noticeably, and the flames diminished.

"Keep doing that," Landon said as he looked in the direction of the parking lot. "Nobody's watching."

I gathered more snow and repeated my first attempt. The air instantly became more breathable.

"There's something weird about this fire," I noted.

"You think?" Landon's eyebrows hopped. "I'm not a witch and even I know." He almost jumped out of his skin when Viola reappeared. One of my newer abilities was allowing him to see the ghosts I called often. I believed he'd always had that ability—long before we knew I was a necromancer, a child ghost had told him where I was and how to save me when I was in deep trouble.

"They're all still in there," Viola announced. "Most of them are unconscious."

My heart skipped ten beats. "Where are they?"

"All over," Viola replied. She was no longer complaining about missing David Boreanaz's bone. "The two girls are still conscious. They're downstairs in what looks like a pantry. The fire is close. The others are in the west wing. I think they've been overcome by smoke. They're all passed out in the hallways."

I swallowed hard. "Dead?"

"I don't know."

I flicked my eyes to Landon. "We have to go in."

He broke from the trees. The fire seemed as if it was ratcheting up again, so I grabbed more snow. Viola stuck with us. I had no idea what had happened to the other ghosts. I didn't really care.

Landon kicked in the rear door.

"I feel like Batman," he said on a nervous laugh as we ducked to see if flames shot out at us.

"Does that make me Batgirl?" I crouched low as I poked my head inside.

"No, you're Wonder Woman."

"Batgirl has the better outfit."

"Only from a female point of view."

The inn was still burning. The flames crawled over the walls and spread across the ceiling. It was almost as if they were watching to see what we would do.

"This is weird," I noted as I reached out to touch a flame.

"Let's not be stupid," Landon snapped as he grabbed my wrist. "I'd rather not test the boundaries of your magic here."

He was right. "Let's get the girls."

I'd visited the inn several times for articles. Still, I had to double back twice to find the kitchen. A wall of flames burned between us and the pantry. On the other side of the room, I heard noises coming from behind a door.

"Grace?" I called out. "Hope?"

"We're in here!" A young voice screamed. "Please don't leave us!"

"It's Bay Winchester. I have my husband with me. We're coming to you. Just sit tight ... and stay as far away from that door as possible. Do you understand?"

"Yes." The girl was sobbing. "We don't know where our mom and dad are."

I didn't want to give them false hope. Instead, I focused on the fire. "Just sit tight. We're almost there." I strode to a spot next to the stove, where a fire extinguisher hung.

"Back up," I ordered Landon.

He watched me as I raised the extinguisher above my head.

"Please work," I whispered to nobody in particular. I briefly shut my eyes and prayed to the Goddess. Then I threw the fire extinguisher into the air and chased it with as much magic as I could.

For a brief moment all sound left the room. It was as if we'd been launched into a vacuum. Then everything sped up as the explosion swallowed the room. The foam inside the extinguisher expanded until it took on a vaguely human form. When it threw itself at the wall of flames, even I was stunned.

"Well that was interesting," Landon said when the foam figure eradicated the flames.

"I didn't know I was going to do that," I admitted.

Landon managed a smile. "You amaze even yourself." He took us both by surprise when he grabbed my chin and planted a kiss on my lips. "I'm going to worship you later. Let's get those girls."

Landon had a little extra swagger in his step when he stopped in front of the door. He warned the girls he was going to kick it open, and when the door was no longer an obstacle, two blonde girls flew out and threw their arms around him.

"You saved us," the older girl shouted. I was fairly certain her name was Grace. "You didn't leave us."

Landon hugged them in return. "Of course not. You're safe now."

Were they? I looked over my head, where the flames toiled effortlessly, and then pointed to the back door. "Get them out," I ordered.

Landon jolted at the order. "Bay—"

"Get them out," I repeated. The girls were safe—and that felt like a huge win—but others remained in the building. "I can handle the rest."

"I'm not leaving you," he hissed, even as the girls tugged on his arms to get him to leave.

"This is one of those times we have to trust each other," I said in a low voice. "I trust you to get them out and get the paramedics to the patio. You need to trust me to do what needs to be done inside."

Landon hesitated, but I recognized the moment he made up his mind. He gripped Grace and Hope by their hands and backed up toward the door. "Be careful, Bay. I can't make it without you."

"Does that mean I can name the dog?" I asked.

"Don't be ridiculous. I will let you rub me in the tub for an hour later, though."

"Be still my beating heart." I watched him for another two seconds, until he had the girls through the opening, and then started for the swinging door.

Viola was still with me.

"Where?" I asked.

Viola pointed to the left when I made it into the inn's interior. Flames roared all around, the fire magical, which made it all the more deadly. The flames chewed through the inn, seemingly with purpose.

"There's a sprinkler system," I said. "It didn't activate."

"Are you going to force it to go off?" Viola asked.

"Yeah. It's going to be like the extinguisher, only with water."

"Will the water look like people?"

"I guess we'll find out." I let loose a breath, one that I didn't even know I was holding, and closed my eyes. Finding the water line with my magic wasn't difficult. Forcing it to activate was another story.

At first, when I flipped the switch, nothing happened. Just like with the extinguisher, all sound ceased. When the water exploded, it sounded like an avalanche was about to take out the inn. It raced in every direction through the sprinklers. It momentarily froze, but the heat from the fire melted it.

The water raced in every direction, and it did look vaguely human when it attacked the flames. I pushed harder with my magic when the fire appeared to fight back, and the energy I expended drained me fast.

I dropped to one knee and pushed with my remaining magic. This was my last chance to douse the fire entirely. It had to happen here.

For a moment I thought the fire would win, but the water expanded and coalesced over me before dropping a giant water balloon.

I sucked in a breath before the water rushed over me, then fell into darkness.

3
THREE

I didn't pass out as much as float—in darkness. Nothing seemed as if it was connected, including my arms and legs.

Then I heard him.

"Bay, I really am going to have a meltdown and take you to the hospital if you don't wake up right now." Landon sounded near tears. "Open your eyes."

I couldn't leave him hanging, even though the floating was kind of nice, so I forced my eyes open. It was like prying open windows that had been painted shut. When my vision cleared, I saw Landon leaning over me.

"You're trying to kill me, aren't you?" he complained. "That's why you do these things."

I tried to leverage myself up on my elbows, but couldn't, which forced him to slide an arm around my back and pull me against his chest. "Hey," I said. My voice was a raspy rattle.

"Hey." He brushed my hair from my eyes. "What hurts?"

"Nothing hurts," I assured him as I wrapped my fingers around his wrist. My limbs still felt disjointed. "I'm fine—I think."

"I don't like that 'I think' tacked on at the end. It makes me want to start screeching like Margaret Little when Aunt Tillie gets her going."

"Sorry." I shot him a rueful smile. "I really feel fine."

"You'd better be." Chief Terry looked ready to take on Landon's inner worrywart along with his own. "We also need to come up with a story, and fast. The paramedics are right behind me."

"I was trying to get to the people upstairs when I was overwhelmed," I replied. My brain was working enough for a story as easy as that. "It's kind of true."

"The fire went out all at once," Chief Terry said. "It was like 'poof' and done."

"Poof?"

"That's what I said." He scowled as he hunkered down. "Kid, your survival instincts aren't great. You need to start worrying about yourself more."

"I don't know that I'm built that way. Perhaps you should blame my mother."

Chief Terry pressed his fingers to my forehead. "You're running hot, Bay."

Landon made a face and pressed his hand to my forehead. "You *are* running hot. We should let them take you to the hospital."

"So I can tell them what?" I demanded. "They won't exactly understand that I used so much magic that I knocked myself out." Was that what happened? I remembered the foam man and the water explosion. It felt like there was something else I should remember, something at the edge of my vision. It was so close to the surface I was one step from recovering it all.

"I still don't like how hot you're running," Chief Terry said.

"Well, it's winter," I said pragmatically. "Take me outside."

"To where all the snow is gone behind the inn?" Chief Terry made his patented stern face. "Do you have any idea how hard that's going to be to explain?"

"Tell them the fire melted it. Your men said the fire burned hotter than normal."

"That might work." Chief Terry didn't look convinced as he rubbed his chin.

"Works for me." I struggled to a sitting position. I was feeling stronger. "I'm okay," I said to Landon when he pressed his hand to my back. "I feel pretty good."

"You should develop a limp or something, because the story of you being in there alone will spread," Chief Terry growled. "People will ask why you weren't injured."

"How does anyone even know?"

"Because Landon dragged two teenagers outside and then ran back inside like an idiot. When firefighters tried to stop him, he threw them off and threatened to throw punches to get to his wife."

I cast Landon a sidelong look. "That might not have been very smart."

"And yet I don't care," Landon fired back. "If they want to file a complaint, so be it."

He didn't mean it. He loved his job. It was as much an extension of who he was as being a witch was for me. His boss was in on the big paranormal secret—as much as he could, given his status as an outsider—so Landon could tell him the truth.

Whatever that was.

"There was something strange about the fire," I volunteered. We didn't have much time before the site was flooded with firefighters and paramedics. "I think it was magical."

Chief Terry blinked. "We'll worry about that later when we can talk freely." His gaze was stern. "You're getting checked out by the paramedics whether you like it or not."

"I'm fine," I protested.

"They're checking the guests," Landon interjected. "It will be weird if you're not checked out too. You don't have a choice."

I'd forgotten about the guests. "They're alive? I never made it up the stairs. Once I dropped the water bomb—"

"You didn't do that," Chief Terry insisted. "That was an act of god ... or delayed sprinkler system activation."

"I was overwhelmed when the water rolled over the building," I said. "That's what I was getting at."

"No, you passed out trying to find a way up to the second floor," Landon corrected. "Don't make it complicated, Bay. They're going to ask you a lot of questions. Just act stupid."

"You mean act blonde."

"Act like the woman who needs to come home with me tonight so I can dote on you," he corrected.

Ugh. When he put it like that. "Fine. I'll act like a moron."

Landon planted a warm kiss against my forehead. "That's all I ask."

THE PARAMEDICS HAD A LOT OF QUESTIONS. Grace and Hope had told the firefighters about the "angels" that had saved them. The story of Landon running back inside the burning inn had spread quickly, already taking on mythological proportions.

That put me at the center of the attention storm.

"Follow my finger, please," Brett Timberland ordered as he waggled his index finger in front of my face. We'd gone to high school together—he was two years older—and back in the day I had a crush on him for a grand total of four months. Teenage Bay would've been thrilled at this turn of events.

Adult Bay was over it.

"I'm fine," I snapped as I slapped his hand away. "I'm not altered. I'm not having trouble breathing. I'm just tired ... and smelly." I wasn't happy that the smoke was beginning to clear, but the scent was lingering because it was clinging to me. "I need a shower."

"Do you want me to help you with that?" Brett teased. He'd been flirty ever since depositing himself in front of me on the rear of the ambulance.

"No, she does not," Landon answered from his spot next to the fire chief. They had their heads bent together and were talking in low voices. He refused to wander too far from me.

"Whoops." Brett switched his charming grin to Landon. "Didn't mean to step on your toes. I still remember when Bay was a hot high school freshman with stars in her eyes whenever she saw me. It's hard to adjust to her being married, and to a guy with Motley Crue hair."

Landon's mouth fell open. "I do not have Motley Crue hair."

Of course that would be the thing he snagged on.

"It kind of looks that way." Brett winked at him before turning back to me. "Your oxygen levels are good. I can't find any burns. You don't seem altered."

"That means I'm free to go home?" I asked forcefully.

"I prefer transporting you to the hospital, Bay. You're running hot."

That was the one symptom hanging around. I didn't feel hot. Actually, I was starting to fight off chills, as if spiking a fever.

"Honestly, I'm fine," I assured him. "I just want to go home and go to bed."

"You want to go home and take a bath," Landon corrected. "No offense, sweetie, but you smell." He managed a smile, but it didn't touch his eyes. He was feeling penned in by all the questions. I didn't blame him. Everybody was naturally curious.

"You smell as bad as I do," I pointed out.

"Not quite, but I'm more than willing to take one for the team and get in the bathtub with you." He sent a challenging look toward Brett. "Something we do all the time."

Brett burst out laughing. "I'm glad Bay got a funny guy. That's one of the things I loved best about her in high school. She had the best laugh."

"I kind of want to punch you for flirting with my wife after a fire, but you somehow come across as charming," Landon said. "What's up with that?"

"It's just the wonder that is me." Brett shrugged. He was serious when he turned back to me. "Take it easy tonight. If you don't feel normal tomorrow—other than the aches and pains—I want you to promise to go to the emergency room."

"I'm fine," I insisted.

"We agree to your terms," Landon added. "If she's not her usual sunny self in the morning—caffeine dependency notwithstanding—I will drive her to the emergency room myself."

"Sadly, I can see that you believe the sun rises and sets on her," Brett said. "I do trust you, which is a bummer because I was going to steal her from you until I decided I like you."

"You can't steal her from me," Landon said. "Some things are too strong to break."

I went warm all over.

Brett flicked his eyes back to me. "Go home. Take a bath. Throw some Epsom salts in. You're going to be achy tomorrow. Get a full night's sleep."

"If it's one thing we do well, it's sleep," Landon said. "I'll take care of her."

"Make sure that you do."

MY ENERGY FLAGGED QUICKLY, BUT LANDON and Chief Terry couldn't escape the scene. People kept stopping them to provide updates, and even though I wanted the oblivion of sleep more than anything, I was intrigued by the updates.

"All the guests at the inn are awake," Clyde told Chief Terry. "They're being kept at the hospital overnight, but the reports are good."

"What about the Milligans?" I asked. They were the only people I hadn't heard anything about.

"They're still unconscious," Clyde replied. "The doctors are guarded. They say it's a waiting game."

"But they weren't burned?"

Clyde shook his head. "Nobody was burned as far as I can tell.

That includes you, even though you ran toward the fire. The flames just went out without burning anyone."

The charge felt accusatory. "Um ... the inn burned." I pointed to the once beautiful building. I was fairly certain the inn would need extensive work. It might even have to be bulldozed, forcing the Milligans to start from scratch.

"I get what you're saying," Clyde said. "I just think it's weird that nobody was injured by the actual fire. It was raging, and then went out like somebody snuffed out a candle. Don't you think that's odd?"

Landon answered before I could. "I'm grateful for it. Otherwise, I might have lost my wife." The statement was so pointed, Clyde had no choice but to shrink back.

"Sorry." He held up his hands. "I wasn't saying that I wanted something to happen to Bay."

"You said it was weird that nothing happened to her while sounding disappointed," Landon said.

Clyde, perhaps sensing there was no way out, took a step back. "The fire inspector will start his investigation as soon as they confirm all the hot spots are out. Surprisingly, they haven't found a single hotspot, which is another weird thing. I'll let you guys worry about that."

"Do that," Chief Terry instructed as he joined us. He looked annoyed. "If you want something to do now that the fire is out, you can sit vigil at the hospital and question any guests who are up for it."

Clyde balked. "I thought they were being held for observation overnight. Can't that wait until tomorrow?"

"The fire inspector seems to think it's arson either way—the building went up too fast for it to be anything else—so those witness reports are important," Chief Terry replied. "I would rather be safe than sorry. Don't you agree?"

Clyde looked as if he didn't agree, but he nodded. "I'll head over."

"Great." Chief Terry waited until he was gone to focus on me. "He's going to be a problem."

"You told me he was lazy," I said. "Since when is he interested in digging into cases that require effort?"

"He *is* lazy," Chief Terry said, "but he's no idiot. Everyone knows there was something weird about this fire. The rumors have already started."

"What are they saying?" Landon asked.

"That it's weird the fire went out the way it did. These guys have never seen anything like it."

"None of us have," I grumbled.

Chief Terry ruffled my hair. "The good news is that everyone is okay. I'm not sure that would've been the case if you hadn't done what you did. You saved everyone."

Was that true? I couldn't decide. "I'm glad everyone is okay. That's the most important thing."

"It is," Chief Terry agreed. "The rest of it, well, we'll have to take it one step at a time. There's nothing more we can do tonight."

"Which means I can take you home," Landon said to me. "Although ... we all drove together." The smile he'd managed to muster diminished.

Chief Terry withdrew the keys to his vehicle from his pocket. "Take her. I'll have one of my men drop me off."

Landon hesitated before grabbing the keys. "Are you sure? I don't want to strand you here."

"It's fine. I want you to take care of Bay." Chief Terry was serious when he leaned over to look in my face. "You take your bath and go straight to bed. I don't want anything else weird happening tonight. Rest, and we'll figure out your end of things tomorrow."

I glanced around to see if anyone was eavesdropping, but we were alone. Even Brett had wandered away. "You don't have to worry about me," I assured him. "I'm fine."

"Keep it that way." Chief Terry straightened. "Straight to bed. No funny business."

"I'll leave your keys in the cubby behind the front desk," Landon promised. "We have to pick up the dog anyway."

"Or you could leave the dog with Winnie—she calls it her grandson—and get Bay straight to bed." Chief Terry was firm. "Tomorrow is going to be a big day, with a lot of things to explain."

My stomach constricted. Was he right to be so worried?

"Fine. I'll put Bay to bed." Landon smirked. "That's where I like her best anyway."

"I'm not rising to the bait," Chief Terry said. "She needs rest. I'll see you two for breakfast. We should know more then."

4
FOUR

Landon, true to his word, forced me into a bath when we got home. He washed my hair, thinking ahead and bringing a glass to the bathroom to rinse it. Then he braided it—something I'd taught him to do on a snowy day—before we tumbled into bed.

My dreams were dark, and I found myself panicking in a strange house as it burned around me. Beyond the flames, I saw shadows. They looked sort of human, but I couldn't make out faces. From some angles they looked like clowns, but I figured that was only the case because of Aunt Tillie's new hobby. I wasn't in the Blue Moon Inn. It was someplace else I didn't recognize. Even though I understood I was in a dream, my fear was real.

I woke after the dream, my breath coming out in a gasp. Landon pulled me to him and kissed my forehead to calm me. Then we slept again. This time my dreams were absurd—Aunt Tillie's pot field was involved ... plus more clowns, only these danced—and I woke feeling refreshed ten hours after we'd crawled into bed.

Landon was up and working on his phone.

"You didn't have to stay in bed with me," I said as I rubbed the crusties from my eyes, my hair still damp in the braid folds. "You could've gotten up."

He put down his phone. "My favorite place in the world is in bed with you." He smiled as he looked me over. "Your color is back, and you're no longer hot."

I frowned. "That was mean."

"You're always hot. That's how you snagged a prime piece of real estate such as myself. You're not burning up, which is what I was worried about."

"I don't think I was still hot after the bath. That seemed to knock it out of me."

"Actually, you were hot after the bath. I was already planning to railroad you into going to the hospital this morning. Your fever—if that's what it was—broke after you woke from the dream."

That was news to me. "How can you be sure it didn't break before then?"

"I guess I can't. I fell asleep pretty quickly after you. When you woke from the dream you were cooler."

"I guess that made you sleep easier."

He nodded. "I was worried." He tugged at the hair that had come loose from the braid. It was wild. "You didn't get a chance to tell me what happened when you tried to go upstairs. I didn't want to leave you."

"I kind of forced your hand," I admitted. "I know that, and I'm sorry. Those girls had to get out, and the people upstairs were out of time. I used my magic to kind of explode the sprinkler system, and the water flew everywhere. It was like a bomb."

"Is that what you were going for?"

I held out my hands and shrugged. "I guess so. I didn't know it was going to do that. As for the fire, it almost acted as if it was moving through the inn with a purpose."

"So you definitely think it was magical."

"It's a very real possibility. It felt very off."

He nodded, taking it all in. "What can you tell me about the Milligan family?"

"Not much," I replied. "They were older than me. My understanding is that they were high school sweethearts. They moved away from Walkerville when they graduated and attended Covenant College. They both graduated about ten years before the place imploded."

"Nobody talks about Covenant College," Landon mused. "People were shocked when the entire campus disappeared. I remember thinking at the time that there had to be some rational explanation. What do you know?"

"Are you asking if I know what happened to Covenant College because I'm a witch?"

"You're magical. It's obvious that something magical took out the college."

"The rumor is that it was a mage." I lifted one shoulder in a shrug. "That mage supposedly lives in mid-Michigan and fights evil with a sarcastic tongue and more power than any of us can dream of. Aunt Tillie wants to meet her."

Landon rubbed his thumb over my cheek. It was obvious his mind was working fast. "So, basically you're saying it's unlikely that the Milligans had anything to do with what happened at the college."

"I don't see how. There were no rumors about them being magical. I've spent some time with them since they returned to the area, and never gotten a whiff of magic off them."

"And yet something magical happened at their inn," Landon pressed. "That doesn't seem normal."

"It's probably not, but that doesn't mean that they had anything to do with Covenant College."

"Fair enough. Continue your story."

"There's not much more to tell." I propped myself on an elbow so I could look down at him. "Sometime after they graduated from college, they moved to the Detroit area. They were there about ten years before they moved back."

"Did they have the kids when they moved back?"

"Yeah. If you're wondering about the girls, I've never heard anything bad about them either. They've had a few fights with the other kids, the normal stuff. Nobody ever suggested that weird things happen when they're around. They're just normal kids."

"Then why did something magical happen at their inn?"

"I don't know. Maybe we can ask Aunt Tillie. She's more familiar with the families around here. Maybe it's the land that's haunted ... or whatever it is."

"Is that possible?"

"We live in a witchy, witchy world, my friend. Everything is possible."

He cupped the back of my head and pulled me down to him. "I want to be more than friends, Bay," he teased before kissing me. "We went to bed uber early and we're up with plenty of time for me to show you how much I want to be more than friends. How does that sound?"

I grinned. "I think I can be persuaded to let you show me your intentions."

WE DROVE CHIEF TERRY'S VEHICLE TO THE Overlook. From the outside, things looked quiet. January was one of the deader months at the inn. My mother and aunts attracted some skiers and snowmobilers, but they rarely hung around the inn. They were more interested in spending their time outdoors.

The family was already seated when we arrived. Landon tossed Chief Terry his keys and then crawled under the table to greet his dog and Peg.

"How are my beauties?" he cooed.

The dog hopped on top of him and started licking his face.

"You really need to name that dog," Mom said as I sat in my usual chair and reached for the juice pitcher. "I don't like having to call him Dog."

"His name is Twix," Landon said.

I glared through the table. "We're not naming him after a candy bar," I scolded. "He's going to have a nice name. Like, how about Zeus?"

"I'll die first," Landon shot back. Apparently, since my fever had broken, he was done coddling me.

"Fine." I emitted a disgruntled huff. "Come up with something that's not related to food."

"Peanut."

"That's a food."

"It's also a comic strip."

"No, and before you ask, I'm not keen on Snoopy either."

"Of course not. He's not a beagle. Are you, my precious boy?" Landon made kissing noises before emerging from beneath the table.

"You're not kissing me with that mouth until you brush your teeth again," I warned.

Landon took it as a dare if his eyebrow arch was to be believed. "Oh, ye of little faith. What about Noodle?"

"No. What about Mario?"

"No."

"You two are driving me insane," my mother complained. "I'm going to name him if you don't come up with something in three days. You've been warned."

Landon didn't look worried. "What's the news on the fire?" he asked Chief Terry as he reached for the bacon platter.

"It was arson," Chief Terry replied. "There were accelerants. The inspector said that despite the accelerants, the fire didn't burn normally."

I shot Landon an "I told you so" look.

"Yeah, yeah, yeah." He rolled his eyes. "Did the inspector come up with a reason for that?"

Chief Terry shook his head. "And I'm really not looking forward to the conjecture that's going to follow the announcement of arson with no familiar burn path."

"There's nothing we can do about that," Landon said.

"Bay's name will be involved with that conjecture," Chief Terry persisted. "Everyone knows that she went into the inn and five minutes later the fire was out. People are talking already."

"Everyone always talks about us," Aunt Tillie interjected. "They'll gossip for a few weeks, then move on to something else."

"They're still talking about the Christmas decorations that terrorized the town for a week," I reminded her. Those Christmas decorations were the product of an Aunt Tillie spell gone wrong. They'd come in handy fighting an evil witch. Other than that, their lone contribution to the daily lives of Hemlock Cove's finest had been to scare the crap out of them.

"You're such a whiner," Aunt Tillie chided. "Nobody is talking about those decorations. You're making that up."

"That's not true," Chief Terry countered. "Margaret Little is telling anyone who will listen that you possessed all the decorations as some sort of war on Christmas. She's trying to rile people up. She's calling you woke."

I frowned. "Aunt Tillie is the opposite of woke."

"I'm awake," Aunt Tillie argued.

"Yes, and we're all thankful for that," Landon teased. His plate was one-quarter eggs, one-quarter hash browns, and half bacon.

"I thought we agreed you were going to limit your bacon intake," I said. "You know, so you live a long and healthy life and get to see that kid you want graduate from high school."

"Okay, Mom," Landon drawled.

I scowled.

"I had a stressful night last night," he continued. "I need bacon to recuperate. I mean ... I was forced to leave my wife in a burning inn while I dragged two teenagers outside to safety. Then, when I returned, my wife—who I love more than anything else in this world because she's just that wonderful—was passed out and potentially dead."

I stared at him for what felt like a really long time. "That's a bunch of crap," I said. "You couldn't have laid it on any thicker."

He smirked. "I get however much bacon I want this morning. You're turning me into an old man. My hair will turn gray before I'm thirty-five."

He did deserve a reward for not turning into a total baby when I forced him to take Hope and Grace out of the burning inn. "I won't give you grief, but only for today."

"I'll take it." He took another bite of bacon. "Bay said the fire did not burn normally, much like the inspector, and she's concerned that it was magical."

"How did you manage to put it out?" Mom asked.

"I used magic. I forced the sprinkler system to start. When it finally did start, it went off like a bomb. It put the fire out in the entire inn right away."

Aunt Tillie beamed. "I taught you that."

"When did you ever teach me how to detonate a sprinkler system?"

"I only heard the word 'bomb,'" she replied.

"Yes, I did learn bombs from you," I agreed. "I don't know how I put out the fire. I was just looking for some water so I could get up the stairs."

"That's weird too," Chief Terry said. "The guests were spread across the second floor. All of them were unconscious, but nobody at the hospital said anything about smoke inhalation."

"What else could it be?" Mom asked.

"I don't know." Chief Terry held out his hands. "Grace and Hope were transported to the hospital last night. Their grandparents are out of town."

"Frank's parents?" I asked.

Chief Terry nodded. "Alice's parents moved to Florida a few years ago. I assume they'll come back because Frank and Alice are still unresponsive. Somebody has to take care of those girls. They're being discharged today."

"We could do it," Mom volunteered. "I mean ... until Barney and Frieda get back. It might take them a bit of time to arrange transportation."

"You just can't help yourself finding little birds with broken wings to take care of," Chief Terry teased. "I don't think that will be necessary, but thank you for volunteering." The look he shot her was flirty. "That's exactly why I can't wait to marry you."

"I think I'm going to be sick," I complained as I sipped my juice.

"Hey, I've had to listen to you and Landon spout nonsense to each other for two years now," Chief Terry argued. "Suck it up."

I glanced at Aunt Tillie.

"I'll curse him to smell like dog crap," Aunt Tillie offered. "Your mother hates the smell of dog crap."

"Who doesn't?" Mom complained. "And you'd better not. You're already on probation for the still thing. And the clown thing."

"Do I even want to know what that means? The still thing?" Chief Terry asked, his fingers rubbing his forehead. Obviously moving in permanently was going to create tension. He wanted to be with Mom—and she would never leave—but Aunt Tillie was a menace when she wanted to be.

And she always wanted to be.

"It means that Aunt Tillie has been warned about making anything other than gin in that still," Mom replied. "Only one batch a season. That's the compromise we reached."

"That's the compromise *you* reached," Aunt Tillie countered. "I do what I want, and winter is the time for whiskey."

"I definitely don't want to hear this." Chief Terry focused on me. "I don't suppose I could talk you into coming to the hospital with me?"

I was instantly suspicious. "Why? What did Landon tell you? I don't have a fever any longer. It broke during the night."

"It broke after you had a dream about being caught in a fire,"

Landon said. "I didn't tell him anything. You handled that yourself with your big mouth."

"She got that from her mother," Aunt Tillie said.

"She got that from all of you," Landon countered. "That's a trait the Winchesters all possess."

"Now I think you're on my list," Mom groused.

"I'm sorry." Landon didn't look sorry as he shoved bacon in his mouth. "I was worried enough about Bay to consider taking her to the hospital against her will. Thankfully, the fever is gone. I don't hate the idea of her checking in at the hospital."

"I can't go to the hospital," I blurted. "I'm not sick."

Landon glowered at me.

For his part, Chief Terry looked genuinely amused. "I'm not asking you to go because I think you're sick. I'm asking you to go to use your witchy abilities to listen to the guests. I have to question them."

I turned sheepish. "I guess I can manage that. I'm not sick, though. And I don't have a big mouth."

Landon shoved another piece of bacon into his mouth.

"I don't," I insisted. "I'm demure, and I think before I speak."

"I love you, Bay, but even I'm calling foul on that one," Mom said. "Don't worry about the dog. We'll keep him with us today."

"Are you sure?" I didn't get Landon a dog so my mother could take care of him. "I promised that you would only have to dog sit now and then."

"He's cute, and he's pretty much already housebroken."

"Only because I cast a spell," Aunt Tillie added. "You can thank me now." When Mom didn't say anything, Aunt Tillie pressed. "I'll head to the Blue Moon Inn and take a look around. If there's magic on the loose there, I'll find it."

Now I was really concerned. "Should you be wandering around out there alone? What if you fall and break a hip?"

"I'll call Thistle," Mom said as Aunt Tillie murdered me with her glare. "She can go with Aunt Tillie."

I couldn't wait to hear Thistle's reaction to that decree.

"You're all on my list," Aunt Tillie warned.

"We'll live in fear," Mom said. "I want to know what happened at the Blue Moon. If it was a magical fire, it could strike anywhere next."

It was a legitimate concern. "We're on it," I promised her. "We'll figure it out."

5
FIVE

When Landon appeared in The Overlook's parking lot, he had a baggie in his hand. He also had a handful of napkins clutched in his fist. The lipstick mark on his cheek told me who had bestowed him with his gifts.

"Plum Pizzaz," I muttered.

"What's that?" Chief Terry asked as he opened the back door for me.

"Your future wife has been kissing my husband." I inclined my head toward Landon's cheek.

Chief Terry stared. "How do you know that's your mother's lipstick?" he asked.

"She has only three shades, and she uses the plum in the winter because she thinks it's festive."

Chief Terry planted his hands on his hips. "You been kissing my wife?"

"You mean your future wife," Landon corrected. "She's been kissing me." He held up the baggie full of bacon. "She sent me off with a to-go bag and made me promise we would agree on a name for the dog."

"She's sneaky," I complained. "Really, really sneaky."

"I don't think bacon will talk Landon into naming the dog Gandalf," Chief Terry said.

"Definitely not," Landon agreed. "I'm thinking Butter. Wouldn't that be a good name for a dog?"

"We're going to end up divorced if you don't get off the food names," I warned as I hopped into the back seat.

Landon didn't look particularly worried. "Our marriage can survive a dog named Biscuit."

"Now you're just trying to rile me," I groused.

"How's it working?"

"A little too well."

"Good to know." Landon winked at me as he climbed into the passenger seat. "Would you like a slice? It's still warm."

"I'm good." I fastened my seatbelt and held back a smirk as Chief Terry cast Landon a dark look.

"If you get grease on my seats, you're licking it off," Chief Terry warned.

"Don't threaten me with a good time." Landon fastened his seatbelt before digging into the baggie. "What are our options, Bay?" he asked. He was all business now. "If the inn was haunted, what do you think the ghosts there wanted?"

"I don't think 'haunted' is the right word for what went down yesterday," I replied as Chief Terry pulled onto the road to town. We had a thirty-minute drive ahead of us to get to the hospital, so I settled in. "Whatever that was yesterday, it wasn't a haunting."

"Poltergeist?" Landon asked. He was familiar with a few paranormal phenomena, thanks to firsthand experience. We'd fought a poltergeist when his parents were visiting. I'd been convinced that would be it for him, that it was too much. Instead, he'd become more dedicated to being the perfect witchy boyfriend. It was another reason I wasn't going to give him grief about the bacon. There had to be a way to hex it and make it healthier, though. I was going to have to get on that because my husband was definitely a glutton.

"I guess I can't rule out a poltergeist," I acknowledged. "I've never heard of a poltergeist being able to control fire like that, though. That is a very specific ability."

"Okay." Landon bobbed his head. "What about Stormy?"

Stormy Morgan, a friend, lived one town over. She was referred to as a hellcat because she was a very specific brand of fire witch. There was no way she was responsible for what had happened at the Blue Moon Inn, but that didn't take fire magic off the menu.

"I don't think Stormy can do what I witnessed," I replied after several seconds of contemplation. "Of course, she's still new at this whole hellcat thing. It's possible she could get to a place where she could control fire like that."

"Aren't there hellcats in her family?" Landon pressed.

"Her great-grandmother has a bit of fire witch in her," I replied carefully. "Nobody else in her family has manifested. Frankly, most of the people in her family are magical duds. I don't think we can look to them."

"Then who do we look at?" Chief Terry asked.

"I don't have an answer for you," I replied. "Aunt Tillie is a menace, but I'm hoping she finds something at the property. All I can say with any degree of certainty is that what happened was magical."

"Then why use accelerants?" Landon asked. "If our culprit has the power to control fire, why use flammable liquids?"

"Maybe whoever it is wasn't powerful enough to start a big enough fire."

"Does that sound right?"

It didn't, but I was out of my element. "No, but there's a lot that bothers me about this. For starters, why didn't the sprinkler system go off? Why did I have to force it?"

"That's a good question," Chief Terry said. "I'll have the inspector look into that. Anything else?"

"I'm curious about why the fire reacted the way it did. I swear it seemed to be searching for something."

"Do you think it was directed at a specific individual?" Landon asked.

"That makes as much sense as anything else."

"Then we have to figure out who."

CHIEF TERRY TOOK THE LEAD WHEN WE WALKED THROUGH the hospital's main door. He stopped at the reception desk in the lobby to announce our presence, flashing his badge and prodding Landon to do the same. The woman behind the desk momentarily focused on me—obviously, she wanted to know why I wasn't flashing a badge—but all I could do was smile in return.

"We need all of our guests to check in," the receptionist said coldly. "That includes your friend back there. She doesn't look like law enforcement."

"She's a consultant," Chief Terry supplied. "She's a child psychologist who specializes in fire victims. We need her for the children."

The receptionist's expression shifted in an instant. "Of course. Those poor little lambs. You know, I've heard their parents haven't regained consciousness. It's a medical mystery."

That sounded dramatic.

"They're still not awake?" Chief Terry frowned. "Does the doctor know what's wrong?"

The receptionist's shoulders hopped. "All I know is that they haven't woken up yet, and people are starting to worry that there's more wrong with them than just smoke inhalation. They're even joking about a sleeping curse."

Chief Terry lobbed a worried look in my direction, but he smiled for the woman's benefit. "Thank you. What floor are they on?"

"Fifth floor. You're looking for Dr. Wooten."

Chief Terry thanked her again and then waited until we were in the elevator to ask the obvious question. "Sleeping curses are real, right? That's not just a fairytale thing?"

"They are real," I confirmed, "but I don't see why they would be a thing now."

"What else could it be?"

They were asking me a lot of questions that I couldn't answer, and I didn't like it. "I don't know."

"Well, you'd better figure it out." He was grim. "This is your area of expertise, Bay. We need answers before we lose them."

"No pressure, though," I said dryly.

"You excel under pressure." He gave me a fatherly kiss on the forehead and then exited the elevator. I followed him to the nurse's station. "Dr. Wooten," he said to the nurse behind the desk.

"Just one second," the nurse said as she registered Chief Terry's badge. "He's been wanting to talk with you. He asked me to call you. You showing up here now is fortuitous."

"Why is that?" Landon asked.

"There's an aunt here for Hope and Grace Milligan, but nobody knows if it's okay to release them to her custody."

Chief Terry rubbed his forehead. "I thought their grandparents were coming for them."

The nurse stared. "You officially know what I know. Dr. Wooten will be here in five minutes. You can wait over there." She gestured to a bank of chairs and couches.

"Thank you." Chief Terry flashed a tight smile before heading in that direction.

"Should we be worried about an aunt coming?" Landon asked. "Maybe the grandparents are having trouble getting back."

"I'm not particularly worried," Chief Terry replied. "I didn't know either of them had a sister who was local."

"Do they even have a sister?" I asked.

"Both of them do," Chief Terry confirmed. "I thought they'd both moved out of state, though."

We sat in the uncomfortable chairs for what felt like a lot longer than five minutes. When a man in a white coat appeared, his brown hair shot through with gray at the temples, I let out a breath.

"This is him," I said as the man stepped forward.

"I'm Jordan Wooten," he volunteered as he extended his hand to Chief Terry. "You're Terry Davenport?"

Chief Terry was grave as he nodded. "I am. You're the doctor in charge of Frank and Alice Milligan?"

"I am. Please sit." His gaze was curious as it bounced between Landon and me.

"This is Landon Michaels," Chief Terry said. "He's with the FBI's Traverse City office."

"You pulled Hope and Grace from the fire," Wooten noted.

"I wasn't alone," Landon said, nodding to me.

"Ah, you must be the angel." Wooten beamed at me. "Grace and Hope have gone on and on about you since they got here. They swear you saved them from certain death; that you even have a halo."

Uncomfortable, I began to shift on my chair. "I wouldn't go that far."

"Bay is my future stepdaughter," Chief Terry explained. "She's Landon's wife. She was with us last night when we got the call. She ran into the building despite me telling her not to."

I frowned. Why was he spinning this tale?

"She wants to make sure the girls are okay," Chief Terry continued. "I know it goes against hospital protocol, but I'd like to take her in with me to see the girls. If it's okay with you."

Ah, that was why. Hospital protocol could be tricky. Chief Terry was trying to get ahead of any potential problems. I guess I could forgive him for categorizing me as a daughter and a wife rather than a hero and a witch.

"I don't see a problem," Wooten said. "There are a few things we need to discuss first."

"So I've been made aware." Chief Terry sat on the couch. "Lay it on me."

"Grace and Hope seem to be okay."

"That's a relief," Chief Terry enthused.

"Yes and no," Wooten said. "They're perfectly fine physically.

Mentally, they seem a little strained. They keep asking to see their parents."

"You haven't let them?" I asked.

Wooten hesitated, then shook his head. "I have not. We don't know what's wrong with Frank and Alice. Normally, I wouldn't admit that so readily, but we're confused. We don't want to introduce the children to them in their current state because ... well ... we don't want to traumatize them further."

"I thought you said they were okay," Landon interjected.

"They are okay *physically*," Wooten replied, stressing the last word. "They show no signs of lasting side effects. Their oxygen saturation levels were fine right from the start. There was no reason to keep them here other than the fact that Social Services would've had to take them."

"It's nice that you allowed them to stay," I said. "A lot of doctors wouldn't have gone out of their way like that."

"Those other doctors would've been wrong," Wooten said. "The girls needed to be someplace safe, and at least here they have people checking up on them constantly."

"I heard an aunt has shown up," Chief Terry said. "Do you know which aunt?"

"That would be Gretchen Whitcomb," Wooten replied. "I believe she's the mother's sister."

"I remember Gretchen," Chief Terry said. "I thought she moved to Arizona."

"She said she lives in Hawthorne Hollow."

"She must've moved back," I volunteered when Chief Terry looked at me. "I don't think I'm familiar with her."

"She's older than Alice," Chief Terry replied. "She was a good seventeen years ahead of you in school. I remember her. She never got in any trouble."

"We need permission to release the girls to her," Wooten said. "She wants to take care of them until their parents are better. I understand the grandparents are trying to get back, but they're in Europe on vacation. The aunt is the next closest relative."

"I'll talk to her," Chief Terry said.

"As for Frank and Alice, we're going to start running tests," Wooten said. "We can find no reason why they haven't woken up yet. There is nothing overt."

My heart skipped. If there was nothing medically wrong with them, was magic involved? If so, why? Were they specifically targeted?

"You don't want the girls to see them with all those tubes," Chief Terry surmised.

Wooten agreed. "Obviously, if we determine the parents aren't going to wake up, the girls will be able to see them. For now, we'd like to release them to their aunt and give ourselves a bit of time to figure out what's going on."

"I'll talk to Gretchen about that too," Chief Terry promised.

Wooten carried on for another few minutes. Then he departed to collect Gretchen. The woman who appeared in the waiting area looked nothing like her sister. She had dark hair and eyes that contrasted with the blonde and blue-eyed Alice. I never would've recognized them as sisters.

"Gretchen." Chief Terry hopped to his feet and extended his hand. "It's been a long time."

"It has," Gretchen agreed. She flashed a wan smile in my direction but kept her focus mainly on Chief Terry. "I assume the doctor filled you in."

"He has," Chief Terry confirmed. "I'm sorry about Frank and Alice."

"I'm not giving up hope," Gretchen said. "I'm sure they'll figure out what's wrong with them. I think it's best I take the girls home with me."

"I have no problem with that," Chief Terry said. "Dr. Wooten said you're in Hawthorne Hollow now. I didn't realize you'd moved back."

"About five years now," Gretchen said. "I couldn't stand the dry air in Arizona. My divorce gave me a reason to come back home. I'm happy to be back in a place that has seasons."

Chief Terry chortled. "If you're happy, that's all that matters. Just out of curiosity, you don't know anyone who had a grudge against your sister or brother-in-law?"

Gretchen looked surprised by the question. "No. I thought it was an accidental fire."

"I don't know who told you that, but the fire was intentionally set."

"Why would anyone do that?"

Chief Terry held out his hands. "I need to ask Hope and Grace a few questions."

Gretchen frowned. "Won't that upset them? Must you really?"

"I have to," Chief Terry confirmed. "It will just take a few minutes."

"Okay, well ... I'll take you to them."

I stayed with Landon until they were gone and then inclined my head to the right, to where I could see Alice through a window. "Can you get me in there?" I asked.

Landon nodded. He talked to the nurse at the station for a few seconds, then motioned for me to follow him. "I told her we just wanted to look in on them."

I didn't say anything until we were inside the room. I moved close to Alice's bed. Her skin was pale. Other than the tube in her nose, she looked peaceful.

"What is it?" Landon asked as he studied my profile.

"There's magic in her," I replied. "I don't know what sort of magic, but I could feel it from the waiting room. Whatever is keeping her under, it's not medical. It's magical."

Landon made a face. "The doctor seems genuinely baffled."

"I am too," I admitted. "I've never felt anything like this."

6
SIX

Once we finished at the hospital—things were growing more uncomfortable by the moment thanks to the magic I was convinced was keeping the Milligans captive in their own minds—we headed back to the Blue Moon Inn.

Almost the entire lot had been emptied of vehicles.

"I had Marcus help tow all the guest vehicles to town," Chief Terry said as he put his vehicle in park. "I figured it would be easier for them to retrieve them there when they're released from the hospital today. We found all their belongings on the second floor ... none of it burned."

"I'm guessing you also didn't want to risk them poking around the inn looking for anything they might have left behind," Landon surmised.

Chief Terry nodded. "It was easier to take that option out of their hands."

Marcus was my cousin Thistle's live-in love. I didn't even know he had access to a tow truck. He had become something of a jack-of-all-trades around town. "When did Marcus have time to do that?" I asked.

"He got two of them last night, after you left, and obviously the rest this morning." Chief Terry inclined his head toward the truck in the corner of the lot. "That's the Milligan vehicle."

I cast him a sidelong look. "How were the girls? I wish I could've seen them."

"It's good that you didn't." Chief Terry sent me a rueful smile. "They kept going on about an angel saving them. I think seeing you in the bright light of day might be a disappointment."

I glared at him. "Thanks."

"Not that you're ever a disappointment," Chief Terry said hurriedly. "I would never say that. Not ever. Not ... um..." He looked at Landon. "I really stepped in it, didn't I?"

"Right up to your knees," Landon agreed. He seemed happy about the turn of events. "I'm just glad it's you and not me for a change." He flashed a charming smile at me. "I'm definitely your favorite today, right?"

There was no stopping my eye roll as I got out of the SUV. "You're both on my list today," I replied as they followed me.

"Okay, Aunt Tillie," Landon teased.

I murdered him with a glare. "You're going to regret calling me that," I warned. "I'm going to make you cry."

"At the risk of earning your wrath, that was also an Aunt Tillie thing to say," Landon noted.

"And I'm done talking to you." I held up my hand, but Landon caught me around the wrist and tugged me to him. I was giggling before he even started tickling me.

"Oh, good," Chief Terry drawled as he walked behind us. "There's little I love more than the two of you fawning all over each other. It doesn't give me even a little bit of indigestion now."

"Blah, blah, blah," Landon said. He skirted Chief Terry's swat. "Who's here from the fire department?" he asked, sobering when he caught sight of a truck on the side of the building.

"That would be me," an amiable voice said from the left, drawing my attention there as Daniel Singer stepped into view. He was dressed in a firefighter turnout coat, a hat and heavy gloves. "Chief Terry," he said with a nod. "Bay." He shot me a wolfish grin.

Behind him, a younger man was dressed in a similar outfit.

"This is Brandon Grant," Daniel continued. His gaze didn't leave my face. "He's my new assistant."

Chief Terry stepped up to shake Brandon's hand. "It's nice to meet you."

Brandon nodded in relief. "I've heard a lot about you."

"This is Landon Michaels," Chief Terry volunteered. "He's with the FBI office in Traverse City."

"Oh, wow." Brandon looked impressed. "I've never met an FBI agent. That must be a cool job."

"It has its moments," Landon replied.

"I bet you don't have an assistant, though," Daniel pressed.

Confusion scattered across Landon's features. "What?"

"I have an assistant." Daniel gestured to Brandon. "You always wanted to date a man with an assistant, didn't you, Bay?"

I frowned when I realized what he was doing. "You would hit on a turnip. Seriously, can't you find a woman who is actually interested in you?"

Daniel was good looking in a Midwest "we only have one stoplight" way. He had dark blond hair, intense green eyes, and broad shoulders. He wore way too much flannel for my liking and boasted the sort of cockiness a man from a small town shouldn't be able to muster. He'd never experienced life outside of Hemlock Cove.

Daniel chuckled. "Plenty of real women are interested in me," he replied. "I've just decided to hunt my prey in a town other than Hemlock Cove. Unless you want to give me a whirl."

"I'm married," I reminded him.

"Definitely married," Landon growled.

Daniel ignored him. "People get divorced all the time."

"Is he really doing this right in front of me?" Landon demanded of Chief Terry.

"It's his thing," Chief Terry replied. "Ignore him. He likes getting a rise out of people."

"Well, it's working." Landon dug into the bag of bacon I thought he'd finished before we got to the hospital. "You're very annoying," he said to Daniel.

Daniel wasn't bothered. In fact, the bag of bacon served to amuse him on about six different levels. "Since you're married—and it's seemingly sticking right now—perhaps you can help me with something else."

The conversational shift threw me. "We're just here to talk about a fire."

"Yes, and we'll definitely talk about the fire in just a second. I'm interested in your friend. Like, legit interested."

I had no idea who he was talking about. "Which friend?"

"The one from Shadow Hills."

"Stormy?"

"Stormy Morgan." Daniel's smile was easy. "She's uber hot."

"She's also uber engaged."

"Engaged is not married," Daniel argued.

"In this case it is." While I found his crush on Stormy kind of cute—and I would tell her all about it—he didn't have a chance of winning her over. There was no sense wasting his time. "Stormy and Hunter have been in love since they were teenagers."

"Hunter Ryan the cop?" Daniel pressed. "I thought he was with someone else until a few months ago."

While technically true, that wasn't the full story. "He was, but they broke up when Stormy came back home. You don't have a shot."

"I just need an introduction. I'll handle getting my own shot."

"Hunter won't be a good sport if you hit on his fiancée," I argued. "They're buying a house together."

"I still like her. I thought about liking your other friend, that badass on the bike from Hawthorne Hollow, but she might actually be too much woman for me."

"She is," Landon sneered. "On top of that, her boyfriend could rip your head off with one hand and would have no qualms about using it as a bowling ball. Don't look at Scout as anything other than that 'hot girl on the bike.' Trust me."

I was suspicious. "Do you think of Scout as the hot girl on the bike?" I asked my husband.

Landon seemed to realize his mistake too late and coughed into his hand. "Let's get to the serious stuff. What have you got on the fire?"

Amusement danced over Daniel's face. "I didn't mean to get anyone in trouble," he said.

"Yes, you did, and we all know it," Chief Terry complained. "Seriously, though, we need to talk about the fire. This other stuff is just nonsense."

"We'll talk about Stormy when it's just the two of us," Daniel said to me.

I couldn't fathom when it would be just the two of us.

"I'm going to send Hunter after you," Landon warned. "You can't creep on his girl."

"Whatever." Daniel's expression said he didn't have a care in the world. As for Brandon, the assistant looked as if he wanted to find a hole to crawl into and die. "Anyway, an accelerant was used. I've never seen anything like it.

"It looks like the accelerant was poured on the stairs first and then whoever did it kept pouring on their way out the back door," he continued. "The fire burned really hot. It didn't spread, which is just ... baffling."

Daniel looked back at the inn. "It's really confusing. I pride myself on being good at my job, but this ... well, this is something I've never seen before."

"Maybe you're not as good at your job as you think," Landon suggested.

I shot him a dirty look, which he ignored.

"I'm good at my job," Daniel said.

"He is," Chief Terry agreed. "He's also good at getting under people's skin."

"That I can believe." Even though Landon kept shooting Daniel dirty looks, he couldn't stop from smiling. "I think growing up in a small town warped your way of thinking when it comes to flirting. You can't help yourself."

"Or maybe you big city guys should stop coming to our small towns and stealing our women," Daniel fired back.

"I'm not a big city guy," Landon argued. "I grew up in mid-Michigan. I came up here to camp when I was a kid."

"The same camp the two of you bought?"

"Yes," I replied. "That's where we met as kids."

"Yes, it was destiny," Landon agreed pointedly.

"For a guy who carries around a bag of bacon, you have a shockingly bad sense of humor," Daniel drawled. He leaned over to get a better look at Landon's baggie. "That smells good, though."

"I have the best mother-in-law in the world," Landon said. "She knows exactly how to make me happy. She's the perfect woman."

"Hey!" Chief Terry and I said in unison.

"After you, Bay," Landon said hurriedly. "That's just a given. As for you, don't get weird," he chided Chief Terry.

"I didn't sign on for this conversation," Chief Terry groused. "If you don't know what sort of accelerant was used, how can you be sure it was an accelerant at all, Daniel?"

"Because the fire only burned where the liquid was dropped, as far as I can tell," Daniel replied.

"Except for the ceiling," Brandon volunteered.

Slowly, I tracked my gaze to him. I had a quick flash of what I'd seen regarding the fire and the ceiling before I exploded water everywhere. "What about the ceiling?" I asked.

"That's an issue all to itself," Daniel said. "There was no accelerant used on the ceiling as far as we can tell. The fire moved over it and yet none of it burned."

"How does that work?" Landon asked.

Daniel held out his hands. "The whole thing is crazy. I heard you guys were inside. What did you see?"

I didn't look at Landon. It would only pique Daniel's suspicions. "Not much," I lied. "We found the girls right away. They were in the kitchen pantry."

"There was a big burn spot in the middle of the kitchen," Daniel said, "but it didn't reach the ceiling and it didn't spread."

"I don't know anything about that," I lied. "There was a fire extinguisher by the sink. We grabbed it and used it to get past the flames and to the girls."

Daniel cocked his head. "Did the fire extinguisher act normal?"

"Define normal," Landon prodded.

"The way a fire extinguisher is supposed to work."

"I guess, mostly," Landon replied. "It jammed a bit, but we'd got enough on the fire to get around it. I threw the extinguisher down and I guess I wasn't paying attention to where I threw it, and it exploded in the fire."

"The extinguisher exploded?" Daniel looked dubious. "I've never seen that."

"I haven't either." Landon shoved another slice of bacon into his mouth. He ate when he was stressed. Actually, he ate when he was happy, too. The guy just liked to eat. I was going to have to help him adjust his eating habits going forward. "I was more focused on the girls than the extinguisher."

"You got them out," Daniel said. "That's the most important thing. For nobody to die in this fire feels like a miracle of sorts."

It felt like something else to me, but there was no sense making Daniel even more suspicious.

"We're going to look around," Chief Terry said. "We need to identify what sort of accelerant was used. We can't start tracking the who until we know the how."

Daniel bobbed his head. "We're going upstairs next. Make sure you get the okay from me before you head up there. We need to test the floor to make sure it hasn't been compromised."

We walked in a different direction, not stopping until we were on the patio. My gaze immediately went to the trees, which were devoid of snow thanks to the magic I'd used the previous evening.

"What are you thinking?" Landon asked.

"I was thinking about the snow monster stories Aunt Tillie used to frighten us with when we were kids."

"You think it was a snow monster?"

I shook my head. "She used to keep us in check with stories about snow monsters. She didn't want us wandering too far from the house when it was cold out."

"That was because your mother always feared that you'd go out on an adventure and get lost," Chief Terry said. "Winter squalls can come out of nowhere and ruin visibility. Aunt Tillie made up that story about the monster to keep you girls from wandering too far from the house."

"I don't believe that's true."

Chief Terry's forehead creased. "Why not?"

I remembered little things from when I was a kid, including Aunt Tillie taking picnic baskets into the woods and leaving them. Then, days later, she would return for the picnic baskets, and they were empty. "I'm not sure it's important," I replied, shaking my head. "It's just ... I can't get the foam monster out of my head. That triggered the memory of the snow monster."

"The foam monster?" Chief Terry looked baffled. "Do I even want to know what that is?"

"Probably not," Landon replied, "but it was there."

I told him what happened with the fire extinguisher, how its contents seemed to take human form and fight the fire.

"What in the hell, Bay? What does that mean?"

"I don't know." There was a lot about this fire I couldn't wrap my head around. "Nothing about this is normal. There's no way magic didn't influence what happened. Plus, the Milligans are still unconscious. I sensed magic when I went in that room. I think they're being kept unconscious."

"Was that the ultimate goal?"

"We don't have enough information to even form a theory right now. We need to keep digging."

"Sure," Chief Terry said. "Where?"

"We need to keep looking here. I don't know if we'll find anything, but we at least need to try to understand."

"The fact that an accelerant was used the way it was suggests this was a deliberate attack," Landon said. "It might not have been a human attack, but that doesn't preclude the possibility a human was behind the attack. We need to know more about the Milligans, including whether or not their marriage was sound and if anybody was having affairs."

It was something I didn't want to dwell on, but it made sense. "Let's start digging. We need to be careful of Daniel and Brandon."

"Because he's a pervert?"

I shook my head. "Because he's smarter than he lets on. He knows something strange happened here. He won't let it go."

"And that won't end well for us," Landon surmised.

"Not even a little," I agreed.

7
SEVEN

The walk through the inn was eerie. Now that the fire was out, it was easy to track the lines of what it had touched. Even though I'd seen the fire creeping along the ceiling, and there were smoke and soot marks, it wasn't burned.

After a few hours of walking the grounds and taking photos inside, Chief Terry, Landon, and I left Daniel and Brandon to do their work. Daniel was smarmy as ever—apparently, he got off on it—but Brandon was shy. Whenever I asked him a question, he turned red-faced and stammered. At first, I thought he had a speech impediment, but he had no problem talking normally to any of the men.

"He has a crush on you," Landon said when we were in Chief Terry's vehicle, headed back to town.

I made a face. "You think everybody has a crush on me."

"That's because I have a crush on you and recognize the signs."

I snorted. "We're married. You can't have a crush when you're married."

"That shows what you know. I've always had a crush on you. That's never going to change."

I turned to Chief Terry for support. "Tell him."

To my surprise, Chief Terry sided with Landon. "I've always had a crush on your mother. That didn't change when we started dating. I still have it now. It hits me at the oddest of times." He took on a far-off expression. "She made me my own batch of Christmas tree cookies the other day. I was crushing hard for two whole days."

"That's kind of sweet," I cooed. "It's gross, but sweet."

"What Christmas tree cookies?" Landon whined. "I didn't see any Christmas tree cookies."

"She made them for me and only me. I just told you."

"Where are you keeping them? I didn't see any in your office."

"Because you're a glutton, I've taken to hiding my goodies. Maybe if you didn't steal other men's Christmas tree cookies, you'd be offered a few here and there."

I would've pointed out how ridiculous they were being, but the Christmas tree cookies were my favorite. "They have cookies in the freezer," I told Landon. "They always make too many and freeze them so we can munch for the next few months."

"I didn't know that." Landon looked scandalized, as if I'd been keeping the biggest secret of them all from him. "I never look in the freezer."

"That's because there's no bacon in there."

"Seriously, Bay, I feel betrayed. Hey, what if we named the dog Cookie?"

"What did I say? No food names."

"Food names are good for dogs."

"What if you give him a normal name?" Chief Terry interjected. "I always like animals with human names. You can call him Stanley."

Both Landon and I screwed up our faces.

"It was just a thought," Chief Terry huffed.

We parked at the police station and headed across the road to the diner. It was lunchtime, and we did our best thinking when our stomachs were full.

Without tourists crowding the town, the diner was almost empty. Unfortunately, one of the few tables that did have people sitting at it was full of the sort of people I didn't want to see. In the middle of the group was Margaret Little, Aunt Tillie's nemesis. In truth, she'd become my nemesis over the past year or so.

"It can't be tolerated," Mrs. Little announced. Her eyes moved to me and narrowed as she sipped from a cup. "We have to put a stop to it. She's turning our town into a hotbed of crime. That will hurt the tourist industry, and we all need the tourists to survive."

"Who is turning Hemlock Cove into a hotbed of crime?" Chief Terry asked as we moved toward our usual table. I wanted to elbow him for engaging with her. Mrs. Little always sought attention, negative or otherwise. It had become my mission in life not to give her what she wanted.

"You know who," Mrs. Little replied darkly.

"No, I really don't." Chief Terry sat across from Landon and me.

"Tillie." Just that one word, delivered with a soupçon of vitriol, had the hair on the back of my neck standing on end.

"Aunt Tillie hasn't been doing anything lately," I argued, twisting in my chair to glare at the woman. "Stop trying to drum up trouble when she's being good."

"Good?" Mrs. Little sputtered. "She doesn't even know what the word means. She's starting her own sex club." She hissed the words.

"Sex club?" Chief Terry looked appalled, his eyes going to me.

"Don't look at me," I complained. "I don't know anything about a sex club. Plus ... there's no way. She's been spending all of her time in Hawthorne Hollow. If she's starting a sex club, she's doing it there."

Aunt Tillie had started dating Whistler, the bartender at the Rusty Cauldron in Hawthorne Hollow. They'd been handsy with one another, in public, but never in Hemlock Cove. As far as I was concerned, that made it my friend Scout's problem.

Of course, she didn't seem nearly as worked up about the groping. When I saw it, I wanted to die. Scout just laughed and said, "Good for them."

"I'm not talking about that old biker," Mrs. Little fired back. "He's a cover. She has those other two she's been ... *doing things* ...

with." Her upper lip curled into a sneer. "You know the two I'm talking about."

"Actually, I don't," I replied. "Aunt Tillie hasn't been spending time with any guys other than Whistler."

"Oh, really?" Mrs. Little arched a challenging eyebrow. "What about the man at the farm on the edge of town? They're joined at the hip ... and I'm guessing other places." She lowered her voice. "They're doing the sort of things you see in those bad movies."

"How do you know what's in bad movies?" Landon asked. "Maybe you're just jealous."

Mrs. Little was talking about Evan, a day-walking vampire who was best friends with Scout. He'd taken over his aunt and uncle's house following their deaths. He needed solitude because he was still getting over some trauma. He and Aunt Tillie might've been spending time together, but they weren't doing it.

"Evan is her sidekick," I snapped. "They're not doing anything sexy." The mere thought gave me the heebie-jeebies. "Get your mind out of the gutter."

Mrs. Little wasn't about to be deterred. "And what about the guy from Shadow Hills? I saw him in town with her the other day. He was wearing a silk shirt. That's all you need to know about his temperament. Am I right?" She looked to her friends for confirmation, as they clucked and nodded.

I had no idea what that was supposed to mean. I did know who she was referring to, though. Easton, Stormy's former familiar who had arrived in the area as a cat and was now a really hot guy. He was Aunt Tillie's second sidekick. She was ranking them these days.

"What's wrong with him wearing a silk shirt?" I asked because I didn't know what else to say.

"Everybody knows that men who wear silk are gigolos," Mrs. Little replied. "Where have you been?"

"Gigolos? That's not even a thing. Right?" I prodded Landon.

"I've always thought I would make a fantastic gigolo," he mused.

"Like, a really awesome gigolo. If I didn't become an FBI agent, I would've done that."

Good grief. "Aunt Tillie isn't doing anything sexy with Easton or Evan. Leave her alone."

"Why would I leave her alone?" Mrs. Little demanded. "She hasn't left me alone." She lowered her voice. "Surely you haven't forgotten the Christmas decorations."

How could I? They'd terrorized the town—Mrs. Little specifically—for an entire week. We still found the odd one-legged Santa stuck in snowbanks after the roads were plowed.

"I have no idea what you're talking about," I lied.

The women with Mrs. Little hissed.

"You have no idea what I'm talking about?" Mrs. Little challenged. "That wasn't you fighting Christmas decorations and keeping tourists safe a few weeks ago?"

"Not that I recall." I was the picture of innocence, although I didn't risk glancing at Landon.

"I'm confused," Chief Terry said. "Are you suggesting that something happened with Christmas decorations? We've had a number go missing—darn kids—but you seem to be talking about something more."

Mrs. Little was incredulous. "The Christmas decorations came alive and threatened to kill people!" she screeched.

"That doesn't sound very Christmasy," Landon drawled.

Mrs. Little was in a fury now. "You cannot sit there and pretend that nothing happened."

"I'm more than willing to work with you," Chief Terry replied evenly. "I just don't know what you're talking about. Perhaps you have video."

He knew darned well Mrs. Little didn't have video. A lot of people had taken video of the incidents. One of the first things we'd done when cleaning up Aunt Tillie's mess was to cast a spell corrupting all the video. People who thought they had film to sell to the highest bidder were sorely disappointed.

"Are you seriously going to sit there and gaslight me?" Mrs. Little seethed.

"I'm not gaslighting you." Chief Terry looked like a man trying to placate a woman in the worst possible way, and I had to bite the inside of my cheek to keep from laughing. "I'm simply trying to understand what you're talking about." He fixed her two friends, Betty and Liz, with a questioning look. "Did you see these Christmas decorations terrorize the town?"

Betty and Liz were fair-weather friends. While they were happy letting Mrs. Little run them, they didn't want to look stupid in front of the town.

"I'm not sure what I saw," Liz hedged.

Mrs. Little glared at her. "You were with me when the reindeer tried to shove his antlers into my rear end!"

"I don't remember that." Liz held out her hands. "I'm sorry."

"You saw that Santa when he tried to honk my hooters!" Mrs. Little was growing more red-faced with each passing moment.

"Santa would never do that," Betty said. "He's the symbol of Christmas for a reason."

"I'm pretty sure that's Jesus," Liz countered. "Don't be sacrilegious."

"Well, he's the other symbol of Christmas."

"Where does the Grinch fit in?" Landon asked, enjoying himself. "He's always been my favorite symbol of Christmas, even if he's a grump. I have no idea why."

"I like the Grinch too," I admitted. "I'm a big fan of Rudolph as well. He just wanted to play his reindeer games, but they were so mean to him."

"You have such a soft heart." Landon leaned in and gave me a sultry kiss. "That's why I fell in love with you."

"It happened!" Mrs. Little started to push herself up but then sat down again. "That snowman packed a snowball and beaned me in the head!"

"Have you considered having a brain scan?" Landon asked. "It sounds as if you might have hit your head or something."

"I hate all of you." Mrs. Little folded her arms over her chest. "I know what happened. You're trying to protect Tillie, as you always do."

"I do love Aunt Tillie," I confirmed, "but if she was doing something truly wrong, I'd stop her. I'm sorry you're having such a rough time of it."

If a person could shoot lasers out of her eyes and kill someone, Mrs. Little would do it to me. She muttered curses, but she didn't leave. She was never the one who gave up and walked away.

I almost admired that about her. Almost.

"What else is going on?" Landon asked.

"What do you mean?" Liz's expression was blank, much as I imagined her brain was most of the time.

"There must be other town gossip," Landon insisted. "Hemlock Cove is always thick with gossip."

"I can't think of anything offhand," Liz replied. "Margaret's fantastical stories about inflatable reindeer saying lewd things to her has been the topic of conversation for weeks."

"That reindeer asked me if I liked doggy style," Mrs. Little growled. "I didn't imagine it."

The fact that we'd managed to unnerve Mrs. Little to this degree made the day a win. We still had a magical arsonist to worry about, but any day I could unhinge Mrs. Little was a good day.

"You guys probably have better gossip," Betty insisted. "Didn't the Blue Moon Inn burn down last night, killing everyone?"

It was no wonder that gossip in Hemlock Cove wasn't reliable. People just made stuff up.

"Nobody died," Chief Terry replied. "As for the inn, there's a lot of damage. It will take months to repair."

"Well, I guess that's lucky." Mrs. Little shifted on her seat. Still irritated from our previous conversation, she didn't want to be left out of the current one. "If they get the right contractor, they can be ready to open again in the spring."

"Yes," Chief Terry agreed, "but they still haven't regained consciousness."

"They haven't?" Interest glinted in Mrs. Little's eyes. "I thought you said everyone was okay."

"I said nobody died. The doctors are running tests today. The girls are fine and will stay with Gretchen in Hawthorne Hollow."

"I heard she moved back," Liz said. "People have seen her visiting the inn. It's good that the girls have her."

"The biggest concern right now is Frank and Alice. The doctors aren't certain why they haven't woken up."

"Well, if they don't wake up, Gretchen can sell the inn," Mrs. Little said pragmatically. "Kevin Dunne has been sniffing around. He made the Milligans a generous offer a few weeks ago. They turned him down, but I doubt Gretchen can run the place herself."

I stiffened at the name. Kevin Dunne was a real estate agent we'd crossed paths with. He'd been cheating on his wife and caused a kerfuffle at a local private school when his two mistresses butted heads. I couldn't stand him. News that he'd been trying to buy land in Hemlock Cove to sell to outsiders hadn't helped matters.

"I didn't know he was interested in the inn," I said. "Has he been asking about other properties?"

"He really wants the land The Overlook is on," Liz said. "Everyone has told him there's no way your mother and aunts will sell, but he's determined. In the meantime, he said he was looking at other properties."

"And you're okay with that?" I turned my incredulous eyes to Mrs. Little. "Why would you want a real estate guy from another town buying up land here?"

"I didn't say I wanted it," Mrs. Little sniffed. "I said that he was looking. Quite frankly, he's not my cup of tea. I would rather people familiar with the rich history of our town buy the land. However, if it gets you lot out of here, I'm more than happy to indulge him."

I narrowed my eyes. "We're not selling."

"We'll see."

I didn't like how chipper she suddenly looked. "We're not selling," I repeated. "You can get that idea out of your head right now."

"We'll see," she repeated.

I opened my mouth to tell her exactly what she could do with her snide "we'll see," but Chief Terry shot me a quelling look.

"It's not worth it," he said in a low voice. "That real estate guy was a turd. Maybe we should pay him a visit."

"I can handle that," Landon said. "I'm the one who can easily move between jurisdictions. I'll take Bay because they already have a warm and cuddly relationship. You can poke your nose into things around here."

Chief Terry didn't look thrilled about being cut out of the action. "If you find anything good, I want to know about it."

"Always," Landon promised. "Right now, we're just kicking over stones."

"Yes," I agreed. "I bet we find a few snakes under them."

Starting with Kevin Dunne. I couldn't stand the guy. That wasn't going to change. If anything, I had a feeling our relationship was about to get worse. Was that even possible?

8

EIGHT

"What are you thinking?" Landon asked as he started his Explorer and waited for warm air to begin coming out of the vents.

"I'm thinking a lot of things." I blew on my fingers, wishing I'd remembered my mittens. "I'm going to target Chief Terry to make sure they have a wedding we all can celebrate. Mom can bully him when she wants, but he can't ever say no to me."

Landon cast me a sidelong look. "Not about *that*. They'll have a wedding just to make you happy because that's who they are. Your mother won't follow through on the town hall threat. I'm talking about Kevin Dunne."

I made a face as I lifted my hands to the vents. "I don't know what to think about that," I said.

"You must have some feelings," he pressed.

I did, but none of them were good. "I don't consider myself a hateful person," I started, choosing my words carefully.

Landon made a face. "Why would you lead with that?"

"Because I hate him." It wasn't difficult to say. Justifying it was more challenging, but I didn't feel any guilt. "I don't like people who betray others so easily."

Landon took my hands in his and breathed on them before he put them back in front of the vents. His Explorer was on the old side and the engine took a bit to warm up. He was talking about getting a new vehicle. It was times like this, when the cold was permeating my bones, that I thought it was a good idea.

"The guy is definitely a tool," Landon agreed. "He's a terrible human being. But he wasn't killing people."

"Maybe not," I acknowledged. "He *was* the one who deranged one mistress enough that she killed two others. That's not even accounting for his wife, who looks as if she's given up on life."

"I'm not saying the guy is a saint—and I hate to think about the message he's sending his kids—but he's not the worst person we've ever crossed paths with."

I sniffed. "I think he might be."

"He's not even close." Landon squeezed my hand. "He pushes your buttons. He's very good at it. Can you ignore his button pushing and remain focused?"

That felt like a trick question. "Don't I always?"

"No, you have a bit of Aunt Tillie in you."

He answered that question far too quickly. "That could be the meanest thing you've ever said to me," I complained.

He grinned. "I didn't say I didn't like it when you reacted. I'm just not certain this is the time you should."

I understood we were about to walk into the lion's den, and it likely wouldn't go well. "I'm sure it will be fine. I mean ... he's likely not a real suspect anyway."

"Why do you say that?"

"Most people don't kill over property."

"I've seen people kill for less than that." He was grim.

"Yeah, but he doesn't have magic at his disposal. He's not capable of causing what I saw."

"But he knows magic is real thanks to what happened," Landon pressed.

"Does he, or does he just suspect? You saw Betty and Liz when we shot down Mrs. Little. The second they faced pushback, they were willing to deny what they saw. Even their fear of Mrs. Little wasn't enough to keep them from backing down."

"That's true." Landon rolled his neck, "but it's possible he knows more about magic than he's letting on. I want you to feel him out when we get there. Don't be too aggressive."

I rolled my eyes. "When am I ever aggressive when it comes to this stuff?"

"Oh, you're so cute." He grabbed my chin and kissed me. "You're also delusional if you think I'm going to fall for that," he said. "You're aggressive to the max when it suits you. I just don't happen to think it suits you this go-around."

"I guess we'll have to see."

KEVIN DUNNE'S REAL ESTATE OFFICE WAS IN TRAVERSE CITY. We were on the road a good thirty-five minutes. Landon stopped at the bakery for hot chocolate—he said it was for me, but I knew he was in love with the snowman-shaped marshmallows they used—and then we were on our way.

During the drive, I asked him how he knew my mother would give in on the wedding. He didn't really have an answer other than, "They both fell in love with you first, Bay. They know how important this is to you. It's going to happen, and it's going to be great."

I wanted to believe him, so I allowed myself to breathe. I was going to put my foot down on the wedding. All of the childhood images I cherished involved my mother and Chief Terry. And the rest of my family.

I would never admit that to Aunt Tillie.

By the time Landon parked in front of the real estate office, I was done with my hot chocolate and hopped up on sugar. "Do you want to be good cop or bad cop?" I asked.

"I knew bringing you was a mistake," he complained.

I ignored him. "I should be bad cop. He already hates me."

"He fears you," Landon clarified. "And yes, he probably does hate you. His private life was blown up thanks to you."

"I want to be bad cop."

"How about I be FBI Agent Landon Michaels and you be intrepid reporter Bay Winchester and we'll see where that gets us?"

"That sounds like zero fun."

"That's definitely something Aunt Tillie would say."

I was still grumbling about being compared to my great-aunt when we walked through the door. The office, still decked in its Christmas finery, buzzed with chatter. That chatter died when they registered who was visiting. We'd been to the office numerous times now.

"Oh, you've got to be kidding me," Kevin complained when he saw us.

Landon's lips turned up at the corners. "That doesn't sound like a warm greeting," he said. "Aren't you supposed to fawn all over us in case we want to buy a house?"

"If you want to buy a house, may I suggest McClintock Realty down the road? They have a few agents who will absolutely go gaga over you."

"I'll keep that in mind." Landon flashed his badge. "We're here on official business."

"Who's dead now?" one of the women who had been laughing just seconds before asked.

"Nobody," Landon replied. "We have a few questions."

"Marcy will handle your questions," Kevin said, pointing to the younger-looking blonde in the corner.

"But we're so much more comfortable with you," Landon replied. His smile was easy. "We understand you've been to Hemlock Cove recently."

Kevin let loose a long-suffering sigh. "Of course it has to be me."

"You're the best, right?" I prodded.

"Don't use that smile on me." Kevin glowered. "I know darned well you don't mean it." He huffed as he led us to his office. "Let's get this over with."

Landon smiled at the other members of the office. His hand landed on the small of my back as he prodded me into Kevin's office. Once the door was shut, the gloves came off.

"How many new mistresses have you picked up in the last few weeks?" Landon asked. "I'm not asking because I encourage the practice. I am curious if you're even more awful than I realized."

The look Kevin shot Landon was withering. "If you must know, my wife and I are in couples counseling."

If I'd had one of those hot chocolate marshmallows, I would've choked on it. "You're in couples counseling?"

"Why so shocked?" Kevin asked blandly. "I've always been a proponent of a strong marriage."

"Is that what you told your mistresses?"

"I don't particularly like that word." Kevin's demeanor was cold. "Mistress." He said it with a lip curl. "It's frankly wasted on me. I happen to love harder than most. Sometimes that means I have to spread that love around. My wife understands that. That's why, after a brief separation, she's agreed that counseling is the way to go."

The separation couldn't have lasted more than a few days. Oddly, even though I despised the man, I felt sorry for his wife. She knew what he was doing and took the abuse because she was too frightened to try to make it on her own. Some women stayed after a cheating scandal out of strength, but not Joanie Dunne.

"I guess it's good you're putting in the effort," I said.

"He isn't," Landon groused.

"Yes, well..." I blew out a sigh. It made me sad to think about the wife he was essentially torturing. "Did you set the fire at the Blue Moon Inn because the Milligans rejected your offer to buy their land?" I blurted.

"Bay." Landon slapped his hand to his forehead. Frankly, I didn't understand why he was so surprised. I'd warned him I wanted to be bad cop.

Kevin barked out a laugh. When I didn't join him, he sobered quickly. "You can't be serious. First you accuse me of killing Enid. Then you accuse me of being involved in Bianca's death. Now you're going to blame me for a fire that put multiple people in the hospital? What is wrong with you? This is persecution, plain and simple."

"You might want to look up that word," Landon countered. "This is not persecution. If you want to go that route, it can be arranged. This is curiosity. The fire at the Blue Moon Inn has been ruled arson."

"I don't understand what that has to do with me," Kevin complained.

"It's been brought to our attention that you have been trying to buy up land in Hemlock Cove."

"I believe I'm the one who told you that weeks ago," Kevin fired back. "Even though I can't stand you, I'm still willing to buy your family's inn." His smile was charming, but there was a predatory glint in his eyes.

"My family will die before we sell our land," I said.

"You'll sell eventually," Kevin countered. "You won't have a choice. When all the other inns in the area are run under the same banner, with the same control over advertising and cross-promotion, you'll either sell or be run out of business."

I sat straighter in my chair. "That sounds like a threat."

"It's reality," Kevin said, "and business. You won't have the funds to compete."

"But we have Aunt Tillie," I replied. "We're renowned for our dinner theater. We have waiting lists of more than a year because our dinner theater is the stuff of legends. People love us."

"Anybody can do dinner theater," Kevin scoffed.

"Not like us." He was starting to irritate me. "Just tell us what went down with you and the Milligans. We know you were in contact with them. We want to know how it played out."

"There was nothing nefarious," Kevin said. "My partners and I went to Hemlock Cove. We tried to set up a meeting, but the Milligans were resistant, so we invited ourselves over."

"Oh, like MLM salespeople," I drawled. "How fun."

"Laugh all you want. It works quite often." Kevin didn't sound bothered by my judgement. "The meeting took about an hour. My business associate did most of the talking."

"Who is that again?" Landon asked.

Kevin smiled. "It's no secret that I'm working with Up North Developments. I recently moved my partnership to Pegasus Developments, though, to move things along faster. We have a plan in place to take Hemlock Cove to the next level. The tourism your town brings in is phenomenal. I think we can double it. Then, when Hemlock Cove has hit peak saturation, the effect will start to expand. The surrounding towns will be engulfed in a wave of witch craziness, so to speak."

Kevin laughed at his own joke.

"Yes, well..." He interlaced his fingers. "The Milligans weren't interested in selling. We told them we would stop by again in six months. They told us not to bother. We reiterated our position—we're going to outlast everybody—and they sent us on our way."

"When was that?" Landon asked.

Kevin shrugged. "About a week ago. Why? Do you think they're interested in selling now? How damaged is the inn? I bet we could get it for half what we offered if they're not interested in dealing with the reconstruction."

"Or maybe you could stop being a greedy pig and remember that two parents were hurt and are still in the hospital," I said, my agitation on full display. "Show a little compassion."

"I didn't realize they were still in the hospital," Kevin said. It was hard for me to ascertain if he was telling the truth or lying. He looked as if he was thinking more than mourning. "The radio said that there were no fatalities."

"Frank and Alice are still getting treatment," Landon said.

"Who's in charge of their estate in the meantime?"

I gripped my hands into fists. "If you go near that family, I'll make you believe the ordeal you went through with your mistresses was child's play," I warned.

"That sounds very much like a threat, Ms. Winchester," Kevin drawled. He looked to Landon for confirmation.

"I didn't hear what she said," Landon said. "Once you're married, it's in one ear and out the other."

Kevin's expression darkened. "I believe I've told you all I know. Now, if that's all, you may go."

"It's not all," Landon replied. "It's pretty far from all. You should know that we're going to be digging. In your business. In Up North Development's business. Pegasus Development's business. We're going to get into every little secret you're keeping."

Kevin merely blinked. "I have bad news for you, Agent Michaels," he said in a flat voice. "I have no more secrets thanks to your wife. I have therapy. I have counseling. The secrets are all gone. Dig all you want. You won't find anything."

He sounded pretty certain of himself.

"We're going through all of your purchase records," Landon said as he stood. "If I find one hinky deal, we'll unravel all of them."

"Now that sounds like a threat."

"Take it however you want." Landon pointed to the door to urge me in that direction. "We'll be seeing you soon."

9
NINE

L andon didn't want to separate, but after visiting Kevin, there was something I needed to do, and he couldn't be present for it.

"I can't just drop you off in Shadow Hills and *hope* you get a ride home," Landon argued.

"You don't have to worry about me," I insisted. "Stormy can take me home. If she doesn't have time, I'll convince Hunter to take me to the halfway point and you can pick me up there. Besides, Evan has been spending a lot of time here. I can catch a ride with him if I have to."

"Why has Evan been here?"

"Well, you didn't hear it from me," I leaned in for a conspiratorial whisper, "but it seems that Evan and Easton are spending some time together."

"Is Easton gay?" Landon asked. "It's none of my business, but if he's gay I won't have to worry about his penchant for getting naked all the time. That dude is uber free with his body."

I had to bite back a laugh. "Stormy said that when Easton was a cat, he saw her naked, but hasn't made a move to see her naked again."

"Which likely proves that he's gay, because Stormy is hot," Landon mused. "Interesting."

"Do you think Stormy is hotter than me?"

"Oh, here we go." Landon burst out laughing. "Nobody is hotter than you, sweetie. You're the prettiest woman in the world."

"That was laying it on a bit thick, but I'll take it." I beamed at him. "I can make it home on my own. You really don't have to worry about me."

Landon didn't look convinced, but he acquiesced. "I need to start digging on the land purchases that our friend has been pulling off. I can't help but think that he's doing something underhanded."

"If people willingly entered into deals with him, I don't know what we can do."

"Maybe we can stop him now and force him to unload the property he already has. Do you really want that guy in Hemlock Cove?"

That was a resounding no. "I want him to find a hole, fall into it, and be forced to live there the rest of his life. And I hope the hole has scorpions."

"I don't know how many scorpions can be found in Michigan, but I'll do my best." Landon navigated into downtown Shadow Hills. "Where do you want me to drop you?"

"Two Broomsticks," I replied, referring to Stormy's family's restaurant. "Stormy should have already finished her shift."

Landon blinked. "You're not going to eat without me, are you?"

It took me a moment to register what he was saying. "Seriously? Why do you seem more upset about the idea of me eating without you than me walking home alone?"

"Because there's no way you would even consider walking home alone in the cold," Landon replied. "And you're right, you have plenty of people to tap for a ride. If that doesn't work, Terry and I are only a phone call away." He hesitated and then continued. "There's always Aunt Tillie too."

We both made faces at that suggestion. "I'm sure it will be fine," I said to him. "You don't have to worry about me."

"Wouldn't that be a nice change of pace?"

STORMY WAS IN HER APARTMENT WHEN I LET myself up. She was in the middle of a pile of boxes—like she'd built a fort or something—and I almost didn't see her when I rounded the corner into her living room.

"I haven't built a good box fort in years," I said.

"Ha, ha." Stormy rolled her eyes. "All of this is Hunter's. Until our house is ready, we're moving in here together because he's selling his house."

"I thought that's what you wanted," I said. "Living with a guy isn't a big deal. I thought it would be—sharing a bathroom is terrifying—but you get over the fear quickly."

Stormy shot me a "give me a break" look. "I don't care about that. Hunter and I practically live together already. I didn't realize he had so many 'necessities.'" She used air quotes. "He said that he didn't have much, and he would store everything else in a unit behind the grocery store until we got the new house. This is just the necessities." She extended her hands as she turned around.

I looked at the boxes—there were a decent number—and then back at Stormy. "I'm supposed to agree with you on this?" I hedged.

She narrowed her eyes. "Are you telling me this isn't a lot?"

All I could do was shrug. "I grew up with Aunt Tillie."

Stormy didn't say anything.

"She tends to hoard things," I continued. "I mean ... she really likes her stuff. There's a section of the attic just for slippers. We're talking dragons, bunnies. She even has a pair that look like penises. Mom has banned her from wearing those when we have guests."

"I'm just not used to the stuff," Stormy said as she rested her cheek against one of the boxes. "I lived out of a hotel for years. I have no stuff."

"And that drives Hunter crazy."

She nodded.

"Well, maybe you can meet in the middle. Moving is a great time to dump stuff. And if you only have five things, that makes it easier to run. Perhaps Hunter wants you to have more because he's afraid of losing you again."

Realization dawned in Stormy's eyes. "That makes sense."

"Yes, I'm practically a couple's counselor." My grin was quick. Then I sobered. "I need to talk to Joanie Dunne."

"Seriously? You want to talk to her after what happened last time."

I cringed at the memory. When investigating Kevin right before Christmas, I'd spied on his wife. Because she was used to Kevin having affairs—so many affairs—she'd assumed I was one of his mistresses. She'd verbally attacked me, then melted down, and then taken off. Thankfully, she didn't turn out to be the murderer.

"I know. I'd rather leave her alone, but her husband is still buying up property in Hemlock Cove. He's going all in with some developers, and they want to buy as many inns as possible."

"Sounds potentially nefarious," Stormy said. "Why do you need to talk to Joanie? She's not likely to know anything about it."

"I think she knows more than she lets on," I said. "Kevin asked about The Overlook again when we were at his office earlier. I told him it wasn't going to happen, and he basically said it will or he'll run us out of the business and then he laughed like a mwahaha-ing buffoon."

"Seriously?" Stormy was incredulous.

"Well, he didn't mwahaha," I conceded. "He wanted to. I tend to exaggerate more the older I get. I think I get it from Aunt Tillie."

Stormy smirked. "We can go downtown. The Christmas festival stuff is still up, and people are hanging around."

I wrinkled my nose. "You can't leave the Christmas festival stuff up three weeks after Christmas."

"We can here," Stormy replied. "We're not like Hemlock Cove.

We don't have forty sets of festival decorations. We have four: Easter, Fourth of July, Halloween, and Christmas. We have to stretch things in Shadow Hills."

"That's another thing Kevin said. He said that once they finish with Hemlock Cove, they're going to try the same thing with the surrounding towns, including Shadow Hills and Hawthorne Hollow."

"Do you really think they'll take it that far?" Stormy was understandably dubious.

"I don't know," I replied. "That's another reason I want to talk to Joanie."

"She's been hanging around the festival, with her kids."

I'd met Joanie's and Kevin's daughter when helping at Stonecrest Academy. The girl had been mortified that her father used her private school as a hunting ground for mistresses. Once the school shut down, Katie had to return home.

"I wouldn't mind seeing Katie too," I said. "I want to talk to her, see how things are going."

"You want to make sure things aren't ugly at home," Stormy surmised. "If Katie tells you Kevin is being a jerk, you can torture him and not feel bad about it."

"It might be fun to aim Aunt Tillie at him," I admitted.

DOWNTOWN SHADOW HILLS WAS CUTE. It wasn't as cute as Hemlock Cove, but it had potential. At the time, the rebrand from Walkerville to Hemlock Cove had been a risk. All of the towns in northern Lower Michigan were struggling. A dying industrial base had made it hard to survive. The only towns thriving were tourist towns, which was why the Walkerville commissioners had decided something needed to be done before the town fell into such disrepair it couldn't be saved. Thankfully for all of us, it had worked. It had also given the neighboring towns a blueprint.

Just as Stormy said, the town square was still decked out for

Christmas. All the booths were still up, and people were milling about.

Joanie was working at the coffee booth. Her eyes immediately zeroed in on us.

"She really hates me," I noted as we sat at one of the tables.

Stormy darted a look in Joanie's direction. "Can you blame her? She'd basically immersed herself in a fantasy world where nothing was wrong."

"But she knew about the affairs," I protested.

"Yes, but as long as she didn't have to talk about them with anyone, she was okay with it. You confronting her imploded her little fantasy world."

"Listen, if I'm being cheated on, I want to know about it."

"Landon would never cheat on you."

"I know. And Hunter would never cheat on you." My gaze fell on her shiny new engagement ring. "Have you set a date?"

"We haven't even started to discuss that," Stormy replied. "Right now, we just want to deal with the new house. The wedding doesn't seem as important. Unless you're talking to my mother. All she wants to talk about is the wedding. She wants to go big."

Stormy's expression told me that she didn't like that idea. "What do you want?"

"I honestly don't know." Stormy held out her hands. "I wasn't expecting him to propose so soon."

"I knew he was going to. You guys just seem to fit with one another."

"Yeah, but I haven't even been back all that long."

"Some things are meant to be."

Stormy's cheeks flushed pink with happiness, and she stared lovingly at her ring. "Yeah. I'm not sorry he did. It just seems like a lot when I'm dealing with gnome shifters who want to kill me."

"We'll handle them," I promised her. I rested my elbows on the table and glanced around. "So, do you think we should order coffee and give Joanie no choice about talking to me?"

Stormy made a face. "That would not be my first choice," she said. "What if we waited until she was done and followed her home? Then she wouldn't have to force herself to be nice to us because there's an audience."

"She could slam the door in our faces."

"It would be less embarrassing for her. I..." Stormy trailed off, her gaze moving to a spot behind me. "Or maybe we don't have to bother Joanie at all."

When I turned to see who had drawn Stormy's attention, I saw Katie scurrying in our direction. The girl had grown attached to me when we'd investigated the death of her school headmistress. The school was closed for the foreseeable future, amid talk of getting new management.

"Bay!" Katie threw her arms around me so hard that she momentarily knocked the breath out of me.

I laughed and patted her arm when I'd recovered the ability to breathe. "How are you?" I asked as she pulled away. "How is ... your family?"

Katie shrugged. "It's pretty bad at home right now," she admitted. She was aware of her father's infidelity. "My dad is sleeping in the guest room. He's not going out like he used to because my mom refuses to feed him if he does."

"I just saw your father. He was ... pleasant."

Katie snorted. "He's in a terrible mood. I guess the fact that all of his mistresses are dead or trying to avoid him because of all the attention that was swirling when Ms. Walters died has put him in a bad mood. He's been spending all his time working."

"He's trying to buy up inns in Hemlock Cove," I said. "What do you know about that?"

"Nothing," Katie replied. "He doesn't talk about work with me. I could try to snoop." Her eyes sparkled at the possibility. "That might be fun."

"I don't want you to get in trouble."

"But you're obviously worried," Katie pressed.

"I'm not worried about your father," I assured her. "It's just ... we had a fire in Hemlock Cove yesterday at one of the inns. Apparently, your father was there within the last few weeks trying to buy the inn. They rejected his offer."

"So, you think he tried to burn it down?" Katie made a face. "No offense, because I know you're an awesome investigator, but I can't see him doing that."

"Because he respects human life?" I was hopeful.

"No. The only thing he respects is himself. He wouldn't want to get his hands dirty that way. He always jokes about how he couldn't survive prison whenever we watch a show or movie that has a prison in it. You don't even want to know the things he said about *Sons of Anarchy* when they did the prison story. I just can't see him doing that because he would be too afraid."

It made sense. And the fire that had raced through the inn had been magical in origin. Kevin didn't have any magical abilities.

"I guess I was just hoping to get a lead."

"I can listen around the house," Katie offered. "They're not sharing a bedroom, so Mom and Dad have been doing their fighting in the garage. It's easy to hear what they're screaming about."

Her words tugged on my heartstrings. "I'm sorry it's so hard for you right now."

"Oh, I'm fine," Katie said. "I like when they fight. I want them to split up. I don't think they're going to, though. My mom is too embarrassed to just give up. She wants to prove everybody wrong."

That somehow made it worse in my mind. "Don't get yourself in trouble. You're right, the odds of your father having anything to do with what happened at the Blue Moon Inn are slim. I would still love to know what he has planned for Hemlock Cove."

"I'll try to find out," Katie said. "I don't want him to ruin Hemlock Cove."

"None of us do," I agreed, my gaze moving to Joanie, who was trying to set us on fire with her glare. "I hope your mom finds a way out of this. I hope you all do."

Katie shrugged. "All I know is I don't want to be like them. There's nothing I can do about the rest of it. I treat it like a game."

That sounded healthier than her other options. "We want some hot chocolate," I said, changing the subject. "If I give you money, will you buy some from your mom? I don't trust her not to spit in it."

Katie laughed. "I can handle that. What do you want?"

I wanted Katie to get a better home life, but that didn't look to be in the cards anytime soon. "Peppermint mocha with extra marshmallows. Don't hold back on the foam."

10
TEN

Katie might've been happy to see us. Joanie was another story. After a bit, her stares got to be too much. Even with Easton and Sebastian joining us, there wasn't enough cover, and eventually I was ready to leave.

"I'll take you," Easton offered as I stood. "I need to see Evan anyway."

Sebastian gave him a sidelong look. "You're going to see Evan?"

"I want to switch days with him," Easton replied, oblivious. It was hard to wrap my head around the fact that he'd been a cat months before. He'd always been something else, but to us he was a cat for the longest time.

Now he was ridiculously hot, ridiculously ripped, and apparently straddling a line with Sebastian, Stormy's best friend, and Evan, the hottest vampire in the world. How had I not realized that was happening?

"How are you going to take her to Hemlock Cove when you don't have a car?" Stormy challenged.

"I'll take yours," Easton replied without hesitation.

"What if I don't want you to take my car?"

"You do, because if I'm in Hemlock Cove, I won't be in the apartment bugging you and Hunter, and you can reenact the proposal to your heart's content ... without clothes."

The look on Stormy's face told me she was indeed interested in the prospect. "Fine." She handed over her keys. "Don't wreck my car. I can't afford a new one, and Hunter will insist on buying me one if something happens. We need that money for the new house."

"I'm an excellent driver," Easton insisted.

"Okay, Rain Man," Stormy drawled. She turned to me. "I'm sorry I couldn't be more help. I wanted you to find answers, but I didn't have anything to offer."

"I have some things to think about." I stood and hugged her. "Enjoy your night of kinky proposal games. Landon and I used to do that right after we got engaged. It's not weird, no matter what anyone tells you."

Stormy looked amused. "What are you going to do?"

"I don't know." That was my problem. "That fire burned weirder than I've ever seen. It was almost as if the fire was a living organism. As if it was thinking about where it wanted to go next."

Stormy lifted an eyebrow. "I haven't been in this long enough to know if it's possible, but I can't imagine it is."

"I don't think it's possible," I replied, "but I'm not an expert on every sort of magic."

"Tillie will know," Easton volunteered. "She's an expert on all things magic."

I scowled at him. "You're one of the reasons her ego is so big. I thought you weren't going to be her second sidekick."

Easton lifted one shoulder in a shrug. "I don't know what to tell you. She makes me laugh."

I sighed. "Just take me home. I need to think."

"No problem. Tillie and I have plans anyway." Easton spun his keys around his finger. "That's what I have to talk to Evan about."

Sebastian made a strangled noise, but nobody looked at him but me. It was obvious he was having some sort of issue. Apparently, they were used to him making strange faces, because nobody found it odd.

"I definitely don't want to know what you have planned with Aunt Tillie," I said. "Just ... keep that to yourself."

"I've been sworn to secrecy." Easton was solemn as he bobbed his head. "I'm not even allowed to tell her what we're working on in case a doppelgänger shows up and tries to get me to squeal."

That sounded like Aunt Tillie. I'd forgotten about the time she warned us that doppelgängers were a thing and explained how they worked. "Just keep her busy," I said. "That will hopefully keep her in little trouble instead of big trouble."

Easton looked intrigued. "What do you consider little trouble?"

"Tormenting Mrs. Little."

"Oh, I guarantee that's on the menu tonight." Easton's smile was smarmy. "What do you consider big trouble?"

"Anything that involves sticking your nose in the investigation at the Blue Moon Inn," I replied without hesitation.

Easton didn't avert his eyes. "Okay, so torturing Mrs. Little is good. Fighting evil is bad. Got it."

"I wouldn't phrase it exactly like that."

"But you did. I've got it," Easton insisted. "You have nothing to worry about."

"ARE YOU SURE THIS IS OKAY?" Easton was dubious when I told him to drop me off downtown. "I don't want to strand you here. I can take you to the inn."

"I'm fine," I assured him. "I'm going to the office." I pointed to The Whistler. "Landon's Explorer is at the police station so he's still downtown. I'll text him not to leave without me."

Easton looked momentarily perplexed but nodded. "Okay. Call me if you need me." He parked in front of the newspaper office.

"Can I ask you something?" I asked.

Easton didn't look thrilled at the prospect. "Is it going to hurt?"

"I hope not," I replied. "Are you and Sebastian a thing?"

Easton shrugged. "We hang out. I like him."

"What about Evan?"

Easton's forehead creased. "What have you heard?" he asked icily.

"I haven't *heard* anything," I replied. "I saw the way Sebastian got worked up about Evan before we left. He didn't like the idea of you visiting Hemlock Cove."

"He's fine with me visiting Hemlock Cove," Easton said. "It's the Evan part that makes him angsty." He rolled his neck before sliding his gaze to me. "I shouldn't be entertaining a relationship with anybody. I came here for one specific purpose."

"To protect Stormy," I surmised.

He nodded. "They sent me because there wasn't a worry about me falling in love with her. It seemed like a good idea on paper."

"Then you met Sebastian," I assumed.

"He was just a little flirty fun. He was feeling down because his boyfriend decided to move out of town. I was bored. I thought maybe..." He looked tired. "I shouldn't be talking about this," he said as he rubbed his forehead. "Stormy hasn't figured it out, and you'll tell her."

"I won't," I assured him. "I don't think this part of it is any of Stormy's business."

"But it's yours?"

"I'm just curious and offering a sounding board. I guarantee you're not getting that from Aunt Tillie. She might not even realize you're gay yet."

Easton let loose a harsh laugh. "You're right. That's why she's so refreshing. She doesn't care about any of it."

"She cares about herself and getting what she considers well-deserved revenge on Mrs. Little," I said. "The other stuff ... well ... she's always been good about that. She's a proponent of 'do what you want as long as you don't hurt others.' That's one of the few beliefs she taught us that I willingly emulate."

Easton nodded. "I'm supposed to be focused on Weston. He's a danger to Stormy. I shouldn't be entertaining anything but the idea of getting rid of him. The fact that I'm so distracted means that ... it means..."

"That you're human," I volunteered. "It means that you're human, and that's okay."

He sent me a rueful smile. "I'm a soldier in Stormy's army. She just doesn't realize it yet."

"That doesn't mean you don't deserve your own happy ending," I argued. "You can't live your whole life for Stormy. She wouldn't want that."

"What she needs and wants are different. She's so happy right now. She's getting the boy, the house, and the happily ever after. She's still working for her grandfather, and we have to get the writing back on track, but she's well on her way."

Stormy had been a writer when she left Shadow Hills. She was forced to move home after being dropped by her publisher. She hadn't touched her laptop since, to my knowledge. She still had stories to tell. We all knew it. Stormy was the only one who didn't realize it yet.

"I'm glad that you put her so high on your list of responsibilities," I said to him. "You can't sacrifice your own happiness in the process. That will make you bitter."

"That's why I was sent here."

"Then your people are misguided." I was firm on that. "You need to find balance. It can't just be about Stormy. It has to be about you, too."

"And what about Sebastian?"

"Do you care about him?"

"Yes."

"But you care about Evan too," I surmised.

"I feel as if Evan and I are like magnets. We've been coming together a lot lately."

I understood his dilemma but had no idea how to fix it for him. "I don't know what to tell you." I held out my hands. "You have to decide that part yourself."

"I don't know if I can."

"Then you're going to keep freaking out like this. Either way, if you choose, it will be over."

"Maybe I could just take a step back and do nothing. Not choosing might make it easier for everyone. They'll both just flitter away."

"Yeah, that's not going to happen." I popped open the door. "You wouldn't be sitting here freaking out if it was easy to walk away. It won't be easy for them either. You're going to have a rough time of it. I'm sorry about that."

Easton hesitated, then nodded. "I understand."

"Good. You don't have to make your decision today, but the longer you drag it out, the more likely someone is to really get hurt. Make sure you really are magnetically drawn to Evan. If it's more than just a brief attraction, I think you have your answer."

"Were you magnetically drawn to Landon?" He looked legitimately curious.

"Like grease to bacon," I confirmed, eliciting a smirk from him.

"You guys really did find each other, didn't you?"

"Yup. Now you have to decide who you want to find."

"I'm not supposed to be finding anybody. That's the point."

"You can't live your life 100 percent of the time for another person. That's not how it works."

On a sigh, Easton nodded. "You've given me something to think about."

"Good. Now don't let Aunt Tillie talk you into anything uber weird tonight. Torturing Mrs. Little is fine. Going to the Blue Moon Inn and trying to set a trap for a witch is not."

"How do you know that's what she has up her sleeve?"

"Because I know her."

"I'll tell Evan. We'll keep her in line."

That was the most absurd thing I'd ever heard, and I burst out laughing. Easton joined in.

"I'll try to keep her from going too far off the rails," he clarified.

I TEXTED LANDON THAT I WAS BACK IN town and needed him to pick me up at the newspaper office before he went to the inn for dinner. He sent me back an emoji of a heart and bacon.

I checked everything for this week's edition. I'd banked articles before Christmas but the fire at the Blue Moon Inn would take precedence this week. I typed up what I had—which wasn't much because I couldn't exactly mention the magical aspects—and led with the fact there were no fatalities. We had photos thanks to the freelance photographer I often tapped. He got some good ones of the fire raging and the aftermath. I sent everything to the layout person and headed back to the lobby.

With nothing more to do, my plan was to go to the police station to see what was taking Landon so long. It was possible he'd gotten some good information and simply forgotten to update me, but that wasn't like him.

Viola was in the lobby. She was agitated because Sonny on *General Hospital* was up to something she didn't like. That was the norm for her, so I listened for five minutes and then told her I was late meeting Landon. That was a lie, but I couldn't bring myself to listen to Viola complain about a soap opera for an hour.

When I exited the office, I found an unwanted face on the bench that looked directly at the building. He wasn't on my property, so he'd managed to get close despite the wards I'd erected to keep him out.

"Warden Childs," I greeted him icily.

"I'm no longer a warden," Brad Childs replied. "I'm simply a man looking for a job."

He'd been fired weeks before Christmas after a prison break at the facility he operated. The break wasn't his fault. Magic had been involved, as well as a group of outsiders helping a specific prisoner. He couldn't have stopped what happened. Somebody had to be blamed, though, and he was the man in charge.

Ever since losing his job he'd become a pain in my backside. He'd figured out that I was magical—it didn't help that Landon and I managed to capture most of the prisoners ourselves—and he'd started making unreasonable demands.

"It's interesting that you're here again," I noted as I pocketed my keys. "I thought you'd decided to stick close to home and let this all go."

"Why would I let it go?" He cocked his head. When I first met him, I liked him. I thought he was a good man forced into an untenable position. Now I recognized he had a few personality defects. He shouldn't have been in his position in the first place. His penchant for following me was becoming an issue.

"Holding onto the past does nobody any good," I replied. "What can I do for you?"

"Well, it's funny, but I can't seem to get closer to your newspaper building than I am right now," he noted. "It's as if there's an invisible barrier keeping me out. I know it's not keeping other people out, because I've been watching for days, and your advertising and layout people come and go freely. I'm the only one having this particular problem. Don't you think that's odd?"

The wards I'd erected kept other undesirables out, but he was correct. "It's a mystery." I held out my hands and shrugged. "I wish I could help you. I'm heading to the police station now." I took two steps. "You have a good rest of your evening."

"Are you all talking about the fire at that inn?" Childs was suddenly on his feet and angling to intercept me.

My stomach clenched. I did not want things to turn physical with this man. It wasn't that I couldn't protect myself—I could—but if he picked a fight with me, Landon would pick one with him. I didn't want Landon to put his job at risk. "I believe Chief Terry and

Landon are working on that. Accelerants were detected. I'm not sure where their investigation stands, though."

Childs stepped closer to me. "It's obvious I make you uncomfortable. If you want me to go away all you have to do is get me my job back," he said in a low voice. "I don't want anything more than that." He sounded utterly reasonable until he tacked on the last part. "You owe me."

I planted my hands on my hips and glared at him. "What exactly do I owe you?"

"I'm keeping your secret," Childs replied. "How do you think the people in town will feel when they find out you're magical enough that you can kill people?"

"Obviously, you don't understand what you're dealing with. The whole town is full of witches."

"You're the only real one."

Not the *only* real one, but close enough for his purposes. "I can't help you, Mr. Childs," I replied. "I wish I could. I'm sorry things are tough for you. Perhaps you should focus on getting a new job instead of harassing me."

"Good luck proving I'm harassing you. I can't wait to see how that plays out."

I shook my head. "You really are losing it. You should consider seeing a therapist. All this misplaced aggression is going to get you in more trouble."

"Was that a threat?"

"Take it however you want."

"Then it was a threat." He showed me his teeth. "I'm not going anywhere."

"Then I guess I will be seeing you around." With that, I determinedly trudged toward the police station. I knew he wouldn't follow me out of fear of running into Landon and Chief Terry. That didn't mean he wouldn't be back.

11
ELEVEN

The moment I walked through the door to Chief Terry's office, I unleashed my story about my run-in with Childs. Landon's annoyance was off the charts, and he threatened to chase after the former warden. Chief Terry stopped him.

"You'll give his story credence," Chief Terry said. "We don't want that, Landon. It's not good for any of us."

Landon glared at him. "He's stalking my wife."

"Childs is a problem, but we can't run off half-cocked and confront him. He'll use it as proof that he's hit a nerve."

"I agree with Chief Terry," I volunteered.

Landon scowled at me.

"You're still my favorite," I assured him. "I get why you're upset. I wasn't happy to see him either. The best way to deal with him is to ignore him. Hopefully, he'll lose interest."

Landon shot me an incredulous look. "Do you really think that'll work?"

I shook my head. "We have to beat him at his own game, but we can't right now."

"What *can* we do?" Chief Terry asked. "I'm not thrilled about any of this, and I wouldn't mind being proactive."

"We need dirt on Childs," I replied. "We need to be able to negotiate with him."

"Or we could use magic to alter his memory like you did with those teenage witches," Landon argued. "Can't we just make him forget what he knows?"

I was leery about that prospect for several reasons. "What if he's written everything down somewhere? If he finds his notes, he'll start looking into us again. He might be sneakier a second time. On top of that, I'm not thrilled with wiping memories." It gave me a sick feeling. "I much prefer putting a stop to this through human means."

"I know you think it's a violation to alter memories," Landon started.

"It *is* a violation," I insisted. "It's like a mental rape. We had no choice with the teenage witches. They kept getting in more trouble. We have a choice with Childs."

Landon looked as if he wanted to argue further. "Fine. We'll give it some time. How do you plan on getting information on Childs?"

"I'll send Viola to spy on him," I replied. "She can track where he goes."

Landon and Chief Terry exchanged weighted looks, nodding in tandem after several seconds.

"You're the big witch in town, Bay," Chief Terry said. "We'll let you pick the route we need to follow. I can't guarantee that I won't want to switch gears at some point. For now, though, you decide what we do."

I let loose the breath I'd been holding. "Thank you. We'll stop by the newspaper office to talk to Viola before going to the inn for dinner."

"We can do that," Landon confirmed. "How did your visit to Shadow Hills go?"

"It was not as illuminating as I'd hoped," I admitted.

"Did you chicken out on approaching Joanie?"

I grimaced. "How did you know?"

"You have a soft core, Bay," he replied. "You don't want to hurt another human being, especially if you think it's unearned. You see Joanie as a victim."

"A victim who sent her daughter away rather than deal with her marital problems," I challenged. "I saw Katie. She's putting on a brave face, but it's obvious things aren't great at home. I want to fix that for her."

"You can't fix everything for everyone, sweetheart," Chief Terry countered. "You can only do your very best."

He was right. Still, I was determined. "Joanie needs a come to the Goddess moment. It will happen eventually."

"I hope for your sake that's true."

THE ENTIRE FAMILY, INCLUDING CLOVE, her husband Sam, their son Calvin, Thistle, and her fiancé Marcus, were in the dining room when Landon and I made our way inside. During the spring, summer, and fall months, we often parked at the guesthouse and walked to the inn for dinner. When there was snow in the forecast—as there was tonight—that wasn't an option. The walk across the grounds could be treacherous.

"Well, this is nice," I said when I found Chief Terry bouncing Calvin on his lap.

Thistle, half a bottle of wine deep, arched an eyebrow. "Oh, there you are," she drawled. "I was starting to think you'd died. I mean ... it's been weeks since we've seen you."

I shot her a dirty look. "It's been three days," I countered. "I've been busy. It's not my fault the Blue Moon Inn caught fire. I had things I had to do today. I was barely in town."

"We saw you at the diner," argued Clove, a glass of wine in front of her. "You had time for lunch but not to stop at the store and talk with your favorite cousins."

I plopped down in my chair. "I would've much rather spent time with you than Mrs. Little. She was in the diner when we stopped for lunch. She's extra malicious."

At the head of the table, Aunt Tillie paused with a glass halfway to her mouth. "What was she doing?"

"Trying to get everybody riled up over the Christmas decorations."

"That was ages ago," Aunt Tillie dismissed. "It wasn't a big deal."

Mom shot her a stern look. "Excuse me? What catastrophe are you remembering?"

"There was no catastrophe." Aunt Tillie looked to me for help. "Tell her. That was a harmless Christmas prank."

It wasn't that harmless. What had started as a mild irritation—and lots of laughs—turned dangerous quickly. "I think I'll refrain from commenting."

"I heard Ernie Stinnett has to have surgery because of those decorations," Clove volunteered. Her cheeks were flushed with pleasure. "They say that one of the reindeer lodged a bell up his you know what."

I pinned Aunt Tillie with a glare. "It wasn't *all* fun and games."

"Hey, Ernie Stinnett believes that a woman's place is in the kitchen," Aunt Tillie shot back. "He once told me that a woman should only be employed until she married and then she should step aside so a hard-working man could have her job. Perhaps that reindeer knew more than we do."

I frowned. "Ernie has always been a bit of a sexist. I hope the bell extraction goes well, but I want to talk to you about something else."

"What have you heard?" Aunt Tillie demanded, an edge to her voice. "Whatever it is, it wasn't me. Especially if you think I hexed Linda Morton's driveway to tilt so she keeps sliding and can't get away from her house. That definitely wasn't me."

Silence descended over the table.

"Ah, Aunt Tillie," Thistle said in a happy voice. "She's definitely the family member you want with you when the government shows up for an interrogation. She'll crack quick and save us all."

"Why is the government going to interrogate us?" Mom asked.

Thistle shrugged. "Why does the government do anything?"

"You get more like Aunt Tillie with each passing day," Mom muttered.

Thistle looked wounded. "That's the meanest thing you've ever said to me."

I cleared my throat to draw attention back to me. "I'm serious, Aunt Tillie. Landon and I were talking earlier, and for some reason that snow monster you warned us about came up. I want to talk about that."

Aunt Tillie's face went neutral. "I don't know what you're talking about." I recognized her tone. She was giving me a chance to talk about something else. Anything else. I wasn't falling for it.

"You used to warn us when a storm was about to hit," I insisted. "You said we shouldn't wander far from the inn. You said there were things out there we didn't understand."

"You're making that up." Aunt Tillie flashed her most manipulative smile. "That is simply not true."

"Yes, it is," Thistle interjected. "Whenever a blizzard was forecast, you reiterated the rules."

"Thanks for your input, Mouth, but you're remembering it wrong too," Aunt Tillie growled. "Let's go back to talking about Ernie's bell retrieval surgery."

"Wait." Mom sat straighter in her chair. "You threatened them with a monster during blizzards? Why is this the first I'm hearing about that?"

"Because they're making it up," Aunt Tillie snapped. "They always made things up when they were kids."

"Not stuff like that," Mom argued. "They're not kids now. They seem to remember it well, and you're acting cagey."

"I don't act cagey." Aunt Tillie turned innocent. "They're remembering it wrong. I don't want them to look stupid for telling a story that is completely untrue. I'm really doing this for them."

"Maybe you told that story because you were afraid they'd get lost in the snow," Twila interjected. "Maybe you knew they'd listen if you conjured something particularly frightening."

"That sounds more plausible," Aunt Tillie agreed. "We'll go with that." She was plaintive when she pinned her gaze on me. "I was saving your lives. You should be grateful."

I flicked my eyes to Thistle. She put her wine glass down and rested her hands flat on the table.

"You're lying," Thistle said. "You didn't care if we got lost in the storm. You would've made our moms go out with a locator spell to find us. You would've laughed if we got stuck in a snowdrift. You specifically mentioned a monster."

"You did," Clove agreed. "I remember because I was afraid of monsters."

"You were afraid of your own shadow," Aunt Tillie fired back. "If you're remembering a story about monsters, you're remembering it wrong. I never told you a story like that."

"She's getting senile if she doesn't remember," Thistle said. "She definitely told us that."

"I am in my prime," Aunt Tillie snapped. "I'm not senile." She seemed to realize that being senile would help her out of this conversation almost immediately. "Or I had a bout of senility when you guys were younger—you really are whiny enough to drive a woman to the nuthouse—and I'm better now. Things got infinitely more comfortable around here when you all moved out."

Her gaze landed on me. "Most of you. One of you still needs to suck at the family teat for some reason."

"I can't believe you just said that," I complained. "That is so gross."

"We pay rent," Landon reminded Aunt Tillie. "I insisted on it when I moved in with Bay. She wasn't paying rent before I moved in, but I am not a freeloader."

. . .

As annoyed as I was at Landon, who was heaping his plate with fried chicken and mashed potatoes, I was more interested in Aunt Tillie pretending she hadn't told us about the blizzard monster. "You told us that story several times. You insisted that we stick close to the house during bad snowstorms."

"Why does it matter if I told you stories to make you crap your pants when you were a kid?" Aunt Tillie demanded, changing tactics on a dime. "I used to tell you stories designed to freak you out all the time. Remember when I told you there were gremlins who would kill you in your sleep if you didn't clean your room? Why aren't you up in arms about that?"

"The more you talk, the more I'm convinced you're hiding something," Thistle said. "You're a crap liar if you don't have time to prepare."

If looks could kill, Thistle would be dead. "You're on my list. Be prepared."

"I'm convinced you're lying too," Mom said. "But I don't understand why. What's the point? It was a story you told them when they were children." She turned to me. "Why do you care? Do you think a snow monster set the Blue Moon Inn on fire?"

"That wouldn't be my first assumption," I conceded, "but the fire was like nothing I've ever seen. It was ... breathtaking how it worked its way through the inn. Like it was actually thinking and searching. It just got me to wondering about other things I couldn't explain, and I remembered the stories Aunt Tillie used to tell about monsters hiding in blizzards."

"In other words, she's a kvetch," Aunt Tillie said. "She likes making something out of nothing. I always knew you were that way, Bay. For a time, I thought Clove was the biggest kvetch, but you are."

I was suspicious, but what was she hiding?

"If you say so," I said. She wasn't going to crack before a crowd. In fact, she would only become more aggressive if I pressed her. I had to think of a different way to get her to own up to the stories, and I wanted to know why she was denying them. "I guess it was nothing."

"Definitely not," Aunt Tillie agreed before biting into a chicken leg with gusto. I thought she would let it go. "You know what your problem is?" she challenged, her mouth full of food. "You think the world revolves around you. Not all information is meant for your ears. Mind your own business."

I glanced at Thistle and found her watching me with a strange look. She was obviously suspicious of Aunt Tillie too.

"Did you find anything that helps explain the fire?" Marnie asked.

"Nothing concrete," Landon replied. He had mashed potatoes on his cheek. "We learned that Kevin Dunne is working with a developer, trying to buy up as many inns in Hemlock Cove as possible. He approached the Milligans. I've looked through their purchases but didn't find anything diabolical. They've bought two properties. Neither are actual inns. They're old houses converted to bed and breakfasts."

That was interesting. "Yet Kevin tried to intimidate us by claiming we'd be run out of business if we didn't sell," I mused. "Did he think we wouldn't look into his dealings?"

"I think he's afraid of you and wanted to talk big," Landon replied. "I'm still looking. Other than that, we have nothing."

"That's not good." Mom looked upset. "Are the Milligans still unconscious?"

"They are," Landon confirmed. "I checked about an hour ago. It's a medical mystery."

"Can we do anything?" Twila asked.

"What is there to do?" I countered. "I'm pretty sure whatever happened to them is magical. We need to figure out what that is before we can reverse it."

"Well, here's hoping that won't take long," Mom said. "The Milligans are good people. We need to help them."

12
TWELVE

"**S**he's obviously lying," I complained as I loaded the dog into Landon's Explorer. The pup didn't seem happy about leaving The Overlook with us when Peg was there for him to play with. He almost seemed depressed.

"Who?" Landon asked as he turned on the heat. His smile was for the dog, not me. "How is my boy? Did you miss me?"

The dog thumped his tail from his spot on the floor. The look he gave me was dark.

"Hey, it's not my fault you can't spend the night with Peg," I said. "You're our dog. You live with us, whether you want to or not."

The dog clearly didn't want to because he hopped up on my lap, bypassing my face for a kiss, and pressed his nose against the window as we pulled away.

"Maybe we should talk to your mom about babysitting him weekdays," Landon said. "He's in love with Peg."

"He's fine," I insisted. "He's been at the inn for two days because we got distracted. It will be easier when the weather is good and they can play outdoors." I wrapped my arms around the dog. "Isn't that right, Atticus?"

"From *To Kill a Mockingbird*? No way."

"What about Boo?"

"I..." To my surprise, Landon cocked his head rather than immediately shutting down the suggestion. "Boo as if he's a ghost and his mommy is a necromancer, or Boo Radley?"

"Boo Radley." Was there any other answer?

"Then no."

I scowled at him. "You're a putz when you want to be," I complained.

"What about Radish?"

"No. What did I say?"

"Radishes are vegetables. You want me to eat more vegetables. That's why I had so many potatoes today. Radish is a good name."

"Potatoes are a starch. I want you to eat more asparagus."

"Blech. I guess I'll keep thinking."

"Me too," I agreed. "As for who is lying, I was talking about Aunt Tillie. She's not a good liar."

"She is when she puts effort into it. Like, when I first met her, she had no problem lying to me."

"You knew she was lying."

"I guess I kind of did, but I wasn't really certain. She has this ability to make you feel foolish even when she's spouting nonsense."

"She is good at that," I readily agreed. "I can see, if you don't know her, why you might give the things she says credence. But you have to admit that she was acting squirrelly tonight."

"She acts squirrelly every night." Landon pulled into our driveway and put the Explorer in park. When he pinned me with a stare, I knew he was about to say something I wasn't going to like. "Why is this important to you?"

"Because she's a big, fat liar."

"She's always been a big, fat liar. That's part of her charm. Why really?"

"Because ... I remember those storms. She was adamant about us not going outside."

"What does that have to do with the here and now? You never saw a monster back then. We haven't seen one on the property, and we roam around at all hours of the night when the weather is good. I don't understand why you're up in arms about it now."

"I remembered it earlier today. I haven't thought about it for years."

"And?" Landon's expression reflected genuine confusion, making me wonder if I was being unreasonable just to be unreasonable.

"It's nothing I guess," I said. "You have to admit that she was acting weird, though. At least give me that."

"She was," Landon conceded. "Have you considered that she's acting weird because she was actually doing something else in the woods around that time? Like, maybe she took advantage of the cold weather to put her still in the woods not far from the house back then. She might not have wanted you guys stumbling across it. That still liquor is strong enough to peel your insides."

It was a perfectly reasonable response, but I wasn't buying it. "That's not it."

"Do you think she has a pet monster that hibernates all year and only comes out in the winter and she was protecting you from being eaten?" He laughed at his own joke. When I didn't laugh, he sobered. "Now I'm going to have nightmares thinking there's a snow monster in the woods. Aunt Tillie ruins everything."

His disgruntlement nudged a smile out of me. "It's probably nothing," I said. "But it's rarely nothing with Aunt Tillie. When she lies, there's a reason."

Landon made a face. "Two months after I came back, when I was fully invested in the relationship and no longer weirded out by the witch stuff, she told me that if I ever tried to arrest her, she would hex my toenail clippings and make them sentient, so they'd come after me at night and leave half-moon marks all over my body. She said they would be like bedbugs, only worse ... and meaner. She said she would give them teeth. There was no reason for that lie."

I grinned. "I have more bad news for you. She could actually do that if she wanted. If you're particularly frightened by that threat, don't remind her. If she knows that she can get to you through toenail clippings, she'll make it happen."

Huffy, Landon grabbed the puppy from my lap. "Your family is the worst." He threw open the door. "I'm definitely going to have nightmares."

"You didn't think my family was so bad when Mom sent us home with enough chicken for a midnight snack," I called after him as he stormed to the guesthouse.

"Don't forget my chicken."

I sighed as I watched him go. Then I tilted my head and looked back to the inn. No matter what anyone said, Aunt Tillie was hiding something. She was always something of an enigma. She liked playing games. This felt different.

THE ANSWER CAME TO ME IN MY DREAMS. I followed Aunt Tillie through The Overlook, watching as she pulled on her boots and combat helmet. Inherently, I knew I was sleeping, but this felt different. It was as if I was one of the ghosts I could so easily command. I could watch, and she didn't know I was watching.

When Aunt Tillie reached the back door of the inn and grabbed her stick and whistle, suspicion had my insides clenching. I followed her outside and watched as she started toward the bluff. She walked with a purpose. When she paused at the edge of the property and looked in my direction a shiver ran through me, and I considered that this wasn't a dream.

She turned back and continued her walk. I stared in her wake, willing myself to follow. I bolted to a sitting position in bed, my eyes wide and sightless.

It took me a moment to adjust to the darkness. Landon's rhythmic breathing brought me back to reality. Next to him, the puppy snored, their breathing in tandem.

I could've stayed in bed next to my warm husband and dog, but something propelled me to rise and dress. I pulled on my boots trimmed with fake fur, my heavy-duty coat, and my warmest gloves. I tucked my blonde hair under Landon's black knit ski cap. Then I headed for The Overlook, and ultimately the bluff.

What would I do if I was wrong, and Aunt Tillie wasn't out there? I would probably laugh at myself and admit to being an idiot. But it felt as if I was walking toward something.

It took me ten minutes to get to the inn. Everything was dark inside the family living quarters, but fresh footprints on the walkway leading down to the bluff trail had me sucking in a breath. Had I really been a silent witness to Aunt Tillie sneaking out? Would I find her conducting some weird ritual on the bluff?

My feet made noise on the path. There was no avoiding it. Between the crunchy snow and the hard-packed ice that caused me to slip a few times, there was no hiding my approach. Thankfully, the wind howled. It was so dark out here that I was convinced I'd made a mistake. Maybe Aunt Tillie hadn't gone to the bluff after all. Maybe the footprints were from earlier. Maybe she was safe in her bed, and I was just an idiot.

Then I saw it, a hint of movement between the trees. It took a moment to focus—there were magical lights swirling, like a strobe light, shining down on the two figures standing together on top of the bluff. When I finally registered the figures, my stomach kicked as if I'd just downed an entire quart of the hottest salsa in the world.

Aunt Tillie, in the same outfit I'd seen her in in my dream, stood in front of a large hulking figure. It wasn't a man, but not a beast. It was humanoid, but not human. It was monstrous, although not entirely a monster.

The creature was validation that I'd been right. Aunt Tillie had warned us about a monster. Were they out here now because I'd asked about it? All that mattered was that I was right.

I almost came out of my skin at the sound of footsteps, and I whirled quickly, prepared to fight.

Evan walked out of the trees. He lifted a finger to his lips to warn me not to scream, and then smiled.

"Nice night for a spy mission," he whispered.

I glared at him. "Are you here as her backup? How long have you known about this?" My voice was shriller than I anticipated, although still muffled by the wind and distance. Aunt Tillie and her monster buddy didn't look up. "What is this, Evan?"

The vampire lifted one shoulder in a shrug. He wasn't wearing a coat, hat, or gloves. He wasn't susceptible to the elements. He should've been susceptible to sunlight, but even that wasn't dangerous to him now, not since my friend Scout Randall had healed him with pixie magic. Now he was a day-walking vampire with a soul and had become Aunt Tillie's sidekick. He said she made him laugh. More than that, I think she was a necessary tether to the land of the living. Even though he wasn't ready to fully engage with the world, Aunt Tillie allowed him to do it slowly, carefully, when she was in the mood for mayhem.

"I'm not sure what it is." Evan stood close to me. He had no warmth to offer, but he was a protective presence. "She's been meeting with this ... *thing* ... for about a week now. She was acting cagey one day when I asked about her plans for the night. I assumed she was hanging with Whistler, but when I followed her, she came out here."

"To that?" I inclined my head toward the creature.

"Yeah."

I rubbed my gloved hands together, debating. "What do they do?"

"They talk. Usually for just a few minutes. Last time, I tried following the creature when they said their goodbyes—the first time I followed Tillie to make sure she was okay—but it disappeared into the trees. I was tracking it, determined to find where it was going, and I lost it. It doesn't leave footprints if it doesn't want to."

"How does that work?"

"I have no idea." Evan cast a curious look toward me. "What are you doing out here?"

"I guess I woke myself because I was suspicious. At dinner I asked Aunt Tillie about the monster she'd warned us about when we were kids, and she lied."

"How do you know she lied?"

I shot him a dubious look. "Seriously? When isn't she lying?"

He chuckled. "Fair point. She does like to spin a tall tale. Why did you ask about this monster now?"

That was a very good question. "I have no reasonable answer. It just popped into my mind earlier."

"What were you thinking about at the time?"

"The fire at the Blue Moon Inn. I've never seen fire like that before. It was as if it had a mind of its own. I don't even know how to explain what we saw."

He cocked his head. "Did you somehow associate this creature with the fire?"

"I didn't know this creature was real until two minutes ago. When we were kids, and big storms were coming in, Aunt Tillie was particularly obnoxious about making sure that we didn't stray too far from the house. She acted worried about us."

"I'm sure she was."

"She used to send us on missions into the woods after dark, on our own, when we were freaking eight. She didn't care about our safety then."

"She followed you on those missions." Evan's gaze was on Aunt Tillie. "You were never really alone. She was trying to make you strong."

"Wouldn't being lost in a storm make us stronger?"

"Not if she worried about you being attacked by something you didn't have the strength to fight off." He was calm. "Bay, have you ever considered that Tillie really does have your best interests at heart?"

"She makes me smell like crap—literal crap—when she's irritated with me. How is that in my best interests?"

"That's just family stuff," he replied. "A friend will look you in the eye and say, 'You're so pretty.' A best friend, someone who truly loves you, will say, 'What's up with your face, Sloth,' and you'll both laugh because you know you're loved."

I frowned. "That was fairly profound, Evan, but this is not Aunt Tillie messing with me because she loves me. This is Aunt Tillie hiding a monster."

"Or protecting her family," Evan countered. "How do you know she didn't strike some sort of deal with this creature? Maybe it only comes out in cold weather. Maybe she protects it when it sleeps, and it agrees to protect you when it's awake."

I opened my mouth to shoot down the idea but snapped it shut. That *did* sound like something Aunt Tillie would do.

Unfortunately, she also wasn't above making friends with some sort of hell beast and hiding it from us. She got bored much too easily.

"What are you going to do?" Evan asked when I was quiet for several seconds.

"I'm going to think about it tonight, and act on it tomorrow," I replied.

He nodded. "No wonder you're the smartest one in your family."

"Are you going to tell her I know?"

"She doesn't even realize that I know. I'm not outing myself, so I'm not outing you. I haven't decided how I want to respond either. Perhaps we can figure it out together."

"Then you'd better come for breakfast tomorrow, because one way or another I'm talking to her about this."

"I might leave this to your family and mind my own business."

"Aunt Tillie would slap you upside the head for saying anything of the sort."

He snorted. "I still make my own decisions. Speaking of that..." He held out his arm. "How about I walk you back to the guesthouse and we leave them to their business? I wouldn't feel good about myself if I let you walk all that way in the dark alone."

"I can take care of myself."

"Yes, but there are monsters afoot now."

"Fine." I linked my arm through his. "You can tell me about your relationship with Easton."

He froze. "Who told you?" He sounded annoyed more than worried.

"Let's just say I have an easier time seeing things than Scout and Stormy, because they're too close to the situation."

"Nothing has happened."

"Do you want it to?"

"I honestly have no idea."

13
THIRTEEN

After Evan dropped me at the guesthouse, I paced the living room for a good hour before finally heading into the bedroom and crawling back in next to Landon.

Lack of sleep made me crabby when I woke the next morning. Landon was up, and I heard him singing "Who's a good boy?" in a ridiculous voice. I tracked the noise to the kitchen, where the dog was eating breakfast, his tail a nonstop blur.

Landon was shirtless, his hair still mussed from sleep, and leaning against the counter. "Nice face you've got there," he said on a laugh as I got coffee. "Did you have bad dreams?"

I said nothing.

"Bay." His fingers were gentle when he wrapped them around my elbow and nudged me around to look at him. "Hey." His smile was warm but turned wan when I met his gaze. "What's up?"

I should've told him. We'd promised to always be truthful. I didn't tell him what had happened the previous evening, but not because I was trying to protect Aunt Tillie. I was trying to protect myself. Landon would be furious when he found out I'd gone into the inky black night without him.

"Bay," Landon said again. He'd forgotten all about telling his dog he was a good boy. "Did something happen?"

Eventually, I would have to tell him, and it would be ugly. I could only tell him part of it now. Maybe I could ease him into it.

"I had a weird dream last night," I said. I looked down at his fingers and kept my gaze there until he released me. "I think maybe it was because I was so suspicious of Aunt Tillie."

"Okay." Landon's tone was carefully neutral. "What did Aunt Tillie do in the dream?"

"She was getting dressed in the inn. She put on her combat helmet, grabbed her staff, took her whistle and went outside. Everyone else in the inn was asleep."

"Did you follow her?"

"To the patio. I was like a ghost or something. I swear there was a moment when she looked right at me, though."

Landon stroked my hair. "Do you think that was real?"

"Do I think I was really a ghost? No. Did I see her in the dream, and was it as if I was a ghost? Yes."

"Okay." Landon managed a legitimate smile this time. "The good news is, it was just a dream. The bad news is, I think you're right and she's likely up to something. How do you want to play it?"

The question made me squirm as I thought about how earnest Evan had been the previous evening. "I haven't decided yet. Can I get back to you after I think a bit?"

"Of course." Landon gave me a real kiss this time. "We are dealing with Aunt Tillie. We need to outthink her."

I forced a smile I didn't feel. "I might ask her some questions over breakfast, feel her out about if she went somewhere last night. Don't be surprised if I sound like an idiot."

Landon chuckled. "Oh, Bay, when Aunt Tillie is involved, you always sound like an idiot." He skirted my hand when I made a move to spank him. "I love when you're an idiot. How else do you think I got you to fall for me?"

The question, although tinged with mirth, had me straightening. "Falling for you was the smartest thing I ever did."

Landon's face flushed with delight as he cupped my chin. "That's how I feel about you."

I waited until he'd finished kissing me to speak again. "I'm going to be on Aunt Tillie this morning. You've been warned."

"Just let me get my bacon first. If the food is going to start flying, I want to make sure that I have enough bacon to sustain me."

LANDON PACKED UP HIS DOG AND helped boost me into the passenger seat of his Explorer even though I was perfectly fine doing it myself. He gave me another kiss—he was feeling playful—and then he practically skipped to the other side of the vehicle.

He smiled the whole way to The Overlook. I did not. I kept thinking about how I was going to trick Aunt Tillie into admitting not only that she was creeping around like a creepy creeper, but that she was hiding a monster. I had to do it in such a way that I didn't get myself in trouble.

"There's the happy family," Evan said from the front desk when we entered the lobby. He was behind the desk, a ledger open in front of him.

"Do I even want to know what you're doing?" I asked.

"It's Twila's month to balance the books," Evan replied. "It takes her five times as long as the others because she's Twila. I can do it in a quarter of that time. I check her numbers for her. This is the third time I've done it."

That was news to me. Evan had become an integral part of our family in a short amount of time, and not only because he was a solid babysitter for Aunt Tillie. He helped my mother and aunts when they needed to change the decorations. As a vampire, he didn't need a ladder to put the lights on the top section of the tree. He also followed Chief Terry at my mother's behest when she was worried about him serving a child custody decree. Evan made sure Chief Terry was safe and never let on that he was following him. Helping Twila with math was going above and beyond, though.

"Better you than me," Landon said as the puppy yipped and danced around Evan. "I tried to help Twila balance the books once, and it was the longest hour of my life. You must be a saint."

"I don't know about that." Evan's eyes flicked to me. "Looks as if you slept poorly, Bay."

He was testing me. I flashed a tight smile that didn't reflect my true mood. "I had weird dreams."

"I hate when that happens." Evan's smile was far from sympathetic. He was suspicious. I really couldn't blame him. All his knowledge of dealing with Winchester witches was based on the time he spent with Aunt Tillie. "Your mother and aunts made pancakes. I'm sure that will perk you right up."

"And bacon?" Landon asked. "I ask because it's Wednesday and I need extra bacon on hump day."

"He's making that up," I said to Evan as I pushed Landon toward the dining room. "He doesn't even like bacon that much. He likes irritating everybody with talk of bacon. That's his schtick now."

"Don't kid yourself, Bay," Landon said. "I love bacon almost as much as I love you. Almost."

"Aw, that's sweet." I patted his arm. "Let's make sure there's some bacon in there for you to make out with, because I'm going to be busy at breakfast. I want you to be happy."

I cast a look at Evan over my shoulder as I walked out of the room. Inside, I was screaming: *Don't screw this up for me.*

Evan was a wild card. I had no idea if he would take my side or Aunt Tillie's when the bell rang and I went in swinging. I was almost as curious about that as I was about the obvious answer Aunt Tillie owed me.

. . .

Only Aunt Tillie and Chief Terry were in the dining room. Clove and Thistle only came for breakfast on special occasions. Clove said getting a baby ready first thing in the morning was tiresome. As much as I would've liked Thistle as backup in setting a trap for Aunt Tillie, Clove would've been a hindrance.

It was better I was alone.

Landon immediately went to talk to Chief Terry about the case, leaving me to hover near the juice station. Evan joined me, making sure to step to the right when the dog and Peg raced by making noises at each other. I was no expert, but I could almost swear that Peg was now barking. I didn't want them underfoot when I started digging the trench to bury Aunt Tillie.

"I can tell by the look on your face that you're going to do something stupid," Evan said. He cast a sidelong look to Aunt Tillie, who was watching us with suspicious eyes. "Don't confront her in front of everybody."

That showed what he knew. "I have no intention of confronting her. I'm going to lay a trap." I poured some tomato juice, and because I needed something to do with my hands—I was surprisingly fidgety—I poured a glass of orange juice for Landon. "I know what I'm doing."

Evan narrowed his eyes. "Bay..." He trailed off, clearly debating how to respond. "You know what? You do you. I'm certain you'll figure it out."

I watched him move to the other side of the table, away from any fireworks that might start exploding. That only served to irritate me further.

I sat in my usual spot, between Landon and Chief Terry, and pinned Aunt Tillie with what I hoped would pass for a friendly look. "How are you this morning?" I asked.

"I'm five by five," Aunt Tillie replied. "How are you?"

"I'm ... awesome."

Mom and the aunts slid in through the swinging doors, carrying huge platters of bacon and pancakes. Mom pulled up short when she saw me. "Are you sick?" she asked.

I frowned. "Why would you ask me that?" I wasn't sick. I didn't look sick, did I?

"She looks constipated," Marnie offered as she placed the bacon in front of Landon and Chief Terry. "By the way, Graham will be here shortly."

Graham Stratton was the police chief of Hawthorne Hollow. He also was the father of Scout's boyfriend Gunner. I'd had limited dealings with him but found him funny and engaging.

This morning, however, I wasn't in the mood for funny or engaging.

"Are things getting serious between you two?" Landon teased. He was either unaware of my mood or trying to ignore it. Likely the latter. He preferred getting breakfast in before arguments most days.

I could oblige him. Hopefully.

"He's just stopping by for breakfast," Marnie said. "Don't make things weird."

The sound of the door in the lobby had her jerking up her head. "That's probably him. I want everybody on their best behavior." She took off for the lobby like a shot, pausing before she left. "Don't talk with your mouth full. Don't mention the word 'grandmother,' because I'm too young to be a grandmother. Also, don't talk about Aunt Tillie's clowns. They freak people out."

"Well, that was strange," Chief Terry noted.

Everyone nodded.

"Seriously, Bay, I have prune juice if you need to loosen things up," Mom offered.

I glared back at her. "I'm not constipated. Stop talking about me being constipated."

"Just making sure. It's a mother's job to worry about her child."

"Not when it comes to constipation," I argued. "Just ... stop. I'm fine."

"You don't look fine," Twila said. "You look as if you're about to explode."

"How about we don't say the words 'constipation' and 'explode' before I have my breakfast?" Landon begged. When everyone glared at him, he sank lower in his chair.

I needed to set a trap, and if they kept talking about constipation, it was never going to happen. I decided to change the subject. Even I didn't know what was going to come out of my mouth until it happened.

In hindsight, I should've seen it coming. Evan had seen the signs, but I was too far gone.

"Aunt Tillie was on the bluff talking to a monster last night," I blurted. The words escaped so fast they almost ran together in one long word.

All around me, it was as if the air had been sucked out of the room.

"What did you say?" Chief Terry asked.

"I thought you said you dreamed of her leaving the inn," Landon pressed. "You didn't say anything about a monster on the bluff."

"Aunt Tillie wouldn't go to the bluff in the middle of the night in winter," Mom said. "She could fall and break a hip."

Aunt Tillie remained silent, glaring.

Because I figured Evan was the only friendly face I had left in the room, I glanced at him ... and found him grinning.

"I have to love this family," he said. "You have the best of intentions, but it's as if you walk around with dynamite in your pockets to blow up bridges at every turn."

"Nobody started, did they?" Marnie asked as she appeared in the dining room with Graham next to her. "It's rude to start ahead of our most important guest."

Graham looked embarrassed. "I wouldn't say I'm the most important guest," he hedged.

"Bay claims that Aunt Tillie was on the bluff last night," Mom volunteered. "I really do think that she might have a bowel obstruction or something. Landon, check her temperature."

Landon glared at me. "Did you go for a walk last night?"

"I didn't lie," I said. "The dream was real. I just happened to go out afterward to see if it meant anything."

"Alone? In the dark?" Landon's tone was frigid. "What would've happened if you'd fallen? What would've happened if the monster you claim Aunt Tillie was with attacked?"

"No offense, but what were you going to do to stop a monster?" Evan asked him. "I was there. She was fine."

"You called Evan to go with you?" Now Landon looked hurt more than angry.

"I didn't call him," I replied. "He was already out there, spying."

Evan shot me a sarcastic thumbs-up when Aunt Tillie turned her murderous glare to him. "Way to take me down with you."

"Sorry. I didn't plan on needing backup," I said to Landon. "I was fine."

"Because Evan was there," Landon argued. "Why couldn't you wake me and tell me what you planned to do?"

"You looked so comfortable with your dog. I didn't want to ruin things for you. I mean ... there was nothing you could've done." I hadn't wanted to wake him, but there was more to it. "And I wasn't sure the dream was real. I didn't want to look like an idiot."

"Well, congratulations," Mom said when Landon focused on his plate, a muscle working in his jaw. "You don't look stupid at all."

"Just constipated," Twila supplied. "I guess we know why you were making that face."

I darted a look to Aunt Tillie. She hadn't denied the charge. She was still glaring. "What's the deal with the monster?" I asked. I'd gone this far, I might as well make things worse, I rationalized.

"Oh, you're going to see a monster," Aunt Tillie said in a low, deadly voice. "A bad, bad monster. You're on my list."

I wasn't surprised.

"As for you, you're on my list too," she said to Evan. "You're going to regret spying on me. You better hope I don't demote you to sidekick number two."

Evan didn't look bothered. "I look forward to my punishment."

How he could say that with a straight face was beyond me. Whatever punishment Aunt Tillie was about to dole out was going to be terrible.

14
FOURTEEN

Landon was angry.

It wasn't that he didn't think I could take care of myself. It was the FBI agent inside him that was angry. I'd once scoffed at the idea that people could go to bed next to someone they loved and never know if that individual left, disappearing never to be seen again. He'd shown me the statistics, however, and I knew that was what haunted him.

The cases he'd never solved because the person really did disappear, never to be found again, was the stuff that chased him in nightmares.

He knew I could fight a monster. I'd taken off into the night without a word, though. When I looked at his point of view, I got it. If I'd never come home the previous evening, he would've woken up alone and always wondered.

Not knowing was worse than knowing.

Aunt Tillie had beat a hasty retreat, never once admitting what she was doing.

"Landon." I chased him to the lobby.

"I don't want to talk right now, Bay." Landon kept his back to me as he grabbed his gloves from the desk. "I have to go to work."

"You can't just leave," I protested. "I'm sorry. I was going to tell you."

"When?" There was no anger associated with the question.

"I don't know." I shifted from one foot to the other. "I thought about it this morning, but I knew you'd react this way."

"So you were trying to figure out a way not to tell me."

"I'm sorry." I meant it. "I couldn't shake the dream and I wanted to see. I was right."

"That's my problem." He was calm when he turned, and that bothered me more than if he had started yelling. "You wanted to beat Aunt Tillie, and that's all you cared about. I didn't factor into the equation at all."

I opened my mouth but didn't say anything. I couldn't.

"Your life should not be about me, but I should be a consideration. That's all I want. Last night, I wasn't even a consideration."

"I said I was sorry. I don't know what else to say."

"I don't know what else you can say either." Landon tugged on his gloves and looked up as Chief Terry walked into the lobby. "I'll meet you at the police station. We can plan for the day there."

"What about me?" I blurted. "Don't you want me with you?"

"I'll handle it alone today." Landon turned and stalked out the door.

I watched him go, frustrated, and then turned to Chief Terry. He would take my side. "Talk to him."

"Absolutely not." Chief Terry took me by surprise. "You were in the wrong, Bay. Do you have any idea how it would've gutted him if something had happened to you? He never would've stopped blaming himself."

"You can't be mad at me too. That's not fair."

"I am mad, Bay." Chief Terry was matter of fact. "I'm mad because you're not a kid any longer. Even when you were a kid, you didn't take off in the middle of the night without your cousins. I'm sure Clove complained the whole way, but you all went together. Last night, you were alone. You could've fallen and hurt yourself and frozen to death before any of us realized you were missing."

I was feeling crappier by the moment. "I would've used my magic to summon help. It was fine." It sounded lame even as I said it.

"Evan was there."

"Did you know Evan was there?"

He had me, and he knew it. "How long are you guys going to punish me?"

"Three days," Chief Terry replied without hesitation.

My eyebrows took a run for my hairline. "You've already sentenced me?"

"Yup, and trust me, you're doing hard time." He left in the same manner as Landon, turning his back on me and walking out without a look back.

I stood there, hands clenched into fists at my sides, and glared at his receding back. "Well, this just sucks," I groused as I turned.

Evan stood there, leaning against the wall, arms crossed over his chest. His expression was impossible to read.

"If you're mad at me, I don't want to hear it," I snapped.

"I'm not mad. I don't appreciate that you ratted me out, but I was going to out myself for spying on Tillie, so it really doesn't matter. You actually did me a favor. She's so mad at you she can't muster much anger toward me."

"Well, as long as I can help," I said darkly.

He laughed—actually laughed—and clapped his hands. "You can't make me feel bad. You forget, Scout is my best friend. She's far more frightening than you ever could be."

"Isn't that the truth?" Graham added as he appeared next to Evan. He didn't look too bad for a guy who had to sit through an uncomfortable family breakfast, complete with a full-on Winchester meltdown. Of course, he was probably used to it. Scout made everybody uncomfortable when she was bored.

"What are you doing today?" Graham asked Evan. "Things are

quiet in Hawthorne Hollow. As quiet as they can be when you have Scout fighting gods and vampires."

"I'm going with Bay," Evan replied.

That was news to me. "I don't even know where I'm going."

"Yes, you do." Evan waited.

I made a face. "I thought maybe I'd go back to the Blue Moon Inn. I want to see if I can find any traces of magic there. If I can find a thread, I might be able to follow it."

Evan's smile was indulgent. "That's why I'm going with you. There's a monster running around the woods, and because you're in the doghouse with your husband and father figure, and I'm on Tillie's list, it's best we stick together."

"So, field trip?"

He grinned. "Let's see what's at the inn."

I DROVE. EVAN DIDN'T HAVE A VEHICLE. He'd had a motorcycle at one time, but now that he was a vampire, he no longer needed it. He could run anywhere he needed to go faster than he could drive.

"It looks like it's still okay from the outside," he noted as we exited my car. He was wearing a coat but didn't need it. People asked fewer questions when he pretended he was affected by the elements.

"Yeah, it's weird," I agreed. "There were a lot of flames. When we arrived, it was fully engulfed."

"The roof looks intact." Evan narrowed his eyes, then looked around. "I'm going up." He held out his arm to me. "Want to come?"

"Are you going to fly?"

"More like run really fast and jump."

"Is it dangerous?"

"For the woman who took off in the middle of the night to spy on her great-aunt, it's nothing."

"Ugh. Let it go." I stepped closer to him and held my breath when he tucked me in at his side.

He ran so fast it was a blur. One second, we were on the ground, and the next, we were on the roof. He deposited me toward one edge, and then he moved to the center of the roof.

"You stay there," he ordered, jabbing a finger. "I want to make sure this won't give out under my feet. I can survive a fall like this, with rubble burying me. You're more delicate."

That shouldn't have come across as an insult, and yet it did. "I'm not delicate. That's the meanest thing you ever said to me."

Evan threw back his head and laughed. "You're a lot like Tillie."

"Now *that's* the meanest thing you've ever said to me."

"You have some of your mother in you too," he added.

"Are you trying to make me cry?"

"You're also your own person. Thistle has a lot of Tillie in her. So does Clove."

It was the last one that got me, and I immediately shook my head. "Clove is never brave. She never picks a fight. She's the one we have to talk into going on adventures. She's nothing like Aunt Tillie."

"She's manipulative like Tillie," Evan countered. He dropped to his knees and pushed on the shingles, cocking his head. "Clove is the most manipulative of your age group. Just like Marnie is for your mother's trio. You and Thistle are blunt, straightforward ... last night notwithstanding."

"Can we stop talking about it?" I whined. "I know I screwed up. I just ... I wasn't sure she was really going to be out there."

"If that was true, you wouldn't have bothered getting dressed and hiking through the snow."

I hated how wise he sounded. "Why are you such a know-it-all? I like you except when you pretend you know everything."

"That's simply who I am." He winked. "You all have a bit of Tillie in you. You all have a bit of your mothers too."

"Don't tell Thistle," I said. "Her mother drives her crazy."

"Twila isn't nearly as scatterbrained as she lets on. As the youngest sister, that's the persona she's adopted. Winnie is the strong one. Marnie is manipulative. Twila's a little ditzy and realized that people reacted to that, so that's who she decided to be."

All I could do was shake my head. "You're an insightful bastard, I have to give you that."

Evan lifted his chin and met my eyes. "There's nothing wrong with this roof."

I moved closer. "I know darned well the fire was going through the roof, Evan. We could see it from the road."

"There are no weak spots. There are soot marks, but no burned pieces."

"What does that mean?"

He shrugged. "It means this was no ordinary fire."

"I think we already knew that." I turned my attention to the ground on the south side of the building, the one side I hadn't visited since the fire. There, two sets of footprints dotted the crusted snow. They led to the woods on the side from which I had not stripped the snow to battle the fire.

"How old do you think those are?" I asked as I inclined my head to the footprints.

Evan stood and extended his arm again. "Let's take a closer look."

I closed my eyes for the trip down. I felt nothing, as he set me on solid ground. I let out a breath I didn't even know I'd been holding and watched as Evan ambled over to the footprints.

"I feel as if I should be more worked up about the fact that I just flew," I admitted.

"Not really, but if you want to tell yourself that, who am I to judge?" Evan pressed his fingers to the footprint. "This snow here is crusty. It's hard."

"The fire could've softened the snow and it could have frozen overnight."

"That's exactly what I think happened," Evan confirmed. "These prints do not head toward the parking lot. They head toward the woods."

"Should we follow them?"

He held out his hand. "It's very icy. I want to keep a firm grip on you."

I took his hand. "Have you thought about what you want with Easton?" I asked as we walked.

Evan kept his eyes on the tracks. If he didn't like a particular section of ice, he nudged me away from it. I hated being infantilized, but it was better than slipping.

"I don't know that I feel anything for Easton," Evan replied. "My emotions are ... tricky ... ever since I regained my soul. When I was first cured, I didn't think I would ever feel anything again. Obviously, I was wrong."

"Obviously. You love Scout."

"I do. I've grown to love Gunner as a brother as well. They're my family. I have no problem interacting with them, or with Tillie. I think she's the one who taught me that I could love outside the handful of people I was willing to let in. She forced herself on me."

"Oh, don't phrase it like that," I complained as we arrived in a small clearing. "That makes her sound like a date rapist."

He laughed again, something he was doing more and more freely these days. "You're so funny. I just meant that Tillie didn't give me an option to wallow, which is what I really wanted to do. I wanted to sit in my uncle's house and feel sorry for myself. She kept forcing me on adventures.

"At first, I fought her, but I found it was easier to do what she wanted and get it over with," he continued. "After that, I realized I enjoyed hanging out with her. She's all kinds of fun when she wants to be. Somehow, I started living again without realizing it."

"You still haven't answered my question about Easton," I pointed out.

"What if I don't have real feelings for him? What if I'm just attracted to him and it doesn't lead anywhere?"

"You don't have to marry everyone you date."

"But our lives overlap in impossible ways. His primary focus has to be Stormy. Right now, Scout needs me as she navigates what needs to be done here. Perhaps this isn't the time to embark on a relationship."

I licked my lips, debating. "You can't go looking for love, you have to be open to it when it finds you. I learned that with Landon. Maybe just let things happen as they're supposed to and don't think about it too much."

"Maybe." Evan motioned for me. "Come here, please." He pointed to one of the footprints. "Put your boot next to it."

I didn't realize what he was trying to see until I placed my boot next to the print and saw my foot was significantly bigger. "These prints belong to children," I said.

He nodded. "How big are your feet?"

"I wear a size eight shoe."

"Standard size. Those boots are much smaller."

"It has to be Grace and Hope," I said.

"Okay, but the snow fell the day of the fire. Otherwise, if they'd been out here before then, the snow that fell that day would've covered the tracks."

"What were they doing out here?" I looked around the clearing. "There's not much of interest to look at."

"Do you feel magic?"

I reached out with my senses and brushed against the remnants of something I couldn't quite identify. "There is some magic," I confirmed. "I'm not sure it has anything to do with the girls. They could have been drawn to the magic."

He nodded.

"I can't tell if it's the same magic I felt during the fire," I added.

"Perhaps we should ask the girls." His eyes were serious when they locked with mine. "I'd like to know if they saw anything strange in the days leading up to the fire."

"Like something they couldn't explain but didn't tell their parents about," I surmised.

"Yes."

"They're staying with their aunt in Hawthorne Hollow," I said. "We can go and talk to her. I can say we're checking in."

"We'll stop at a store and buy a few things for them, act as if we're concerned and want to make sure they're okay. That should be appropriate cover."

"What if they did see something?"

"Then we'll have to figure out what it is and go from there."

15
FIFTEEN

We went to the Rusty Cauldron. Scout was inside with Gunner, arguing with her boss, Rooster Tremaine.

"I don't see how you can say this is my fault," she complained, hands on her hips.

Gunner moved away from her and to the pool table. He wanted no part of this problem.

"You don't see how Marissa getting covered in the guts of a jackalope is your problem?" Rooster challenged.

"No, I do not," she replied primly. "It's not as if she doesn't know how things work at this point."

Marissa Martin poked her head out of the hallway that led to the bathrooms. She was unpleasant to the *n*th degree on a normal day. She looked as if she was ready to go nuclear today. She was related to Mrs. Little, and it wasn't difficult to imagine the two of them plotting like demented *Gossip Girl* characters as they chuckled their way to what they thought was triumph.

"Really?" She pointed to her face, which was covered with some sort of fur. "Really?" She pointed again, to her hair.

"Is that jackalope?" I asked, shaking my head. "I thought that was a hat. I'm actually glad it's an exploded animal and not a purposeful choice."

Marissa's eyes were glittery slits of hate. "Do you think you're funny?"

Was that a trick question? "I have it on good authority that I'm often quite hilarious," I replied blandly.

"Then you're being lied to," Marissa hissed. "As for you, I'm sick of this crap," she said to Scout. "I don't want to be sent on a job with her again. That's it. I'm done."

"You don't really get a say in that," Rooster said, feigning patience. "I dole out the assignments."

"Yes, and you keep sending me on jobs with her even though each and every time—*each and every time!*—I end up being thrown in stinky swamp water, having sprites detonated over my head. And that's not counting the time that jackal bit me."

"This is Michigan," Scout replied evenly. "We don't have jackals."

"Then what was that thing?"

"I think it was some sort of golem dog." Scout looked momentarily thoughtful. "If it hadn't been so intent on ripping out our throats it would've made a nice pet."

"I can't even." Marissa held up her hand to obliterate Scout's face. "No more. This is my line in the sand. I refuse to go on any more assignments with Scout."

"What's your solution to this conundrum?" Rooster asked. "Scout can't go out alone."

"Send her parents with her," Marissa growled. "They seem determined to spend as much time with her as possible." She pointed at Evan. "Send the freaking vampire with her. She never tortures him."

"There are different types of torture," Evan replied. "I'm fine going with Scout. Perhaps Marissa should do all of her assignments with Gunner. That might be a better twosome."

The look Gunner shot Evan could've melted iron. "Let's not be hasty."

Evan smirked. I'd heard numerous stories about Marissa trying to seduce Gunner and knew from where the discomfort originated.

"You have a bit of Aunt Tillie in you too," I said to Evan in a low voice.

"She does have a certain spark," he agreed. "Before this conversation continues, we're here for a reason. I need to know where Gretchen Whitcomb lives."

Rooster blinked several times before he shifted to look at Evan. "Why do you care about Gretchen? Has she done something?"

"She's the aunt of the two girls who were in that fire in Hemlock Cove," I volunteered. "We need to talk to the girls. She's their aunt. She's watching them because their parents still haven't woken up."

"Still?" Rooster looked concerned. "Were they burned? The news made it sound as if there were only minimal injuries."

"We don't know what's wrong with them," I admitted. "The doctors are baffled. The fire was magical in origin, and whatever is afflicting them has to be magical too. Evan and I were just at the inn. We found a set of footprints leading into the woods. They were child sized and had to have been there since before the fire."

"I'm not sure why that's important," Rooster said. "Do you think the kids had something to do with the fire?"

I wanted to say no. Believing two girls had a hand in a fire that had left their parents incapacitated was a hard thing to swallow. Unfortunately, I'd dealt with my fair share of evil teenagers. I held out my hands and shrugged. "They didn't seem evil. I didn't sense magic emanating from them, but I was distracted by the fire."

"What was different about the fire?" Scout asked.

I explained to them what happened, leaving them perplexed.

Gunner leaned on his pool cue. "There was nothing wrong with the roof?" he asked Evan.

"I'm not a structural engineer, but the roof was solid," Evan replied. "There were no weak spots. Nothing suggested the fire had burned through the roof."

Gunner rolled his neck. "Maybe we should head to Hemlock Cove and take a look around," he suggested to Scout. "You might be able to detect something with your pixie magic that Bay might not necessarily pick up."

"Are you just saying that because you want to be near The Overlook in time for dinner?" Scout challenged.

Gunner adopted an innocent face. "I hadn't even thought of that. If we are, though, why not have dinner with the Winchesters?"

Gunner's love of my mother's pot roast was legendary. "I'm sure they would love to see you for dinner," I assured them. "Landon and Aunt Tillie aren't talking to me, so you might make a nice distraction."

Gunner laughed. "Landon is whipped. There's no way he's not talking to you."

"He's mad." I looked down at my shoes. "Aunt Tillie is always mad about something, but she's mad too."

"Why?" Scout asked. She looked more curious than judgmental.

I had to tell them the second part of the story. When I got to the part about the monster on the bluff, explained how it was fuzzy but somehow rubbery looking at the same time, Rooster practically came off of his stool.

"I've heard stories about that thing for years," he said. "There have been stories about something that looks kind of like an orc running around between Hawthorne Hollow, Shadow Hills, and Hemlock Cove for years. A few deaths have been blamed on it."

I considered the information for several seconds, then shook my head. "I don't think that's right," I said. "I have never heard those stories."

"They were much more prevalent twenty years ago. You would've been a kid."

"I don't remember those stories either," Gunner argued. "My father is a police officer. I think I would've heard."

"Your father ate breakfast at the inn this morning and was there for the fight," I offered.

Gunner straightened. "With Marnie?"

"Ignore him," Scout said with a hand wave. "He keeps sticking his nose in his father's business, and they're about to come to blows. I've told him a million times to let it go. Marnie is cool, but he likes to give his father a hard time."

"If Marnie is going to be my new stepmother, I want to know about it," Gunner said. "What if her pot roast isn't as good as Winnie's?" He sniffed. "I'm just trying to be practical."

I turned away from him because I couldn't contain my laughter.

"I'll leave you to fight that out with your father," I said. "I want to talk to Grace and Hope. It's possible they were playing in the woods. There was nothing in the clearing that felt nefarious."

"It's also possible they stumbled upon something bad, and we need to know about it," Rooster said. "Hold on." He pulled up his phone and started typing. "The address is 12432 Crescent Street. That's on the east side of town."

Evan nodded. "If you two end up in Hemlock Cove, text me. I'm sure dinner at The Overlook this evening will be the stuff of legends."

"Now that you've mentioned it, I'm sure we'll have no choice but to attend," Scout said. "I wouldn't mind looking around the property for that inn. Keep in touch," she said to me.

"I will," I promised. "I'm hoping this visit is nothing to worry about."

"It's better to know either way."

WE STOPPED AT A STORE TO BUY a few gifts for the girls. I selected flavored hot chocolate and pretty mugs, as well as a few books. I was still nervous when we parked in front of Gretchen's house.

"How do I explain who you are?" I asked.

"Just say I'm going back to Hemlock Cove with you, and you decided to stop by," he said. "Don't do that twitchy thing you do when you get nervous because you're lying."

"I don't do a twitchy thing," I muttered as I shoved open the door. "I'm not twitchy."

"You're not calm when you lie. That's why everyone thinks you're constipated."

"Just ... stop talking."

Gretchen answered the door. She wiped her hands on her apron as she registered us. "Bay?" she questioned. "I met you at the hospital."

"That's me." I flashed a smile I didn't feel—now I was suddenly worried I was going to be twitchy. I held up the shopping bag. "I was here to pick up my friend Evan—his car is in the shop—and decided to stop in and see the girls. They've been on my mind."

Gretchen looked momentarily sad. "It's hard for them. They keep asking about their parents, but I don't know what to tell them. The doctors have no idea what's going on. They say there's no reason to panic yet."

"Then let's not panic. Hopefully, they'll wake up tomorrow."

"That would be nice." Gretchen moved away from the door and motioned for us to follow her. "They're in the den. I'm sure they'll be happy to see you. They've been talking nonstop about the angel who saved them."

My cheeks colored. "I'm no angel."

"No? From where I stand you are. You and your husband rescued them."

"Anyone would've done it."

"That's not even remotely true." Gretchen led us into the den. "Hey, girls, look who's here to see you."

Grace hopped to her feet and raced to me. "Have you seen our parents? Have you woken them up?"

She knocked the wind out of me with her hug. I tried to return it with as much gusto as possible. "I haven't seen your parents. I know they're getting the best possible care, though. They're going to be okay."

The look Evan shot me read "you shouldn't have said that last part." I already knew that.

Hope was a bit less exuberant with her hug but still earnest. "They won't let us see them," she whispered. "I'm afraid they're dead."

"They're not," I assured her. "I promise."

"You're an angel, so you have to tell the truth, right?"

"I'm not an angel." I was uncomfortable with them saying that. "I'm a woman."

"You're way more than that," Grace said. "Way more."

"I'll leave you to visit and go finish with the dishes," Gretchen said. "You can give the girls their gifts and have a nice chat." She looked as if she needed a break, so I nodded.

I waited until she was gone to hand over the shopping bag. "Just a few things," I said as the girls squealed over the unicorn mugs.

"I love marshmallows," Hope said as she clutched the bag of snowflake-shaped marshmallows to her chest. "We're going to make this before bed tonight."

"That sounds fun." I smiled and glanced at the door. Gretchen wasn't there, so I pushed forward. "I was at the inn a bit ago. There's some damage, but I don't think it's bad enough for the entire inn to have to be torn down and rebuilt. Your parents will be able to fix it up."

"I wish they wouldn't," Grace said. She was focused on her mug, but her forehead had puckered in concentration. "That's a bad place."

I shifted on my chair. "What's bad about it?"

"Ghosts," Hope said.

"You've seen ghosts?" I tried to keep my voice neutral. "What kind of ghosts?"

"What other kind are there?" Grace asked.

Tricky question. "I was just wondering if the ghosts looked like your parents, or if they looked like Casper." My smile felt like the constipated one from this morning, and I immediately wiped my face.

"We've never seen them," Grace replied. "We just hear them, and it's kind of like when you see something out of the corner of your eye. It's there, but it's gone so fast."

"I know what you're talking about." I looked to the door again. Still no Gretchen. "Do you think the ghosts started the fire?"

Evan sent me a nod to tell me it was the right question.

"They told us bad things were going to happen," Hope whispered. "They told us to run when the fire started. We were trying to get out when we heard them outside. We were too tired to go, so we hid."

"And almost died," Grace added.

"The important thing is that you didn't die," I assured them. "You're both good, and your parents are going to be good." I rubbed my hands over the arms of the chair. "Just one more thing and then we have to go."

"Are you going to check on my mom and dad?" Grace asked.

"Of course."

"What's the thing?"

"Did you ever see anything else in the woods around the inn?" I asked. "Not a ghost, but something you might see in a scary movie."

The girls exchanged looks.

"No," Grace said, averting her eyes. "We just heard the ghosts."

I wanted to press her, but Gretchen picked that moment to return. "Everything okay?"

"Everything is fine," I assured her as we stood. "The girls have made me promise to check on Frank and Alice, so we should be going."

"Thank you so much for stopping by. I know the girls appreciated it."

"It was no bother," I said. "I'm sure we'll be back."

I waited until we were in my car to speak. "That wasn't maliciousness," I said. "She was lying, but not because she wanted to mislead us."

"She's afraid," Evan said. "They saw something, and they're afraid."

"Aunt Tillie's monster?"

"Bay, I know she drives you crazy, but there's one thing you have to keep in mind when it comes to Tillie. No matter what, she always has your best interests at heart. Her family is the most important thing to her. She loves you. If she's keeping secrets, maybe there's a reason."

"The problem is, she keeps secrets about her still, and pot field, and wine. It's hard to gauge what is and isn't important to her."

"That's not true. Just give her the benefit of the doubt."

"You really are the minion with the mostest," I teased. "As for those girls, they've seen something, but forcing them to admit it in front of Gretchen won't get us anywhere."

"Well start thinking, because now we have to ensure that Frank and Alice wake up. You promised."

"Yeah, that was stupid."

"Not if you can follow through."

16
SIXTEEN

E van looked distinctly uncomfortable as we entered the hospital.

"What's wrong?" I asked him as I tugged off my gloves.

"Why do you think something is wrong?" he asked.

I shrugged. "You're acting as if you want to run right back out the door. Are you afraid of hospitals or something?"

He scoffed at the notion. "I might not like hospitals. I wasn't all that fond of them before the whole vampire thing. Now, though..." He leveled his gaze on me. "I have these dreams about being transported to a hospital after a job for some reason, and when they poke and prod me, they find out I'm not human and want to experiment on me."

"I didn't realize vampires dreamed. Heck, I didn't even know you slept."

"Everyone needs restorative sleep, Bay. I don't need it as much as a human, or a normal vampire, but I still sleep several hours every night."

I pursed my lips. "I don't think you have to worry about them trying to experiment on you today. Just act normal."

We stopped at the front desk, which was manned by the same receptionist from the day before. Recognition sparked in her eyes when I asked if it was okay to go up to the fifth floor to see the Milligans. Her gaze stuck on Evan.

"What happened to the hot FBI agent?" she asked, sounding almost disappointed.

"He's working in Hemlock Cove today," I replied. It wasn't a lie. It wasn't the whole truth either. "This is my friend Evan. We visited Grace and Hope, and they asked us to check in on their parents. I was hoping that wouldn't be a problem."

"Your friend?" She looked Evan up and down. "Which are you friendliest with?" she asked.

"I'm not sure I understand the question." I understood the question. I just wanted to hear her say it.

"They're both very attractive. You must be magic to have both of them as 'friends.'" She drew air quotes with her fingers.

I glanced at Evan, who appeared ready to burst out laughing, then sighed. "I'm married to the hot FBI agent."

The receptionist's face fell.

"He really is just a friend." I gestured to Evan. "You might have a shot. I'll leave you two to discuss it while I head upstairs to see the Milligans. If that's okay."

The receptionist perked up. "That's a great idea."

I started toward the elevator without looking over my shoulder. I heard the frustration in Evan's voice when he called out to me. "Bay, I thought you wanted me with you. You know, moral support."

"I'm okay," I called back. "I can handle seeing them without you."

"Bay." There was an edge to Evan's tone.

"I'll see you up there when you're done."

"More and more like Tillie each passing day," he hissed to my retreating form.

The fact that I was smiling when the elevator door closed was enough to tell me he was right ... and I was fine with it.

Mostly.

Dr. Wooten was on the fifth floor. He looked up when I said his name and offered a weary smile. The lines around his eyes were more pronounced than they had been only twenty-four hours earlier.

"I take your expression to mean you don't have good news," I said.

Wooten held out his hands. "I thought Agent Michaels and Chief Davenport were coming."

My stomach did a little flip. "I'm here on my own. I was in Hawthorne Hollow seeing the girls, and they made me promise to check on their parents."

That was as good an explanation as anything, I told myself. If Wooten believed I was enough of a sap, he would fall for the story without questioning it.

"You're very sweet." He patted my shoulder. "It's obvious you have a good heart."

"The girls are worried about their parents. Shouldn't they have woken up by now?"

"Yes." Wooten bobbed his head. "The fact that they haven't is a mystery." He gestured to the couches. "I was going to go over this information with Agent Michaels and Chief Davenport but I'm sure you can share it with them. I'm going to head home and get some sleep. I've been on for almost thirty-six hours."

I felt sorry for him. He didn't want to abandon the Milligans, but he was coming up empty at every turn. "I can tell them," I promised. I left out the fact that they weren't speaking to me. That would be smoothed over before dinner.

At least I hoped it would.

"We've been running a lot of tests." Wooten pulled out his phone. "We've done everything we can think of. We've run heart tests. Those came up fine. We've run tests for brain activity. Those seem normal."

"Does that mean they're dreaming?" I wasn't certain why I asked, but it felt important.

Wooten arched an eyebrow. "I believe so. They make faces. They seem agitated. They're in there, they just won't wake up."

"Could it be poison of some sort?" I asked.

"We've run numerous toxicology tests. Nothing out of the ordinary. Frank is on high blood pressure medication, but that wouldn't cause this."

I rubbed the back of my neck. "The whole thing is very odd."

"We've tried numerous medications. We've tried outside stimuli. Nothing has worked."

His tone wasn't positive. "What are our options?"

"We're calling in specialists from Detroit. They'll conduct their own tests."

"Your tone tells me you don't think that's going to work."

"I'm just afraid that we're dealing with something that's slipped past all of us, and if we wait too long, we're going to lose them."

I looked toward Alice's room. "The girls are okay with their aunt for now. I can tell she's afraid."

"It's the not knowing," Wooten said. "That rocks people in ways they can never get over."

I agreed. I was about to say something else but was distracted as the door to Alice's room opened to allow a solitary figure to exit.

Joanie Dunne was fixated on a point in front of her and didn't look in our direction. Wooten was still focused on our previous conversation and hadn't noticed the way my body had gone ramrod straight.

"What is she doing here?" I blurted with all of the finesse of a Kardashian trying to pretend she wasn't looking for a camera.

Wooten looked in the direction I was staring. "That's Joanie Dunne. She's best friends with Alice. We told her to go in and talk to her. We were hoping the stimulus might help."

"They're best friends?"

"That's what Joanie said." Wooten fixed me with a peculiar look. "Do you have reason to believe otherwise?"

I couldn't answer that without putting myself at risk. "I guess they could be best friends. I know Joanie through a friend in Hawthorne Hollow, and Alice through the inn network in Hemlock Cove. I didn't know they knew each other."

"Ah." Wooten nodded knowingly. "Isn't it strange when those things happen?"

"Very strange," I confirmed.

"She was in there about thirty minutes," Wooten said. "Hopefully, she said a few things that will jog Alice back to reality."

"I can go in and check for you," I offered. "I'll sit with Alice for a bit. I have an hour or so before I have to head back to Hemlock Cove."

"I don't want you to get your hopes up," Wooten cautioned. "The odds of Alice waking up out of the blue are slim. I think it's going to take outside intervention at this point. I just don't know what sort will work."

"I'm sure you'll figure it out."

"I certainly hope so. I don't want those children to lose their parents, especially to something that we can't figure out. Medical mysteries still occur, but not like they did fifty years ago. I can't help feeling that we should already have the answers."

I wanted to ease his burden, but there was no way I could do that without casting a spotlight on myself. "You can only do what you can," I assured him. "I'm sure everything will work out."

"I certainly hope so. The alternative is heart breaking."

It was also terrifying on a whole other level. "It will be fine. Have faith."

"I'm trying. It's not as easy as I'd like."

I TALKED TO WOOTEN FOR A FEW MORE MINUTES and then excused myself to visit Alice. The first thing I did upon entering her room was look around. Whatever story Joanie had spun for Wooten was false. She had a reason for being in this room, but it wasn't friendship.

Evan walked into the room right behind me. I felt disapproval from five feet away without meeting his gaze.

"I'll never forgive you for that," he announced. "That was the sort of maneuver Scout would pull."

I didn't have time for games. "Do whatever you think is best."

Evan immediately picked up on my dour attitude. "What is it?"

"Joanie was here."

"Who is Joanie?"

"Joanie is Kevin Dunne's wife. She was the one who knew her husband was having multiple affairs and melted down when I tried to talk to her at the Shadow Hills festival a few weeks ago."

"Right." Evan bobbed his head. "Forgot all about her. Why was she here?"

"Dr. Wooten said she introduced herself as Alice's best friend."

"I'm guessing you don't believe that."

I shook my head. "I was in Shadow Hills with Stormy yesterday. I saw her. Joanie did not look happy to see me."

"And now she's visiting Alice." Evan looked at the bed. Alice, no longer with the tube going to her nose, was breathing easily. She looked peaceful, but the room felt stagnant and unfriendly. "Why would she be here, Bay?"

I didn't have an answer. "I don't know, but something doesn't feel right."

We started snooping around the room, Evan taking the right side and me the left. There was a pitcher of water on the nightstand. The angle it had been placed looked odd. On a whim, I reached for it ... and found the handle damp.

"Here's something," I announced.

Evan looked over at me. "Water?"

"The handle is wet."

"Well, water is wet."

"That's the Scout in you," I shot back, causing him to grin.

He crossed over to me. "I don't understand why you're worked up about water, Bay. It's not as if she's drinking it." He inclined his head to Alice, who was still out cold in the bed.

"Exactly, so why would the handle of the pitcher be wet?" I pulled off the lid and peered inside. The liquid was clear.

The second the contents were unmasked, Evan snatched the pitcher from me and jerked it out of my reach.

"Hey!" I gave him a dirty look. "What the hell?"

"You don't smell that?" His forehead creased. "How can you not smell that?"

I inhaled deeply. "I don't smell anything other than the same old sanitary hospital smell."

"This is poison! Smell it." Evan carefully lifted the pitcher, and I obediently sniffed again. This time I picked up a faint musty odor.

"You smelled that when I didn't pick it up the first time?" I challenged.

"I'm a vampire. I can pick up a single droplet of blood from a mile away."

I watched as Evan carried the pitcher to the bathroom. I tried to stop him before he dumped it, but it was too late.

"We needed that as evidence," I complained, frowning when a bit of smoke arose from the drain. "What was it?"

"I'm not certain. It wasn't straight hemlock. There was something else in it."

I braced my hand on the door frame as I debated what we were supposed to do. "It had to be Joanie."

"That's my guess," Evan agreed. "You never mentioned her being magical."

"She wasn't. At least not the first time I met her." I thought of our more recent interaction. "And I didn't go to her yesterday. I chickened out. I intended to talk to her but spoke with her daughter instead."

"Did she see you?"

"In Shadow Hills? Yeah."

"Today. Did she see you today?"

I shook my head. "She was focused on getting to the elevator. She didn't even look at me."

"You didn't sense anything magical about her?"

"No, but I wasn't that close."

"Well, I agree that it had to be her, but there must be magic involved. That concoction in the pitcher was deadly. I can tell you that. Call Landon and tell him what we found."

I made a face. "Or I could text him and tell him. He's mad at me. I don't want him to send me to voicemail."

"I very much doubt he will."

"You don't know. He's a baby when he's crabby."

"And you're a baby when he's crabby," Evan said.

"I'm not a baby."

He arched an eyebrow.

"I'm not," I insisted. "I would rather text him."

"And then what?"

"We have to confront Joanie."

"If she's poisoning people she may have had some sort of psychotic break. We should check on her daughter."

"And if she's a danger?"

"You'll have to call in Landon and Terry. We have no other option."

17
SEVENTEEN

I let Evan drive, even though I had no idea if he was competent behind the wheel. I had a call to make and needed to concentrate on that.

Landon didn't answer. I tried twice more, with the same result.

"Well, that is immature," I complained as I stared at my phone.

"Landon isn't answering?" Evan looked surprised.

"He's punishing me."

"Or he's doing something else and can't answer."

"He always answers."

"You rarely have to call him for anything important because you're always with him," Evan replied pragmatically. "He's probably doing something and can't answer right now."

"Why are you taking his side?" I demanded. "He's being a baby."

"I very much doubt that he wouldn't answer his phone, no matter how angry he is with you. You're still the thing he loves most in this world, and you find trouble on a regular basis. He wouldn't ignore that."

He had a point. Still, I was annoyed. "Fine. I'll go above his head." I held my breath as I hit Chief Terry's name in my phone.

He answered on the third ring and sounded annoyed. "Do you need something, Bay?"

"You're not still mad at me, are you?" I huffed.

"If you need me to stop by the newspaper later because you've been having trouble with vandals, I'll certainly find the time," Chief Terry said.

My frown grew deeper. "I didn't say anything about vandals." That's when it hit me. "You're talking about vandals because somebody is there and you can't speak in front of them," I said.

"That's it exactly," Chief Terry said. "I can be at your office in an hour or so. I figure I'll be done with the state police then."

The state police? Why would they be in Hemlock Cove?

"I'm not in Hemlock Cove," I replied. "I'm with Evan. We're going to Shadow Hills. We found something in Alice Milligan's room today but obviously we can't talk now."

"That doesn't sound likely," Chief Terry confirmed. "I can be there in an hour."

His ability to be free in an hour wasn't helpful. "Is Landon caught up in the same thing?" I asked.

"Yup. Yup. I can manage that."

"I'll call you when we're finished in Shadow Hills. Or I'll give you a heads-up in an hour."

He hesitated. "Just wait at your office," he said.

"Yeah, we're already on the road. I'm not waiting."

"Bay—"

"Do what you have to do," I insisted. "Call me when you're finished."

"Fine." Chief Terry sounded agitated. "I'll call you when I'm on my way."

Evan's eyes were on the road, but I could read his worry when he tightened his grip on the wheel. "I heard."

"You do have that superhuman hearing."

"Why would the state police be bothering them?"

"It's possible the hospital contacted them. The other possibility is Brad Childs."

Evan's forehead creased. "The warden?"

"Former warden. He's been hanging around."

"Why?"

"He has figured out I'm magical."

"And he's blackmailing you?" A muscle worked in Evan's cheek as he stared forward. "I'll handle him."

"Don't." I shook my head. "That's not the smart way to deal with this."

"He's threatening you, Bay."

"He doesn't understand," I clarified. "He thinks I can just wave my hand and make anything happen. He doesn't understand there are limitations."

"But he is threatening you," Evan insisted.

"He has made a few threats," I confirmed. "I don't think he'll follow through."

"Why not?"

"He believes I'm his only chance of getting his job back. He thinks I can snap my fingers and make what happened to him go away. It's frustrating and sad, but I can't help him."

"What if he gets to a point where he blows up and outs you because he has no other move?"

"I've thought about it." I leaned back in my seat. "How will it play out if a disgraced warden, a man who was so crappy at his job there was a prison break, starts throwing around accusations at one of the people who helped capture most of the escaped prisoners?"

"It'll look like sour grapes," Evan responded. "But people will ask questions about how you managed to bring in so many prisoners."

"I'm from Hemlock Cove. What if I just embrace the witch thing and keep saying I'm a witch, but act goofy?"

"You mean act like Twila," he surmised.

"Pretty much," I confirmed.

Evan focused on the road as I directed him to Joanie's house. "I hate to say it, Bay, but that's the best possible way for you to play this. Childs will end up looking like an idiot."

"That's another worry," I said. "What happens if we push him too far? What happens if he loses everything and realizes he's not getting his job back? He strikes me as the sort of man who will lose his tenuous grasp on reality."

"So what are you going to do?"

"I keep hoping he'll lose interest and go away."

"Do you really think he will?"

"At first, I thought it was a legitimate possibility. Not so much now."

"Maybe you should let me talk to him," Evan suggested. "I can show him things. I can put on a display. Maybe if he realizes the paranormal world isn't as bright and shiny as he thinks, he'll back off."

"Doesn't he already know that?" I challenged. "He's one of the few people who realizes that the prisoners were being controlled magically."

"But he also saw you swoop in and win the day," Evan pointed out. "You secured a happy ending. Maybe he needs to realize there's no happy ending for him."

I pointed at Joanie's house. "For now, let's deal with her."

Evan nodded. "How do you want to do this?"

"I thought I would be sly."

"And when that fails?"

"I figured I would just wing it."

"Good plan."

NOBODY ANSWERED THE DOOR. THERE WAS A CAR IN THE driveway. If it was one of the kids, I didn't want to drag them into this. If it was Joanie, I had no intention of letting her hide.

I slid my eyes to Evan, who leapt to the roof hanging over the porch. He was gone a few seconds before returning.

"She's in the kitchen at the back of the house," he said. "She's sitting at the kitchen table drinking tea."

"Does she look angry?"

"She looks broken down."

My heart hurt for Joanie, but I was at my wit's end with her. "Let's get this over with," I said. "She can't go around poisoning people."

"I still haven't figured out why she poisoned Alice Milligan."

"I'm trying to work that out too," I admitted.

We circled the house, not bothering to hide our approach. In a town the size of Shadow Hills, it was a waste of time. People would see us, and it would be obvious that we were sticking our noses in business that wasn't ours. Trying to hide ourselves would only backfire.

Once we reached the patio, I moved closer to the windows. Joanie was at the kitchen table, just as Evan said. I raised my hand to knock on the door and then thought better of it. I pulsed a bit of magic into the handle to open it even though it was locked, and pushed my way in.

"Normally, I'd apologize for behavior like this," I noted. "But not today."

Joanie gave me a dull look. "What do you want? I didn't invite you in." Her voice was rough, and she was so pale I wondered if she'd finally sabotaged her immune system to the point of no return.

"Alice Milligan didn't invite you into her room at the hospital," I said.

"Smooth," Evan noted. "Way to be sly."

"Hey, I gave it a good shot." I never moved my eyes from Joanie. "We know you tried to poison Alice."

"Tried?"

"We found the pitcher. Alice is unconscious. It's not as if people are filling glasses of water for her right now."

"I thought when she woke up. That's supposed to happen any day now."

"Aren't you the one keeping her asleep?" I challenged.

Joanie screwed up her face. "Why would I?"

"Why would you poison her?"

"She's trying to break up my marriage. She has it coming."

I was surprised. "Why do you think she's having an affair with Kevin?" I asked. "Other than the obvious answer that he'll stick his little Kevin in anyone and tell you he has a glandular problem."

"They've been seen together," Joanie said tiredly. "He's been at her inn. Twice. I know what they were doing. I always know what he's doing."

She was digging her fingernails into her palms so deeply I was almost certain there were small flashes of blood under the nails.

"She is wrapped really tight right now," Evan warned.

"I'm not sorry." There was a distance to the way Joanie was holding herself. It was almost as if she was somehow separate from the whole thing, looking back on us as if we were part of a past that she didn't want to lay claim to. "She should learn to stay away from other people's husbands."

"Maybe your husband should learn to keep it in his pants," Evan suggested. He edged around the room, positioning himself directly in front of Joanie. She had no choice but to look at him. There was no recognition on her. "You know one person can't steal someone from another person."

"I know that she's married and should stay away from other people who are married."

Evan slid his eyes to me. They were bubbling with turmoil. I wanted to ask him what he was seeing but decided to handle things in the only way I knew how. That meant honesty.

"Alice Milligan was not having an affair with Kevin," I said.

"He was there!"

"Yes, because he and his development group are trying to buy inns in Hemlock Cove. The Milligans rejected his offer."

"Did Kevin tell you that?" Joanie let loose a hollow laugh. "You can't believe him. He lies. He always lies."

"I'm sure he does, but this time I think he's telling the truth. He told me weeks ago that they're determined to buy inns. They approached the Milligans and were told no. That's why he was there. He had no intention of backing down. He told me and offered to buy my family's inn."

"No!" Joanie slammed her hand down on the tabletop. "They were together. He lies."

I took a step toward her, determined to unclench her hand because I could see the blood had started to drip from her palm. Evan stopped me.

"Don't touch her," he ordered. His grip on my wrist was strong as he nudged me back.

I was confused. "She's in distress. We need to get her to the hospital."

"It's too late for that." Evan took a step back from Joanie, using himself as a barrier to keep me back. "She's not human any longer, Bay."

My initial instinct was to laugh, but he was deadly serious. "Evan, she's human. I've talked to her before." I looked at Joanie, determined to prove it, but when the woman lifted her eyes to me, they were black. "Oh, crap!"

Evan wrapped his arm around my waist and pulled me further from Joanie. "Don't let her touch you."

"What is she?" I was breathless as I watched Joanie's face grow paler. Her hair grew duller, and her eyes lost all semblance of humanness. Her fingernails were even worse. They'd grown to the size of claws during our discussion.

"She's a banshee," Evan replied.

I'd never seen one this close. "How?"

"Banshees are former humans," he replied. "They're usually transformed by a great loss. Death is normally the trigger. In this case, I'm guessing it was the loss of her faith. She let the bitterness get a foothold and now, well, she's no longer the person she used to be."

Joanie got to her feet, forcing Evan to shove me back again. "I don't want to deal with you people," she announced as she started for the back door.

"What the hell?" I tried to give chase, but Evan held me in place. "Where are you going?" I yelled at Joanie's back.

"Does it matter?" Joanie lifted one eyebrow. She'd gone from sullen and sickly to frighteningly beautiful. "I know what needs to be done."

"Joanie, you need to stop ... whatever this is. You need to sit down and take a breath. You need to..." What? What did she need to do? I was in way over my head. "Evan, I don't know what to do."

"Just stay back." He took a tentative step toward Joanie, but when she turned her black eyes on him, I knew that there was no getting her back. At least not without a plan.

Joanie opened her mouth and emitted a terrible scream. The windows rattled before several of them shattered. The glass blew inward, and Evan clambered on top of me to protect my face.

"Get your head down!" he ordered.

The glass settled over us, and when silence stretched more than a few seconds I risked lifting my chin.

"Where did she go?" I demanded, looking around.

The door was open. Evan pointed. "She took off."

"Should we go after her?"

"We're not in a position to go after her until we figure out what we're going to do." He sat up and looked around. "We're going to have to explain this."

I was already resigned to that and pulled out my phone. I had tiny cuts on my exposed skin. "I'll call Hunter."

"And I'll call Landon." Evan retrieved his phone.

I made a face. "Why are you calling him?"

"We need help coming up with a story. The neighbors have likely already called the police. We need to get ahead of this. Right now."

He was right. "I don't look my best right now, Evan. I want to be pretty when I see Landon."

Evan rolled his eyes. "Witches," he muttered. "Call Hunter. We don't have much time. We also need to figure out what happened to the girl in this house. I'm hoping she's just out."

My stomach did a tight roll. "You don't think she killed Katie?"

18

EIGHTEEN

Hunter was understandably flummoxed when he walked into the Dunne house.

"What in the hell?" He dragged a hand through his hair and looked between Evan and me. "What did you do?"

"It wasn't me," Evan replied.

I scorched him with a dirty look. "That is totally something Aunt Tillie would do. You are spending way too much time with her."

He shrugged. "Survival of the fittest, baby."

"Now you're on my list."

His smile was easy. "You're nowhere near as terrifying as Tillie."

"Ugh." When I turned back to Hunter, I found him watching me with an incredulous look. "Sorry. You want to know what happened here."

"I want to know what you did," Hunter growled.

"Wait! Wait!" A harried female voice came from the back door and Stormy appeared in the opening. "Whatever it is, I did it. Don't blame Bay."

I had to hold back a sigh. It was so Stormy to be a martyr for the cause. "She wasn't even here," I said to Hunter.

He shook his head as he glared at his fiancée. "Don't take credit for something you didn't do. This is on them." He waved his hand at Evan and me. "I want to know what we're dealing with here. Then I'm going to figure out a way to keep you out of jail."

"We didn't do this," I assured him. "It was Joanie."

"Joanie broke every window in her own house?" Hunter was dubious. "Why do I have trouble believing that?"

"You're probably going to have trouble believing the story regardless." Before I could tell him what happened, another figure appeared in the doorway. I inadvertently let out a little squeak when Landon stepped into the wrecked kitchen. "Hey, buddy," I said lamely.

Landon lifted one eyebrow. "*Buddy?*"

"Your wife completely destroyed this house," Hunter said.

"It wasn't me," I protested.

"It definitely wasn't me," Evan said.

Landon gave the vampire a "whatever" look and took a step toward me. The glass on the floor crunched under his boots. "Are you okay?" He looked me over, his expression carefully neutral.

"I'm fine," I said automatically. I couldn't even feel the tiny cuts now.

"She's injured," Evan countered. "The glass flew around us like we were in a snow globe. She has a million little cuts. You really should be nicer to her," he admonished Hunter.

Stormy checked my arms. "You do have a lot of little cuts."

That prodded Landon into moving closer. He took my wrists and held out my arms for a better look, frowning when he saw the marks. "I'm no longer mad," he announced. Then he pulled me in for a crushing hug. It knocked the breath out of me, and I leaned into him. It wasn't just relief; it was the need for tactile contact. Evan was a good partner, but it wasn't the same as being with Landon.

Landon's hand cradled the back of my head. After exhaling a shaky breath, he pulled back and stared into my eyes. "Don't get up in the middle of the night and go looking for a monster without telling me again."

I nodded. "I'll try my best."

"No, you'll wake me up." He was firm. "I don't know what I could've done to help you, but I would've liked having the option. I don't want to ever wake up and wonder where you are."

I swallowed hard at his earnestness. "Okay. I really am sorry."

"You're going to have to make up with Terry on your own."

I wasn't looking forward to that, but I wasn't that worried. "He'll forgive me."

"He always does." Landon kissed my forehead. "Tell me what happened. If you didn't do this, who did."

"Joanie Dunne."

"Joanie Dunne destroyed her own kitchen?" Landon was as dubious as Hunter.

"I'm not making it up."

"She's right," Evan confirmed. "When we got here, Joanie was ... not herself."

"Why did you come here in the first place?" Landon asked. "I knew when you called Terry that something was up, but with the state police breathing down our necks..."

"Why were the state police there?"

"Acting on an anonymous tip regarding the fire," Landon replied. "I can't be certain who called in the tip, but they asked a lot of questions about why we ran into the building."

"What did you tell them?" I asked.

"I said you were worried about the girls and ran in before I could stop you, so I had no choice but to follow," Landon replied. "If they question you, stick to that story. Say you can't remember the details all that well because the smoke and fire freaked you out, but that you were afraid for the girls."

That wasn't all that far from what really happened. "I can sell that."

"Just don't do that blinky thing you do when you lie."

"I don't do a blinky thing." Hunter and Evan grinned. "I don't," I insisted.

"I don't really care about the blinky thing," Hunter said. "I do care about this mess. What happened here?"

"It started in Hawthorne Hollow. We went to see the girls."

"Actually, it started at the Blue Moon Inn," Evan corrected. "We were on the roof and saw footprints leading into the woods."

"You were on the roof?" Landon blanched.

"Evan was with me," I quickly added.

"I watched her," Evan confirmed. "Besides, there's nothing wrong with the roof. The structure is still sound."

Genuine puzzlement flooded Landon's features. "How is that possible? We saw flames shooting through the roof."

"I only know that the structure is fine," Evan said. "It didn't even look burned."

"That is just all kinds of freaky," Landon muttered.

"From our vantage point on the roof, we saw footprints leading into the woods," Evan explained. "The prints were old and crusted over, suggesting they'd been there since before the fire. We followed them into a clearing, and then realized they were smaller than those of an adult."

"Meaning it was the girls," Landon surmised. "Do you think they set the fire?"

I shook my head. "Not even a little. I think they know more than they're letting on. We visited them. We brought gifts. The girls said they were afraid but wouldn't tell us what they were afraid of."

"You think it's whoever set the fire," Hunter guessed.

"The fire was magical in origin and the girls saw something magical in the woods," I replied. "I also think the girls realize the fire wasn't natural. They said they'd been hearing voices. They were warning them that something bad was going to happen. They think it was ghosts."

"What do you think it was?"

I shrugged. "I only know the girls were frightened. They asked us to check on their parents, so we went to the hospital. That's when I saw Joanie."

Landon's shoulders jolted. "You saw Joanie at the hospital?"

"She was coming out of Alice's room," I confirmed. "She told Dr. Wooten that she was Alice's best friend."

"That was a lie." Landon shot a look to Hunter, who nodded.

"We went into the room and looked around. The only thing of interest was a pitcher of what we thought was water. It was wet, indicating someone had recently held it. Evan took the pitcher from me and dumped it down the drain. It smoked."

"Hemlock," Evan added. "I could smell it. Bay couldn't at first, but she picked up a faint whiff when I pointed it out."

"So Joanie poisoned Alice's water?" Hunter said. "Why would she do that? What good would it do? She's unconscious. It's not as if she's going to suddenly wake up and reach right for the water."

"I'm not sure Joanie is thinking clearly," Evan replied. "She seems ... out of it."

"Now we're getting to the part of the story that I care about," Hunter said. "I'm sure you called Terry about the poison."

"We did, but he told me to handle it myself," I acknowledged.

Landon made a face. "He did not. I was in the room with him when he got the call. He was trying to tell you not to do anything until we were done."

"That's not what I heard."

Landon shot me a stern look. "You are really too much sometimes."

I beamed at him, which caused him to shake his head. "We came here to confront Joanie. She didn't answer the door, so we came around back."

"And just let yourselves in?" Hunter pressed.

That felt like a "gotcha" question. "She was sitting at the table, and I swore she motioned for us to come in."

Evan ducked his head, likely to hide his smile.

Landon narrowed his eyes. "You guys had better work on your delivery, because nobody is going to believe that."

"We'll practice," I promised. "Anyway, we came in and confronted her. She didn't deny trying to poison Alice. She thought Kevin was having an affair with her. She knew that Kevin had been to the Blue Moon twice in the past few weeks. She assumed they were sleeping together."

Realization dawned on Landon. "I assume you told her that Kevin isn't having an affair with Alice."

"She didn't believe me. Then she turned into a banshee."

It was as if all of the air had been sucked out of the room.

"What?" Hunter asked.

"She looked strange when we arrived," Evan said. "She was pale. She was digging her fingernails into her palms hard enough to draw blood."

"Then her eyes turned black," I added.

"Sounds lovely." Landon moved his hand to my shoulder and squeezed. "Did she hurt you?"

"She didn't seem all that interested in me," I said.

"Isn't that weird?" Landon asked. "Three weeks ago, she assumed you were sleeping with her husband."

"But then she realized I wasn't."

"But you're still a danger to her. She realizes you're magical."

"She has to at least suspect it," Evan said. "She heard us talking."

"What's a banshee?" Hunter asked. He was new to the paranormal game.

"It's a screechy woman," Landon replied.

I sent him a stern look.

"Am I wrong?" Landon demanded.

"It's a traumatized woman."

"Who screeches," Evan added. "That's the deal with banshees. They screech. That's how the windows broke."

"She did this by screeching?" Hunter looked around. "That's terrifying."

"Be nice to Stormy and you won't have to worry about her getting all traumatized and screeching at you," Evan said matter-of-factly.

"I'll take that under advisement." Evan's tone was dry. "Is she coming back here? What about Kevin? Is he in danger?"

"Kevin is definitely in danger," I said. "He's the reason she turned. We have to track him down and..." And what?

"Are we supposed to tell him the truth, Bay?" Landon looked perplexed. "That won't go over well."

"Do you see another option? How else do we explain this?"

"We tell him that you came here to question Joanie about her visit to Alice and she freaked out and broke the windows in her haste to escape," Hunter replied. "We'll say she's unbalanced, and that we fear for him and Katie. We want to move him to another location."

"Like a safe house?"

Hunter nodded, his eyes going to Landon. "Do you know of any safe houses we can move them to?"

"I can arrange that," Landon confirmed. "We're going to have to put out an alert for her. Are we going to say she's wanted for attempted murder?" He didn't look comfortable with the suggestion.

"What else can we do?" I asked in a soft voice.

Landon rolled his neck. "It's our only option. My question is, can we save her? Can we make her return from being a banshee?"

I looked at Evan. "This is your area of expertise."

"I've only crossed paths with a few banshees," he said. "I've never heard of one being turned back. You might want to talk to Tillie."

Now it was my turn to make a face. "I'm mad at her. She hasn't owned up to hanging out with a monster. I got in trouble, but she's the one doing crappy stuff."

"You did some crappy stuff too, Bay," Landon argued. "Besides, you got in trouble because people love you. There's a difference. Aunt Tillie can't avoid answering your questions forever."

"I would try to bring her in on this," Evan said. "She knows more than she's letting on. I'll hit up my team at the Rusty Cauldron. You can put Kevin and Katie in a safe house so Joanie can't find them. I think that's all we can do tonight."

It didn't feel like enough. "We should put someone on Alice's room at the hospital."

"I can get people stationed at the hospital," Landon said. "But they won't be able to fight Joanie off if she shows up."

"Maybe just seeing them will be enough."

"And maybe Joanie's rage will be focused where it should've always been focused going forward," Evan said. "She'll be obsessed with finding Kevin and doling out her revenge. That will at least keep her busy."

"Well, we have a semblance of a plan," Hunter said. "Stormy, I need you and Bay to go upstairs and pack a bag for Katie. I'll send a unit to the festival to collect her, and then we'll send someone to get Kevin at his office. They can't come back here."

"Agreed," Landon said. "Kevin will fight us. He won't understand that we're trying to protect him. As much as I hate the guy, we need to keep him safe for Katie's sake. She's our primary concern now."

19
NINETEEN

Landon sent Evan and me back to Hemlock Cove. He didn't want us around when they started spinning lies to protect the Dunne family.

"If Kevin sees you, he'll know that something otherworldly is going on." Landon rubbed his thumb over my cheek. "It's best you're not here for that. I'll take care of it."

My stomach gave a little lurch. "Are you totally not angry any longer, or mostly not angry any longer?"

"We'll talk when I get to the inn."

"You're supposed to say you're totally over it."

He smirked. "We're not arguing, Bay. I'm over that. I still want to talk about what happened last night."

"Because you want to punish me?"

"No, although a spanking isn't out of the question." He gave a devilish wink, then sobered. "We're fine. I do have some questions, but those can wait. For now, I don't need people asking questions about why you're here."

I kissed him. "I'm holding you to that not being mad thing."

"Try making up with Terry before I get there," Landon suggested. "That will make all of us happy."

I wasn't certain who he was considering "all of us," but I nodded. Now that Landon was back on my side, Chief Terry was my main target. "Try not to be too long."

EVAN ACCOMPANIED ME TO THE INN. IT ALMOST felt as if we'd grown up with him. We'd known him less than a year, yet he'd infiltrated every corner of our lives.

"That smells divine," Evan cooed as he planted a kiss on my mother's cheek. "Pot roast?"

"Indeed it is," Mom confirmed. The look she gave Evan was fond. "I didn't realize you'd been here all day. You could've hung around with us if you'd wanted."

"I was with Bay." Evan looked at Aunt Tillie's recliner in the corner of the kitchen. Normally, about this time, you could find her in her chair overseeing my mother and aunts. She was suspiciously absent today. "Where's Tillie?" Evan's tone was deceptively mild, but only an idiot couldn't have read between the lines of his question.

"Aunt Tillie has been surprisingly evasive today," Mom replied. She went back to looking at the bread on the cooling rack in front of her. "She's spent the better part of her day in her greenhouse."

I was instantly suspicious. "In the snow?"

Mom shrugged. "I know you have questions about whatever she was up to last night," Mom started.

"She was with a monster."

"Or she was messing with you," Mom argued. "Maybe she knew you were following her. It's possible she conjured that thing to teach you a lesson about spying."

On any other day I might've agreed. There was just one little problem. "Evan has been watching her for days. He saw that thing before I did."

Mom's forehead creased. "Is that true?" She turned to Evan. "Did you see the monster before last night?"

Evan didn't look happy about being put on the spot. "You know, you have a real problem sacrificing people to make a point, Bay," he groused.

"Well, Aunt Tillie has a pet monster none of us knew about," I shot back. "We need to figure it out, and you have information."

"That thing isn't out there all the time," Mom insisted. "We would know. We're on the bluff all through summer, dancing under the full moon and sometimes just walking out there. We would know if there was a monster."

She was right. That's what made this so confusing. "She warned us away from the woods during storms in the winter," I said to Mom. "This has to be why."

"I don't remember her telling you to stay away from the woods," Mom argued. "I think I would remember, even if she was making up a story."

I looked to the door that led to the family living quarters. "When was the last time anyone saw her?"

"Breakfast," Marnie replied. "She's been gone ever since."

"That's not like her." I flicked my eyes to Evan. "Can you find her? I'm guessing she's somewhere on the grounds."

"I could," Evan confirmed, "but I won't."

I frowned at him. "We need to talk to her."

"Maybe so, but I'm not inserting myself into your squabbles, Bay. I have loyalty to every member of this family."

"But Thistle the least, right?" I pressed.

Evan smirked. "You all have qualities I adore. Even Thistle. I'm not going to step between you."

I narrowed my eyes. "Your unerring loyalty is extremely frustrating," I muttered. "I prefer when Aunt Tillie's minions can be bought."

"I'll keep that in mind," Evan replied dryly. "As for the thing on the bluff, I've never seen anything like it. Part of that is because it was shrouded. It was as if there was some sort of camouflage surrounding the creature."

I tapped my fingers on the counter. "Is it possible there's a plane door here, and the creature comes through only in winter?"

"Why would it bother?" Marnie asked. "It's not as if winter in Hemlock Cove is the happiest time of year."

"Then maybe the creature hibernates."

"It's not a bear," Mom argued.

"Then you tell me what it is," I snapped.

Mom extended a spatula in my direction. "Don't take that tone with me. It's not my fault you're fighting with your husband and Terry."

I turned sullen. "Landon and I made up. Only Chief Terry is still mad at me."

A small smile played at the corners of Mom's mouth. "I bet you want to make up with him before dinner. You never could take it when he was angry with you."

"I definitely want to make up with him," I agreed. "I also want to find Aunt Tillie. She has some questions to answer."

"We all know Aunt Tillie won't show up until she feels like it," Mom said pragmatically. "Terry, however, is in the library. He's having a drink and taking some downtime. Perhaps you should go make nice with him before you try to pick a fight with Aunt Tillie."

"Maybe I want to do it in the opposite order," I fired back.

"You won't allow Terry to stay mad at you. When people are mad at you, you get the trots, Bay. I'm your mother. I remember these things."

I glared at her. "If we could stop talking about my bowel movements, that would be great." First constipation, now the trots? This day really did suck. "I'll go talk to Chief Terry. You find Aunt Tillie," I ordered Evan.

"I'm not tattling on her," Evan insisted.

"Because you don't want to be cursed?" Twila asked knowingly.

"That and I'm drawing a line in the sand. You all need to understand that I won't be used as a pawn in your skirmishes with one another. If you want to fight, fight it out on your own."

It was a reasoned response. We would all try to break him eventually, though. "Find Aunt Tillie. Make sure she doesn't skip dinner. I'll talk to Chief Terry."

"I'll find her, but I won't manipulate her." Evan's stare was heavy.

"Duly noted."

CHIEF TERRY WAS IN THE LIBRARY, a glass of bourbon on the small table by the couch. His eyes were turbulent when he lifted them to look at me. "I didn't realize you were back. Is Landon with you?"

"He's still in Shadow Hills. I expect him soon."

"I heard the chatter on the radio. Something happened with Joanie Dunne."

I nodded. "It's a long story. I'll tell everyone at dinner."

"Is it dinner time now?" He put down the book he'd been flipping through.

"Ten more minutes."

"Okay." He picked the book back up, leaving me staring at him.

I didn't like when he was angry with me. It was rare that he yelled at me. It had happened twice in recent weeks, though. "Don't you want to forgive me?" I asked.

He looked over the top of the book. If I wasn't mistaken, he looked as if he was going to start laughing. "I'm not angry with you, Bay. Why would you think that?"

"You were annoyed earlier today."

"I sided with Landon and said that you shouldn't have done what you did."

"That's the same thing."

"It's really not." Chief Terry shook his head. "I'm not angry."

"You seem angry."

"I believe you made a grave error in judgement when you took off in the middle of the night the way you did, but I can't be mad about it. You don't know any better because you and your cousins learned that from Tillie. That's simply part of your makeup."

"Why didn't you tell Landon that?"

"Because I don't think he's making an unreasonable request. It's not too much to ask that you don't sneak out without telling him."

I hated—*absolutely loathed*—how reasonable he sounded. "Have you seen Aunt Tillie?"

Chief Terry smirked. "Just think ahead about seventeen years from now, to when you have a teenager and you put her to bed, and then you wake up to learn she was sneaking around the countryside in the dark."

I was appalled. "Why would my kid do that?"

"Why did you?"

"We were going on adventures."

"You don't think you're going to have an adventurous kid?"

He was full of points I didn't want to entertain tonight. "Can we just be back on good terms? I don't want to argue. Landon and I made up, and he'll be here any minute. It's pot roast night. On top of that, we need to deal with Aunt Tillie."

"Do you think the monster you saw on the bluff has anything to do with the Blue Moon fire?"

"I honestly don't know. It's not out of the realm of possibility."

"But you're not leaning in that direction," Chief Terry guessed.

"I'm not. Joanie being a banshee and trying to poison Alice Milligan suggests she's to blame, but we can't rule anything out."

Chief Terry arched an eyebrow. "It sounds like I've missed a few things."

"I can catch you up at dinner."

"I look forward to that."

"You say that now. You'll change your mind when I'm done."

. . .

AUNT TILLIE SHOWED UP AS dinner hit the table. I wasn't at all surprised to find Gunner and Scout already seated.

"You smelled the pot roast from Hawthorne Hollow, didn't you?" I teased as I sat.

"There's no way we were missing dinner, no matter what it was," Scout said as she watched Gunner ladle a huge portion of meat, potatoes, and gravy onto his plate. "Don't you think you should have at least one carrot to pretend you're eating healthy?" she demanded.

Gunner's response was to shove a huge forkful of food into his mouth.

Landon entered the dining room, and his stomach let out a ruthless growl as he sat next to me. "This is exactly what I was hoping for." He beamed at my mother before turning to me. "Everything is taken care of."

"You got Kevin and Katie into a safe house?"

"I did." Landon grabbed my plate and dished food onto it before giving himself double the portion he gave me. "Kevin was upset, but when I explained that Joanie appears to be having a mental break, he didn't seem all that surprised."

"Turning into a banshee didn't happen in a vacuum," I said. I grabbed a hunk of warm bread. "I wonder if he's been noticing changes in her demeanor. She's obviously been building to the transformation."

I had every intention of cornering Aunt Tillie before she finished dinner. Apparently, she'd decided to insert herself into the conversation before I could make my move.

"Are you sure she's a banshee?" Aunt Tillie demanded.

"She screamed loud enough to break all the windows in the house." I kept my gaze on Aunt Tillie. "Why? Do you know something?"

"How would I know anything about Joanie Dunne?" Aunt Tillie demanded. I could tell by the flash in her eyes that her fuse was dangerously close to lighting. "I've been dealing with my own stuff today. I haven't had time for your stuff."

"You mean your friend on the bluff?"

Aunt Tillie didn't respond. "Did Joanie go after you? Once she transformed, did she try to go after you? Banshee scratches are dangerous. They can transform someone who might not make the transformation herself. It's just a little push, really." She leaned over Landon to look at me. "Were you scratched?"

Was she really concerned about that? It was always so hard to tell with her. "She didn't get near me."

"She didn't," Evan confirmed. He was positioned next to Scout and had a bit of pot roast on his plate. Scout had told me that Evan's eating options were still up in the air. He could sustain himself on blood but also eat food. It was all very odd for a vampire.

"Good." Aunt Tillie sagged against her chair. "That's something at least."

"The reason we knew to go after Joanie at all is because she tried to poison Alice Milligan with hemlock."

"Where did she get hemlock?" Mom asked.

"I have no idea."

"But how did she know to get hemlock?" Mom persisted. "When humans want to poison someone, they normally go for rat poison, or cleaning solutions, or arsenic. Hemlock is a very specific choice."

"The witch stuff has permeated the entire area," Scout pointed out. "It's possible that she read about hemlock when you rebranded from Walkerville to Hemlock Cove. It's right in the name."

Mom still looked troubled. "What's the plan? I've never dealt with a banshee."

"I've dealt with a few," Scout replied. "I've found beheading works best."

I cringed at her blasé tone. "I was kind of hoping we could save her," I said.

Scout didn't laugh. She also didn't look excited at the prospect. "I've never heard of a banshee being saved, Bay. In theory, I guess it's possible, but I don't think you can just turn her back into a mother and wife. The stuff that turned her in the first place grew to be too much. It consumed her."

"We have to try."

"I'll handle it," Aunt Tillie announced.

All eyes turned to her.

"Did you say you'd handle it?" I asked after a few seconds.

"Are you suddenly hard of hearing?" Aunt Tillie barked. "I've got it."

"Would you like to share with the class why you should be left to your own devices to deal with the banshee?"

"No, I would not," Aunt Tillie replied primly. "I've got this, Bay. You can go back to arguing with your husband over naming your dog. That seems like the most important thing you have to deal with right now. I'll handle the heavy lifting."

I didn't like her tone. "Aunt Tillie—"

She cut me off with a growl. "I said I've got it. I don't want to hear another word about it."

I glanced at Landon. He looked as troubled as I felt.

"Let's talk about the pot roast," Gunner suggested. "It could be the best you've ever made." He winked at Mom. "If you weren't already engaged to this guy, I would try to steal you away." He gestured to Chief Terry.

"You really are my favorite," Mom said to Gunner. "If Landon hadn't gotten to her first, I would've wanted Bay with you."

"Where does that leave me?" Scout demanded.

"Oh, we would've found somebody for you," Mom assured her. "I need a son-in-law who appreciates my cooking. Thankfully Landon is easy to please."

"Yes, we're all thankful for that," I agreed.

20
TWENTY

Aunt Tillie did what she always did, evaporating into thin air after dinner. She didn't even hang around for dessert, although when Mom brought the huge chocolate cake into the dining room from the kitchen a hefty slice was missing.

"Aunt Tillie?" I asked, staring at the cake.

Mom nodded. "Yup."

"She knows something," I insisted.

"We don't know that," Mom argued. She was often the only one who could keep Aunt Tillie in check. There were times she made excuses for her too. "It's possible she's just messing with you."

That felt unlikely. "How does that work?" I demanded. "I saw her with something on the bluff last night. Something not human."

"Maybe it was an optical illusion," Mom said.

She drove me crazy sometimes. One day she'd make up elaborate conspiracy theories to assign to Aunt Tillie. The next she'd bend over backward to make excuses for her. This was a byproduct of mama bear ferocity, family loyalty, and a short fuse. It was enough to give me whiplash.

Chief Terry cleared his throat. "Maybe you should describe what you saw, Bay," he said. "It's possible there's a perfectly rational explanation."

"You're just saying that because you don't want to tick off Mom and take my side," I argued.

Chief Terry's cheeks flushed. "I want a chance to think about the evidence you're presenting."

He was full of it. "Is this how it's going to be?" I asked, something terrible occurring to me. "Are you going to take Mom's side over mine?" Something even worse occurred to me. "Is it going to be Mom, Landon, and then me in the pecking order?" I was horrified. "I think I'm going to be sick."

Amusement running over his features, Landon rubbed my back with his right hand while determinedly shoveling cake in with his left.

"It's not about picking favorites, Bay," Mom argued. "It's about getting to the truth."

"It's easy for you to say that," I shot back. "You're the current favorite." I stuck out my lower lip and glared to my right. "I can't believe I'm not your favorite any longer."

Chief Terry looked appalled. "You're always my favorite." He seemed to realize his mistake right away and darted an apologetic look to Mom. "After you, of course."

"Perhaps we should make a list," Landon suggested. He had cake in his mouth but didn't seem to care. "You can rank all the women in the house from top to bottom and then everybody will know where they stand."

"You're not helping," Chief Terry growled. He looked as if he wanted to start throwing punches.

"I'm pretty sure he's not trying to help," I assured Chief Terry. "He's enjoying himself."

"That's a cruel thing to say, Bay." Landon's fork headed toward his plate, but he'd finished all of his cake. I could hear the gears in his mind working as he stared at the empty plate. He darted his eyes to me.

"If you want another piece of cake, have it," I offered.

Landon was instantly suspicious. "Just like that?"

I nodded.

Landon reached for the cake plate but froze halfway there. "You're about to trick me." He drew his hand back. "What's the catch, Bay?"

"Who said there's a catch?"

"You want something. Before I take that cake, I want to know what it is."

"I have no idea what you're talking about," I sniffed. "But we did agree that you would try to moderate your sugar intake."

"There it is," Landon muttered.

"I want you to live a long and healthy life. We both agreed that it wasn't too much to ask that you embrace the concept of moderation."

"This is a trap," Landon growled.

"I'd be willing to overlook the concept of moderation this evening if you're willing to overlook the concept of home safety when we get back to the guesthouse," I said.

Landon frowned. "I should've seen that coming."

"She was smooth," Chief Terry said. "She knew she was going to bamboozle you with frosting before she even started. Aunt Tillie would be proud of her masterful performance."

"Aunt Tillie is the last one I'm worried about right now," I replied. "I have to deal with her, but that feels like tomorrow's problem. Right now, I'm wondering what our conversation will be like when we get back home." I sent Landon a pointed look. "Will it be an hour of you explaining to me why I made a mistake—something I readily admit—when I went exploring on my own last night? Or, will it be you and I stripping to our underwear and eating the piece of cake I plan to take home while sharing a fuzzy blanket and watching *Diehard*?"

Landon's mouth fell open. "I love *Diehard*."

"You said that was your dream scenario," I said. "I said I wanted to live in the house the Owens witches get to call their own in *Practical Magic,* and you said you wanted to be Bruce Willis in *Diehard* ... with better hair."

Now Landon was caught, and he knew it. "That was sly, Bay," he complained.

I didn't bother to hide my smirk. "Do we have an agreement?"

"No." Landon's head shake was fast and firm.

It was not the response I was expecting. "What do you mean no?"

"We're going to have a rational discussion about why I was angry about you sneaking off. If you want to lecture me about the potential dangers of too much sugar and fat, I can't stop you. As you've repeatedly told me, you lecture me about that because you love me."

This was taking a turn I hadn't expected. "Landon—"

"We're talking about it."

I threw up my hands. "Fine, but I don't have to like it."

Chief Terry tapped his fingers on the table to draw my attention. "As much fun as it is to watch you guys fake fight your way through foreplay—and don't think that won't give me an aneurysm someday—I want to talk about what you saw on the bluff last night, Bay. What sort of creature are we talking about?"

"Please tell me it wasn't Bigfoot," Marnie pleaded. "It's getting to the point Clover will come out with the baby twice a week. If she thinks Bigfoot is hanging around, I'll have to keep visiting the Dandridge, and that's just not as convenient."

My smirk was fast. "We can't have that. As for what I saw on the bluff last night, it wasn't Bigfoot. It was..." I trailed off, uncertain. "It was misshapen. It was tall. It looked as if it had been human at one time.

"I couldn't hear what they were saying," I continued, "but it looked like a serious conversation."

"Maybe it's something new," Mom suggested. "Maybe Aunt Tillie created a golem." Her forehead creased with frustration. "After that incident in 2003, I told her that wasn't allowed again."

"Yes, because Aunt Tillie always follows the rules," Marnie drawled.

I rubbed the back of my neck as I considered it. "I can't rule out a golem, but that doesn't feel right. This was ... different."

"Meaning?" Chief Terry asked.

"I'm telling you; this has something to do with the stories she told us as kids," I said. "This thing, whatever it is, is out there, but dangerous only when it storms in the winter. I don't know if it hibernates. I don't know if it crosses from a different plane. I don't know if it's a Dr. Jekyll and Mr. Hyde situation. I only know Aunt Tillie is keeping a big secret from us."

"And she's interested in the banshee situation," Twila volunteered. "She seemed agitated when Bay mentioned Joanie Dunne had turned into a banshee. There's something she's not telling us there, too."

Mom scratched the side of her nose. "Well, you worry about being in trouble with your husband tonight, and I'll worry about Aunt Tillie," she said.

I shifted on my chair. "You're going to handle Aunt Tillie?"

"I believe that's what I said." Mom's eyes flashed with warning. "I don't need your help. You need to finesse the situation with Aunt Tillie sometimes. You're not very good at finessing. You like to ram your head against brick walls. You lack nuance."

"What a really weird way to insult me," I groused.

Mom smirked. "Just give me a chance to talk to Aunt Tillie. It's possible the thing she's hiding isn't what you think."

"And it's possible you're making excuses for her because that's what you like to do sometimes," I fired back.

Mom's eyes narrowed. "I said I've got this, Bay. Let me handle it."

I didn't like that she was basically relieving me of responsibility. As a control freak, that didn't leave me with enough options. I nodded all the same. "Fine. Do your worst. Just know, Aunt Tillie is definitely up to something bad."

. . .

AT HOME, I WENT to the bedroom and changed into sleep pants and an oversized T-shirt. Landon remained in the kitchen—probably praying to the slice of cake I'd brought home. When I heard him come in from outside with the puppy, I made my way into the living room.

It was time for the fight.

"Just do it," I said as I flopped on the couch and stared forlornly at the wall.

"Do what?" Landon picked up his puppy and carried him to the chair next to the couch. The puppy looked ready for bed and allowed Landon to cuddle him to his chest as his eyelids drooped. Landon was going to make a great father, I realized. He was going to get up to tend to babies crying in the middle of the night. He was going to want to be involved in their feedings. He would never miss a Christmas pageant or a special program at the school.

He was a good man.

Still, I wasn't in the mood to be lectured. "I want to get this done, so if you want to yell about last night, let's get it out of the way."

"I don't want to yell. I'm not your father, I'm your husband. We do things together. It would be great if you wanted to include me in these adventures. I don't want to be invited simply because you don't want to get in trouble."

"I didn't want to wake you in case..."

"In case you really did find a monster and there was a magical fight, and I ended up hurt in the process," he said. "I get it. You're stronger than I am."

I shook my head. "I have magic. Last night seemed like a magic thing."

"I want you to remember that I love you. Waking up to find you gone would've gutted me. I'm not sure how we would've finagled things with him here." Landon gestured to the puppy. "We couldn't have taken him, and I wouldn't have been keen about leaving him behind."

"It's something to think about for when we have kids," I mused.

"I'm hoping Aunt Tillie won't still be hanging out with monsters on the bluff when we have kids," Landon said. "She's hiding something big. I'm not your mother, who wants to believe the best about Aunt Tillie at the oddest of times. I would've liked to have been included."

"That's it?" I was dubious. A year earlier, Landon would've huffed until he ran out of breath.

He shrugged. "The longer I'm in this, the more I realize I won't always get my way. You're strong—far stronger than when we first met—and you have certain things you need to do. We have to come to a compromise, though.

"I have to be less demanding when it comes to how you approach magical problems," he continued. "You have to remember that we're an 'us' and no longer a 'you' and a 'me.'

We haven't been married all that long. We're still figuring it out."

"But you were angry," I pressed.

"I was upset," Landon clarified. "I can't wake up and have you be gone, Bay. That's going to freak me out. Even if you think I'll get in the way or be irritated, I still want you to wake me and tell me."

"It wasn't about you getting irritated," I hedged. "It was about me not knowing if I was being irrational and not wanting to look like an idiot. Plus, you were so comfortable with your dog."

"As much as I love the dog, I love you more." Landon was matter of fact. "I just want to be included. I don't want to be left behind."

The naked emotion on his face caused my heart to ping. "I'm sorry. That was not my intention."

"I know." He grinned at me. "Now, can we eat the cake?"

"No." I glanced at the clock on the wall. "We have a few hours before bed. We should wait."

His lips curved down. "You're kind of mean."

"We both know I'm going to have to be bad cop when we have kids because you're going to be the indulgent father."

Landon opened his mouth—was he really going to argue that point?—and then shrugged. "I'm a softie, but Terry bent over backward to make you, Clove, and Thistle happy. He still had a firm hand when it was necessary. I think that's how I'll be."

"A softie for ice cream and a hard-ass when they want to date?"

"They're not dating." Landon vehemently shook his head. "Boys are pigs."

"Not all boys," I argued. "We met when we were kids, and you were a little gentleman."

"Yes, but that was before my hormones kicked in. You would not have wanted to know me as a teenager. I was mouthy, full of myself, and hot to trot for certain girls."

"I doubt I would've been one of them."

"Don't sell yourself short." Landon wagged a finger. "I've seen photos of you. You totally would've been my type."

I couldn't stop from smiling. "What do you think our lives would've been like if we'd started dating as teenagers?"

"I wish I could say we would've hooked up back then and lived happily ever after, but that's not realistic. We would've had drama. I needed time to grow into a man for you, Bay."

"And I needed time to realize that I wanted to be here," I agreed. "I always thought I wanted to be anywhere but here. I was wrong."

"This is our home," he said. "In a few years, we'll have our house. We can add a kid. If that kid is really well behaved and self-sufficient, we can add another. I don't want adult playtime interrupted too much."

I burst out laughing. "That sounds pretty good."

His smile slipped after a few seconds. "What do you really think Aunt Tillie is up to?"

"I don't know," I replied, "but I'm going to find out. She can run but she can't hide."

21
TWENTY-ONE

I was down for the count the second my head hit the pillow despite the late influx of sugar. I barely registered Landon rolling in next to me and getting the puppy comfortable. I was lost in dreamland, and intent on staying in bed.

That's why, when I woke around midnight knowing that something was wrong, I was confused.

A figure sat on the rocking chair in the corner of our bedroom. It was dark, so I couldn't make out the individual, but I felt a set of judgmental eyes on me.

"How can you two sleep all wrapped around each other like that?" Aunt Tillie demanded.

My shoulders came down as I relaxed—marginally—and glared at her. "What are you doing in our bedroom?"

Landon stirred. "No more adventures tonight, Bay." He patted my wrist. "Sleep first. I'll romance your socks off in the morning."

Aunt Tillie angled her head, so it was visible thanks to ambient moonlight. "He's kind of a putz."

"I won't sit here and listen to you insult my husband. Get out."

Aunt Tillie flashed the sort of smile I wanted to smack right off her face. "I need to show you something, Bay." She was serious enough that I didn't immediately turn her down.

"Are you going to tell me what that thing on the bluff is?"

"I'm going to introduce you."

"Are you serious?"

"What else would I be?"

"It's hard to tell with you. I can see you leading me to the bluff just to hex me with a snowball spell and have me run all the way home trying to avoid snowballs thrown at my head."

Aunt Tillie's eyes lit with interest.

"That's not supposed to give you ideas," I complained.

Aunt Tillie's chuckle was light. "Your ideas are always a good jumping off point," she said. "They need time to percolate." She waved her hand. "Come with me."

"Because that thing is out on the bluff?" I wasn't going unless she gave me a compelling reason.

"Yes. And it's not a thing. It's a ... friend." She seemed to reconsider the statement. "Maybe not a friend but an acquaintance I see a handful of times a year. Think of her like Santa but with claws."

"Her?"

There was an edge to Aunt Tillie's voice. "There's a story, but it's not mine. Come along."

I grumbled as I tossed off the covers. Then I remembered Landon. I could not leave him behind again. "Hey." I nudged his shoulder.

"What are you doing?" Aunt Tillie hissed. "We don't need him."

Landon's eyes were open. "I was wondering if you were going to sneak out. Is this where you tell me that you want to handle this alone?"

I flicked my gaze to Aunt Tillie. "How dangerous is this going to be?"

"It'll only be dangerous if he goes."

I didn't understand. "You're just trying to cut him out of the action."

"That's what it sounds like to me," Landon agreed, annoyance knitting his eyebrows together. "I'm going." He moved to get out of bed, but Aunt Tillie stopped him.

"No!" She frantically waved her hand. "If she sees I've brought a man..." Aunt Tillie looked momentarily helpless. "Let's just say that it won't end well."

"Because he's a man?"

"Only we can go. I promised her, Bay. Don't make a liar out of me."

"Evan has been watching you on the bluff," I said. "He's been out there and nothing bad happened."

"He's not really a man. He's a vampire, and he's not interested in women. That makes him kind of neutral."

"To whom?"

"It's better I show you."

I slowly tracked my eyes to Landon. If he didn't want me to go, after the previous evening, I would stay. To my surprise, he didn't look as if he was going to stop me.

"Obviously, this is serious," he said in a low voice. "I think she's truthful when she says my presence might make things difficult. You should go."

I would've liked a bit of unreasonableness to prop my position from my previous adventure.

"Fine." I planted a kiss on Landon's cheek. "I don't plan on being gone long."

"Keep her out of trouble," he ordered Aunt Tillie. "If something happens to her, I'll blame you."

"Oh, listen to the big man and his puppy dog," Aunt Tillie scoffed. "I'm not afraid of you."

"If something happens to Bay, you'd better get afraid of me." Landon flopped back on his pillow. "Be careful, Bay. Aunt Tillie wouldn't willingly lead you into trouble, but she doesn't always think like a rational person."

"Says you," Aunt Tillie snapped. "I'm the most rational person in this family. Heck, I'm the most rational person in the world. If they gave out medals for rationality, I'd win the titanium one."

"Why not the gold?" I asked.

"Titanium is better than gold."

"Whatever. Give me five minutes to pull on some clothes. This had better be worth it."

"It is." Aunt Tillie turned grim. "It's also important to what's going on with Joanie."

"How?"

"Just ... come on. You'll find out soon enough."

"Fine, but you're in big trouble."

"Don't push it. I can still make you smell like tofu."

"What did I ever do to you?" Landon demanded. "I'm staying behind like a good boy."

"You make me tired," Aunt Tillie complained.

"She'd better come home smelling like bacon."

Aunt Tillie eyed him for what felt like forever, then offered a curt nod. "I'm sure something can be arranged."

THE WALK TO THE BLUFF WAS COLD AND uncomfortable, and I was glad I thought to layer before bundling myself into my heavy coat.

"How long has this been going on?" I asked.

"About twenty years or so."

"Has it been worth it?"

"Maybe you should wait to talk to her before you start casting judgments." Aunt Tillie's tone told me she was more worked up than I realized.

Aunt Tillie took the lead when we reached the bluff. Something told me to look up as we passed under a tree. I found Evan perched on a branch, watching us. He lifted a finger to his lips. It made me feel better to know he was close.

. . .

The creature was visible on the bluff when we crested the final hill, and my heart began to hammer. It seemed bigger, and less human. Aunt Tillie referred to it as a she, but it looked like a lumpy mass.

"Hey," I said lamely when we drew to a stop. "Fancy meeting you on a dark bluff in the middle of the night."

Aunt Tillie shot me a glare. "Don't embarrass me. I told her you were the smart one in the family. Next to me, of course. You're not acting smart, Bay."

"I'm way smarter than you," I grumbled as I leveled my gaze on the creature. "What..." I caught myself. "I mean, who are you."

When the creature spoke, it was with a husky rasp that reminded me of those old ads for telephone sex operators. She might not have looked human, but she sounded human.

"Donna O'Malley," was her simple response.

I waited for her to expand. When she didn't, I looked at Aunt Tillie. "I don't know who that is."

"Of course you do," Aunt Tillie said. "I've talked about Donna a million times."

"I'll take one time you mentioned her."

"This is like when I told you about the garden imps biting ankles and you thought I was making it up. What happened then?"

"You left out the part of the story where you created the garden imps by hexing regular garden gnomes and introducing them to bee venom."

"Someone has to protect the bees," Aunt Tillie sniffed.

I pressed my gloved hand to my forehead and forced myself to focus on the creature. "I don't know who you are. I'm sorry. I don't recognize the name."

"I knew you when you were a child," Donna replied. It was hard to think of her as a who instead of a what because of her looks. "I was friends with your mother."

I searched my memory and came up with a vague face. "Dark hair. Curls. You wore Doc Marten boots. They were black but you'd painted the soles pink."

The creature nodded. "That was me."

"I don't remember what happened to you," I admitted. "I vaguely remember you. I kind of remember you having tea with my mother."

"I had a lot of tea with your mother," Donna confirmed. "We were very good friends ... until we weren't." She looked sad.

"I'm trying to remember the circumstances," I admitted. "I'm guessing this is part of it." I motioned to her and then sent her a rueful smile. "I'm sorry. That came out horrible."

"It's fine." Donna smiled, but it made her look even more frightening. "This is all because of me. I've come to terms with it."

"Come to terms with what?"

"I was married when it started. My husband's name was Alan."

The name stirred a memory. "Alan O'Malley? He was the guy killed in his house when we were kids. I remember rumors he was clawed to death, and people believed..." I trailed off as the rest of it came into focus.

"And people believed his wife did it," Donna finished.

I looked at her with fresh eyes. "I'd better hear the whole story."

Donna turned from me and stared at the moon. "I was a very unhappy woman. I didn't realize at the time that it was a problem of my own making. My husband liked to cheat. After a few years, he didn't even try to pretend he wasn't cheating. He would tell me what he was going to do, and then leave me at home to stew."

"Sounds like a real prince," I drawled.

"It was no great loss when he died," Aunt Tillie said. "I thought about throwing a party."

I pinned her with a quelling look. "Just because he was a douche nozzle doesn't mean he deserved to be murdered."

"I happen to believe differently," Aunt Tillie replied. "That's neither here nor there. You need to hear the story to understand, Bay." Her voice softened. "Just listen."

"Alan was a terrible man, but I enabled him because I didn't stand up for myself," Donna explained. "The first time I caught him he apologized. There were no repercussions, so he just kept doing it.

"Over and over and over again," she said. "Each time, he grew colder. I think he wanted me to fly off the handle. I took it ... and I grew more pathetic in his eyes as the years went on. He had no respect for me at the end."

I was starting to get a better picture of what we were dealing with. "And you grew bitter," I said.

"Not with him. At first, I blamed the other women. They knew he was married. They didn't care. It was easier to vilify them, because if I made him the villain, I would've had to look inward and ask myself why I stayed with him."

"You turned into a banshee," I said. She didn't look like a banshee, but it made sense.

"I turned into a monster. I just ... lost it one day. It had been building up. I noticed signs that I was changing but ignored them. I was afraid."

"She turned into a banshee and killed Alan," Aunt Tillie said. "I went looking for her because ... well, you know why."

"Because if you didn't, she could've infected others, and more people would've died," I said. "It would've been a bloodbath."

Aunt Tillie nodded. "I found her. I was going to kill her. But she was ... different."

"Different how?"

"There were still bits of Donna in her. She was horrified by what she'd done. Normal banshees don't care. They have no remorse."

I rubbed my hands over my thighs, which were growing numb from the cold. "She was aware," I said. "The banshee didn't completely overtake her."

"I wasn't aware when I killed Alan," Donna corrected. "I remembered doing it, but it was as if I was watching someone else do it. I came back to myself later and was regretful."

That didn't explain why she looked as she did, or why she was running around in the winter. "I need to know the rest of it," I insisted.

"I worked up a potion," Aunt Tillie replied. "I managed to cure her, but only partially. A byproduct of the potion was that she turned into this." She gestured to the misshapen hulk. "I was going to reverse the potion and try again, but Donna didn't want that."

"I deserved to look as ugly on the outside as I felt on the inside," Donna explained. "I didn't want to live any longer, but Tillie convinced me that killing myself wasn't the answer. So, instead, I sleep most of the year. I come out when the land is barren and gather my strength. Then I return to sleep for nine months."

"That doesn't seem like much of an existence," I pointed out.

"Do you think I deserve a better one?"

"I'm not the judge and jury, but Alan sounds like a real jerk."

"Oh, he was," Aunt Tillie agreed. "She's paid for what she's done."

"I don't believe I'll ever pay enough," Donna said, "but I don't believe in suicide. I stay away from others, except for Tillie, and I ... exist. That's my penance. Occasionally, if there's another monster that needs to be taken care of, I'll throw myself into that fight. I can't be around men sometimes. I still lose my cool. I want to be better."

I had so many questions. "Where do you hibernate?"

"A cave not far from here. Tillie warded it. I sleep for long periods. I get up. I wander and look at the world I can't be part of. Then I go back to sleep."

"Sounds very lonely. What does that have to do with what's going on now? We're totally talking about this later," I warned Aunt Tillie. "I'm not saying you did the wrong thing, but this doesn't feel right for anyone concerned."

"You mind your own business," Aunt Tillie fired back. "As for why it's important now, it's Joanie."

"I figured as much. Because Joanie is a banshee doesn't mean she's like Donna."

"Actually, it might," Donna countered. "Joanie's mother, Carrie, was my sister. She died a few years ago, while I was sleeping. I look in on Joanie whenever I wake. She was always a good girl."

"You saw that her husband was a righteous jackhole," I surmised.

Donna nodded. "Each year that passed I grew more and more concerned. I was here last night talking to Tillie because I saw what was happening to Joanie. I knew what she would become. I thought I had more time."

I stared at her for what felt like a really long time. "You believe there's something in your family blood that will make Joanie different. Like you are."

"Tillie says she hasn't killed anyone yet."

"She tried. She tried to poison Alice Milligan."

"But she hasn't killed anyone," Donna persisted. "We can still save her."

"How?"

"That's what we need to figure out," Aunt Tillie replied. "We have to do better than I did last time. Now do you see why I brought you here?"

I shook my head and stared into the sky. "Can you find Joanie?" I asked. "Can you get us to her?"

Donna shrugged. "I can try."

"If you find her, come to the guesthouse and tell me. We'll go from there." With that, I turned on my heel and stalked away from them. "And don't think you're not in trouble, Aunt Tillie," I yelled back to her. "You're in big, big trouble."

22
TWENTY-TWO

I was freezing when I got back to the guesthouse. I double-checked the locks. When I crawled into bed with Landon, he was warm, and I pressed myself to his side.

"Hey." He wrapped his arm around me and drew my cheek to his shoulder. "You okay?"

Was I? "I'm fine," I said. "We have a direction to look tomorrow."

"Because of the monster?"

"The monster is a woman. Or she was."

Landon stared into my eyes. "How does that work?"

"It's a long story. Can we talk about it in the morning? I just want to sleep." And think. I desperately needed to think.

Landon closed his eyes again. "How much trouble are we in?"

Weirdly, the meeting with Donna had eased a little of my anxiety. "We might have a way out, but things are going to be ugly at breakfast."

"I can't wait."

. . .

LANDON WAS UP AND SHOWERED when I stumbled into the bathroom the next morning. I felt hungover even though I hadn't had a single drink the night before. He gave me a concerned once-over and kissed my cheek.

"I want to know what we're up against before you go after Aunt Tillie," he said.

"Just let me shower. I'll tell you on the drive to the inn."

"Okay. I'll take Sausage out."

"We're not naming him Sausage!" It almost came out as a shrill scream.

He smirked. "Good to know I can still get a rise out of you even when you're exhausted." This time the kiss was on the lips. "I'm taking Dog out. I'll be ready when you are."

I showered on autopilot and dressed in jeans, furry winter boots, and layered with a T-shirt and flannel before pulling on my coat. Landon gave me a head-to-toe scan when I met him at the door. He had the puppy on his leash.

"You look as if you're getting ready to play a very rough-and-tumble game today, Bay." There was no censure in his tone, but I felt his worry.

"I need to be prepared in case I have to search through the woods for a banshee," I assured him. "I have no idea what I'm going to be doing today, so don't panic yet."

"I want to hear about your mysterious adventure on the drive."

"No problem." I needed someone to bounce theories off of anyway. I spent the five-minute drive filling him in. He didn't say anything, but the way his eyes widened periodically told me he was concerned. He was practically spitting when we parked at The Overlook.

"Are you serious?" he demanded as he put the Explorer in park. "She knew that thing was out there but didn't warn anyone."

"That thing used to be a person," I argued. "I don't think she's dangerous."

"She killed her husband. You know I'm going to have to pull that case file."

I hadn't thought about it. "Landon, he's gone. You can't change that."

"She needs to go to jail."

"Okay, but ... you can't take someone that looks like a monster and put her in jail."

"Why? Are you worried the other murderers will tease her?"

"I'm worried she still has some banshee in her and not only can kill anyone who looks at her funny, but also infect them. Then we'll have an even worse prison break than we had last time."

"Is that possible?"

I held out my hands helplessly. "I didn't stay out there asking questions. It was cold. And I wanted you." It was the last part that had me turning sheepish. "I know why Aunt Tillie didn't want you there—she's worried men might still trigger Donna. I was thrown. I would've done better asking questions if you were there."

Landon's hard expression softened. "That is very sweet. I still want to hurt Aunt Tillie."

"Join the club."

He grabbed my chin and gave me a fierce kiss. "Let's deal with this."

We took the dog in on his leash. Peg was waiting for us, and Landon immediately let the puppy loose to play with the pig as we made our way into the dining room. To my surprise, in addition to Aunt Tillie and Chief Terry, Thistle was present. She had a big glass of juice in front of her and what looked like expectation on her face. She'd also given up the Christmas red and dyed her hair a pink I'd never seen.

"Is that on purpose?" I asked, inadvertently wrinkling my nose as I took in her hair.

"Oh, don't even," Thistle shot back. "I look fierce, and you know it."

"Okay, Tyra." I wasn't in the mood to argue about Thistle's hair.

Well, mostly. "It kind of makes you look like a cupid," I said. "You're not very tall. You have the short hair. All you're missing is the bow and arrow, and a diaper."

If looks could kill, I would be dead. "And here I showed up for moral support and everything. See if I ever do that again."

I was confused. "Why would I need moral support?"

"Aunt Tillie said you need help today because you can't handle the banshee yourself," Thistle replied. "That's what she texted. She said the banshee is stronger than you, so you need me and her to fix whatever you screwed up yesterday."

My mouth fell open. "Really?" I demanded of Aunt Tillie.

She sat in her chair, which looked more like a throne today, and cocked her head. "We're family, Bay. You don't have to be ashamed to ask for help. What happened yesterday with Joanie wasn't your fault. You couldn't have foreseen it."

Yup. I was going to kill her. It was going to hurt, too. Before I could launch myself at her claws first, Landon caught me around the waist and kept me anchored at his side.

"It's not worth it," he said. "You had to know she would do something to save face. The fact that she is trying to make you look bad to bolster herself shouldn't come as a surprise."

Mom and the aunts swooped through the swinging door from the kitchen, and he immediately let me go.

"What is that?" he asked, his eyes wide when he saw the iron skillet Twila placed on one of the protective trivets in the middle of the table.

"That is a corned beef hash medley of sorts," Mom replied. "We thought it would be a nice change. It's corned beef hash, and we added a bit of onions and green peppers."

"Hmm." Landon pursed his lips. "It kind of looks like dog food."

Mom's eyes narrowed. "Is that so?"

"Very good dog food," Landon assured her. "I bet it's great with bacon."

"Uh-huh." Mom rolled her eyes until they landed on me. "What's going on?" she asked when she finally registered that my agitation had nothing to do with the corned beef hash surprise.

"Do you want to tell her, or should I?" I challenged Aunt Tillie.

"I'll tell her." Aunt Tillie's affect was flat. "Thistle and I have to go with Bay today to look for the banshee. Bay isn't strong enough to fight her, and she feels guilty for pushing the woman to the edge. Now she's a killer, and it's all Bay's fault."

I made a strangled sound in my throat. Mom, of course, shook her head and clucked her tongue.

"Bay, you can't take the weight of the world onto your shoulders simply because you decided to accuse Joanie Dunne of poisoning Alice Milligan. It's not entirely your fault."

"Really?" I seethed at Aunt Tillie. "Is this how you want to play it?"

Aunt Tillie's expression didn't change. "You know I'm a stickler for the truth."

That did it. I had planned to tell Mom her friend was still alive in a much softer manner. All of that went out the window thanks to Aunt Tillie's machinations. "Donna O'Malley is still alive," I said. "She's a banshee. She killed her husband but felt guilty about it, so Aunt Tillie used magic more than twenty years ago to try to cure her and instead turned her into a misshapen monster.

"Then she warded a cave somewhere on the property, and that's where Donna lives," I continued. I was furious. "She hibernates nine months a year because of Aunt Tillie's spell. She spends the other three months feeling sorry for herself because she's a murderer."

I was breathless.

Mom's eyebrows hiked. "Is this true?" she asked.

"You're so on my list," Aunt Tillie growled. "I'm going to need a new list, in fact, because you're going to be every single name on it."

"Fair is fair," I fired back.

"This stuff is great," Landon enthused. He'd sat down without me even realizing and was elbow deep in the corned beef hash medley. Of course, because he was Landon, he was dipping bacon in it.

"At least have some eggs and juice," I complained as I grabbed the scrambled egg bowl and dished two scoops onto his plate. "You can't have huge piles of meat for every meal."

"That's what she said," Thistle offered.

"And you." I turned on her with more vehemence than I realized. "How could you believe Aunt Tillie when she said that I'd screwed up and you had to come save me?"

"Multiple scenarios were possible," Thistle replied. "You do tend to flog yourself when you feel guilty."

"That is true, Bay," Landon said around a mouthful of food. "I can see you blaming yourself for the Joanie thing. You should've tipped me off about that right away. I can't believe you took Evan instead of me. I feel so abandoned."

"Evan is a much better sidekick," I snapped. "I might keep him as my permanent sidekick, in fact."

"You can't have Evan," Aunt Tillie argued. "There's a reason he's my number one sidekick. You need to find your own day-walking vampire with a soul. And before you even think about getting cute, you can't have Easton either. He's a gnome shifter, and all of his powers haven't even come into being yet. He's going to be awesome when he's done percolating. They're both mine. You can have that blonde with the fake boobs that's always hanging out at Whistler's bar."

Marissa? She was giving me Marissa? "I'm going to kill you," I announced.

This time it was Chief Terry, passing behind me on his way to the juice carafe, who caught me before I could wrap my hands around Aunt Tillie's neck.

"Pick your battles," he intoned, his eyes serious when they locked with mine. "This is not a battle worth fighting, Bay. She knew what she was doing when she set you up."

That was probably true. "Let me go," I ordered. "She has it coming."

"I'll hex you to within an inch of your life," Aunt Tillie warned. "I'll do that snowball curse."

"I came up with that," I fired back.

Aunt Tillie pretended I hadn't spoken. "You'll wish you'd never crossed me if you're not careful."

There were so many things I wished for right now. Before I could tell her where she could stuff her snowball hex, the sound of someone—a very uncomfortable someone—clearing his throat in the open doorway behind me drew our attention. There, Fire Inspector Daniel Singer stood with his assistant Brandon Grant, watching with open-eyed wonder.

"Sorry to interrupt," Daniel started. He didn't look sorry. After several seconds, he glanced at me. "You know, when we were younger, people said meals at your house were like really crazy movies. I didn't know what they meant. I get it now."

I wanted to punch him. Clearly sensing that, Chief Terry tugged on my flannel sleeve. "Sit, Bay."

"What a nice surprise," Mom said, recovering quickly. "I haven't seen you in a bit, Daniel. Would you like some breakfast?"

Only my mother would worry about food when two outsiders had likely heard us yelling at each other about banshees, bacon, and wards.

"Well, I probably shouldn't." Daniel took in the feast. "If you have enough..."

"We always have enough," Mom assured him. "We have to feed Landon. We triple our recipes."

Daniel laughed. "Awesome." He took the open chair next to Thistle. "This looks amazing."

Brandon continued to hover in the doorway. He looked as if he was about to crap himself.

"This is Brandon Grant," Chief Terry said. "He's Daniel's

assistant. I think they're training him to be the new fire inspector because they expect Daniel to move up to chief at some point."

"Is that true?" I asked. It sounded more judgmental than I'd meant, but there was no hauling it back. Sometimes I thought that was my curse from Aunt Tillie.

"What? Are you worried you married the wrong guy?" Daniel teased. "I'm definitely moving up in the world."

I didn't bother to hide my eye roll. When I glanced at Brandon, he was watching me with an emotion I couldn't identify. It almost looked like adoration. "You should eat while it's warm," I said to him. "It's good."

Brandon gave me a shy smile. "Of course it's good. You cooked it."

Landon and Chief Terry snorted.

"Bay doesn't cook, dear," Mom said as she settled in her chair. "She has other ... gifts. Thankfully, Landon was thinking with something other than his stomach when he fell for her, because his love of food and her lack of cooking acumen make for an interesting combination. What are you going to do when you move away from the inn and into your own house, Bay?"

Landon paused with a slice of bacon halfway to his mouth. "I never considered that. We might have to get up early to drive here for breakfast every day."

"I can cook breakfast," I argued. "I'm just not good at anything other than frozen waffles."

"Maybe you could take lessons from your mother," Thistle offered.

I glared at her. "Maybe you could take lessons from yours," I shot back. That was the meanest thing she'd ever said to me.

"Marcus is okay with the fact that I can't cook. I'm a dynamo in bed. That's all that matters."

"Finally, one of my lessons took," Aunt Tillie noted.

I needed this conversation to shift, and fast. "Have you found anything about the fire?" I asked Daniel. He seemed more interested in the corned beef hash medley.

"We have," Brandon answered when Daniel kept chewing. I noticed he took much smaller portions than his boss. "We found a compound from a strange herb when we ran the tests. We're trying to figure out why anyone would include it in an accelerant."

"You found an herb in the accelerant?" I asked.

"It's called alder."

I swallowed hard even though I'd yet to eat anything.

"What's alder?" Landon asked, looking to me. He seemed to notice a shift in my body language.

"It's a witch herb," I replied. There was no reason to lie about it. Even a simple Google search would turn up the answer.

"It's apparently a fire element herb or something," Daniel agreed. "It doesn't grow anywhere around here that I've been able to find. Even if it did, it's winter, so it's not as if somebody could go outside and pick it. Whoever used it had to grow it."

He thought we grew it. We did. I'd seen alder in Aunt Tillie's pot field. Now that she'd created a dome to protect her pot so she could grow it year-round, alder grew there as well.

"You have a greenhouse, don't you?" Daniel asked. "I know you grow witch herbs for the tourists. Do you have any alder?"

I lied quickly. "I don't think so. There's nothing but Aunt Tillie's still in the greenhouse right now. You're welcome to look."

"Still?" Daniel's eyes lit up. "You have a still?" His gaze moved to Chief Terry. "Isn't that against the law?"

"Don't start," Chief Terry warned. "After breakfast, we'll check the greenhouse. It's possible someone could've broken in and stolen the herbs, but I don't think Tillie keeps fresh herbs there this time of year."

"I don't," Aunt Tillie confirmed. I could tell by the way she was holding her hands that she was agitated. She wouldn't bring up the pot field. Not in front of guests. "You're welcome to test anything in the greenhouse, but I don't grow alder."

Daniel shrugged. "We'll have a look and cross you off the list."

I forced myself to fill my plate. When I looked up, I saw Brandon watching me from the far end of the table. He was smiling ... and it was creepy.

"Dig in," I instructed him. "It's not as good when it's cold." *Plus, as soon as you're done searching, we can start our own search,* I silently added.

23
TWENTY-THREE

Daniel and Brandon wanted a tour of the inn after breakfast. Mom took control, and she and Twila started upstairs, which gave us a few minutes to talk.

"You have alder in the pot field," I hissed to Aunt Tillie, keeping my voice down in case the fire investigator or his assistant were eavesdropping on the stairs. "Don't bother denying it."

"Why would I deny it?" Aunt Tillie shot me a "this is going to end badly for you" smile, the one she usually held in reserve for Mrs. Little. "It's a helpful herb. It can heat things up when they grow cold in the bedroom."

Landon leaned forward. "Why did you look at me when you said that?" He glanced at me. "Why was she looking at me? I'm red hot, baby."

"Oh, geez." I rolled my eyes to the ceiling and prayed for the Goddess to figure out a way to save me from my current predicament. "She's trying to irritate you."

"It's working."

"She's doing it because she doesn't want to get called on the carpet for keeping a freaking banshee on the property." I placed my hands palms down on the table and willed Aunt Tillie to look into my eyes. When she did, there was no guilt. And that was the problem.

"Did it ever occur to you that having a banshee on the property is dangerous?" I asked in my most reasonable voice. It would irritate her more if I didn't fly off the handle. If I attacked, she could play the victim.

"Of course it did," Aunt Tillie replied, "but she was different. She wasn't a regular banshee. She was more like the Hulk."

I must have misheard her. When I focused on Thistle, though, my pink-haired cousin was bobbing her head.

"She's going somewhere important with this," Thistle intoned. "Just wait."

"The Hulk?" Chief Terry asked. "How is she like the Hulk?"

"Because she only banshees out when she gets angry. We don't kill the Hulk because he occasionally loses his temper."

"The Hulk isn't real," I pointed out.

"You don't know that. All movies are based on reality."

"Yes, I know when I feed my Gremlin after midnight, all hell breaks loose," Landon said.

"The gremlin is a metaphor," Aunt Tillie replied. "The Hulk isn't real, but the philosophy behind the Hulk is. Anger is a beast. In this case, it happens to be an actual beast."

"I hate to say it, but I was right about her going somewhere with this," Thistle said. "It kind of makes sense."

The betrayal flowing through me was real. It had teeth. "And what would've happened if we'd stumbled across the banshee when we were kids?" I demanded. "Would we have accidentally triggered her, angered her, and ended up banshees ourselves through a scratch? I know that the virus—or whatever it is—can be passed that way."

"You're such a drama queen," Aunt Tillie lamented. "I told you not to go into the woods when she was out. I had it under control."

"Yes, because all kids and teenagers listen to their great-aunt, the almighty Tillie the Exaggerator," Thistle agreed.

"I don't exaggerate." Aunt Tillie turned her ire on Thistle. "You know what? You're on my list too. You're all on my list." She got to her feet. "I don't need this abuse. You can't abuse the elderly. There are laws." She looked to Chief Terry for confirmation. "Elder abuse is real."

"It is," Chief Terry agreed. "This, however, is not elder abuse."

"Besides, I thought you were in your prime," Thistle taunted.

Aunt Tillie leaned over the table and glared holes into Thistle. "You know that eggnog left over from Christmas that you tried to drink the other day?"

"The rancid eggnog?" Thistle nodded. "I could've died."

"That's what you're going to smell like when you wake up tomorrow morning."

"Keep it up, old lady," Thistle sneered. "I've been reading up on spells, and I know how to do that one now. If you're not careful, I'll fix it so you wake up smelling like Bengay tomorrow."

Aunt Tillie's eyes were narrow slits of hate. "Excuse me?"

"That's right." Thistle wasn't backing down. That was always her greatest mistake. "You're going to smell like Bengay, and I'll make it so everyone asks you how your AARP membership is going."

"AARP is for old people!" Aunt Tillie slammed her hand on the table.

"You're old," Thistle shot back. "Deal with it."

"Rancid eggnog is too good for you." Aunt Tillie lifted her chin at the sound of footsteps. Mom and Twila were leading Daniel and Brandon back through the dining room. When she saw Twila, she straightened. "Say goodbye to your offspring. She's pushed me too far. I'm going to kill her with a paper cut curse and then bury her in a shallow grave."

If Twila was bothered by the threat, she didn't show it. That was normal for Twila, though. She was often in her own little world. "Bye, Thistle." She waved at her daughter. "It was a genuine pleasure being your mother at least thirty percent of the time." With that, she disappeared into the kitchen.

Mom's chest heaved but she forced a smile for Daniel and Brandon. "That's just more of our dinner theater that we were talking about."

"It's awesome," Daniel said. "I can see why the tourists love it so much." He glanced at me. "Now I really am kind of sad that you settled for the FBI agent. I would love to be the one hanging out here with you in all this chaos."

From behind him, Brandon glared.

"That's very flattering," I said, not meaning it. "But Landon got here first."

"And I'm staying forever," Landon agreed. "And nobody is getting cold when things are supposed to be hot," he added for Aunt Tillie's benefit. "Now you're on *my* list. I'm going to join with Thistle on that Bengay thing. I hope it makes you cry."

"I see how it is." Aunt Tillie gripped her hand into a fist on the table. "I want to file a report," she barked at Chief Terry. "I'm being abused. I want them all arrested and charged with elder abuse."

"Until they strap you down to a bed and steal your Social Security check, I don't think you have much of a case," Chief Terry argued.

"Then you're on my list too." Aunt Tillie turned and headed for the kitchen. "I hate you all," she yelled before pushing through the door.

Daniel broke into applause in her wake. "This is magnificent. Are you sure you and Landon are forever, Bay?" He looked hopeful that I would give him an opening.

"I'm sure," I said. "Thanks for bolstering my ego, though."

Daniel winked. "That's what I'm here for."

When I locked gazes with Brandon, the younger man looked as if he wanted to remove Daniel from the equation altogether. "I hope you enjoyed your breakfast and tour. Thank you so much for stopping by."

"Yes, thank you," Chief Terry agreed. "We'll take it from here."

. . .

MOM DIDN'T LET DANIEL AND BRANDON LEAVE without ladening them down with bags of cookies and bread. It was thirty minutes before they finally cleared out, and by then we'd lost Aunt Tillie.

"She's in her pot field," Thistle said as we hiked to the field. "She's going to try to get rid of the evidence."

I didn't actually believe that. "Or she's trying to figure out if someone got past her wards to get the alder."

Landon and Chief Terry were behind us, their heads bent together as they whispered back and forth. "Alder isn't illegal to grow," I called back to them. "You can't arrest Aunt Tillie for growing it."

"That's not what we were talking about," Landon said.

"Definitely not," Chief Terry agreed. "Landon is still upset that Tillie suggested he might be falling down in the bedroom. I told him this was the one conversation I never wanted to have with him. He doesn't seem to care that I'm uncomfortable."

"You're my best friend," Landon argued. "If I can't talk about this with you, who can I talk about it with?"

"I'm not your best friend," Chief Terry said. "I'm Bay's father figure. Keep that in mind."

"Whatever." Landon waved off the statement. "You have to be my best friend. Marcus is kind of my friend, but we don't spend enough time together for me to confide in him. That only leaves you."

"I could be your best friend," I offered.

Landon's smile was sweet. "In some ways, you're my best friend. But I need a dude best friend to talk about dude things. You can't understand the dude things."

Well, now he had my full attention. "Do I even want to know what the dude things are?"

"You know: dude things." Landon looked at me as if I'd grown another head.

"I think he means they talk about shaving their chests and manscaping," Thistle offered helpfully. "Like, they probably have discussions about whether or not they should shave their pits to make their muscles pop. I know Marcus struggles with it."

The look Landon shot Thistle was withering.

"Marcus considers shaving his pits?" I asked. "If I were a guy, I wouldn't shave my pits. It's annoying."

"It is annoying," Thistle agreed. "Plus, it makes them look a little too smooth. Like they're dolphins or something."

"It's not like dolphins," Landon snapped. "Rocky shaved his pits."

"Sylvester Stallone is like five-foot-three," Thistle argued. "Nobody is short enough to look up at his pits and think they're weird."

"Chris Hemsworth shaves his pits." The look of triumph on his face suggested Landon thought he'd won the battle.

"Do you think you're on the same level with Chris Hemsworth?" Thistle challenged.

"Bay!" Landon's voice was a roar. "I can't deal with your family another second."

"Just ignore her." I waved him off. "Although, I am curious. Do you want to talk to Chief Terry about shaving your pits?"

"I can't even." Landon planted his hands on his hips and stared into the sky as if trying to combust. "That's so shallow, Bay. Men talk about things other than armpit hair."

I looked to Chief Terry. "Is that true? What do you talk about?"

Chief Terry looked far too amused with the conversation, especially considering what we were up against at present. "Do you know what Landon talks about when we have a beer, just the two of us?"

"I'm kind of afraid to know what dude things are."

"He talks about how much he loves you," Chief Terry continued, unruffled by my indecision. "He talks about how you're his favorite person in the world, and he wonders if he ever would've been happy if he didn't stumble across you in that cornfield the day you met."

"That's so sweet." I beamed at Landon.

"He believes you were destined to find one another, and he has deep thoughts after two beers," Chief Terry continued. "He wants to know what would've happened if he'd found a way to live up here and be with you as teenagers. He wants to know what would've happened if he'd found you later, when he was more set in his ways. He's terrified he would've accidentally settled for a woman who doesn't have a mother who can keep him in bacon the rest of his life."

I smirked as Landon glowered at Chief Terry. "Is that true?"

"I did that once," Landon complained. "He's never let me live it down. It was after four beers, not two."

"Aw," Thistle and I teased.

Landon shoved past us. "This whole family drives me crazy."

Months ago, if Landon and Chief Terry had tried to cross the wards into Aunt Tillie's pot field, they would've been knocked down by the worst cases of the trots known to man. They would've been bedridden for days. Landon had forced his way past the wards to help save me from an escaped prisoner and knew firsthand the horror that Aunt Tillie could wield. That day, however, we'd laid down the law with her. There had to be exceptions for Landon and Chief Terry. She'd reluctantly agreed. That's why the four of us could cross through the glamour dome she'd erected and enter her private domain without consequence.

Aunt Tillie was a strong witch. She didn't always use her magic for good. In this particular case, however, turning the field into a climate-controlled dome that we could access all winter—it was balmy and lovely beneath the dome—felt like the best magic imaginable.

"We should come back for a picnic when this is done," I told Landon, briefly closing my eyes as the warmth washed over me.

Outside, the starkness of a Michigan winter made me feel lethargic. Here, though, I felt amazing.

"We should," Landon agreed. He snuggled up behind me and offered a hug. "I really do say corny stuff to Terry about you," he whispered. "The truth is, you are my best friend. But I still have dude stuff to discuss occasionally."

I had things that I could discuss only with Clove and Thistle. "It's okay." I patted his hand. "I'll try not to tease you about your pits."

"I don't shave my pits," he growled as he released me.

"If that's your story." I gave him a wink before plunging deeper into the field. "The alder is over here." I led them to the east. "I saw a row a couple of weeks ago."

To nobody's surprise, Aunt Tillie was in front of the alder when we arrived. She looked annoyed.

"It came from here, didn't it?"

Aunt Tillie moved her jaw back and forth and nodded. "Here." She pointed to a section of the field that had been picked clean. "They took a whole plant."

"What does that mean?" Landon asked as he moved closer. He seemed content to give the alder a wide berth.

"It means that someone—I have to think someone with a firm grasp of fire magic—took the alder to set some fires."

"More than just the inn fire?" Landon asked.

"I didn't see that fire," Aunt Tillie cautioned. "From what Bay described, though, I think we're dealing with a fire wielder who gets a little help from my herbs."

"A fire wielder who is also a thief," Thistle mused. "Just out of curiosity, who would've known this was here?"

"It's not the leap you're imagining to think that Tillie has a whole garden of witch herbs here," Chief Terry argued. "There have always been whispers, and about more than just pot. Why else do you think Daniel came straight out here? I'm more concerned about the fact that whoever stole the alder managed to cross the wards. How did they do that?" he asked Aunt Tillie.

"I don't know." Anger sparked in Aunt Tillie's eyes. "There were footprints on the south side of the field. I think they tried to get in from that direction first. Then they circled around."

"Somebody came from the woods?" Thistle asked. "That means it's your banshee, doesn't it?"

Chief Terry answered before Aunt Tillie could. "Not necessarily. It could've been someone who assumed there was an entrance on that side. They could've parked on Elder Road and hiked in."

"They would had to have been reasonably assured we had what they were looking for," Thistle said. "Is that Joanie?"

"It's possible she researched our family after we met," I said. "Kevin likely knows we're magical, even if he doesn't realize to what extent. Then there's Childs. He's been hanging around. There's also Donna."

"It could also be someone we're not considering," Landon said. "They could be watching from afar."

"I need time to put together a spell," Aunt Tillie replied. She plucked some alder from a different bush. "We're going to search for my potion ingredients. It's possible whoever we're dealing with managed to shield themselves. It's also possible they didn't."

"How long will it take you?" Landon asked.

"At least a few hours," Aunt Tillie replied. "It's a precise spell." Her eyes moved to Thistle. "I have another spell to work on while I'm doing that."

"Don't waste time with nonsense," Chief Terry ordered. "Just focus on the locator spell. The Winchester hijinks can wait."

"It's as if you don't even know me," Aunt Tillie sniffed. "I'm going to do what I want, and there's not a thing you can do to stop me."

Chief Terry glowered at her. "Are you trying to kill me?"

"No, but keep pushing me and I might decide that's my ultimate goal."

"You're too much," Chief Terry groused.

"That's what keeps me young."

24

TWENTY-FOUR

We had a lot of questions and not enough answers. That meant starting from the beginning.

"We're reasonably certain that Joanie went after Alice because she thought Kevin was having an affair with her," I said back at the inn's dining room. Only Aunt Tillie was missing. She'd gone to her greenhouse to start work on the spell. "She tried to poison her. There was no fire involved."

"You think that the fires might be separate from Joanie's banshee problem," Landon surmised.

"It makes a weird sort of sense."

Landon didn't immediately answer. He swirled his spoon in his coffee and debated. "I don't know, Bay," he said finally, causing me to deflate a bit. "I have to think the fire was part of it. Otherwise, why would someone want to go after Frank and Alice? Why set their inn on fire? From everything you've told me, they're good people. So if it wasn't the idea that Kevin and Alice were having an affair, what was it?"

"The land deals," I replied. It was all I could come up with. "The fire burned hot, and it should've taken the entire building down.

That's what we assumed was happening. But the damage looks mostly cosmetic."

Landon ran his tongue over his lips. "You think Kevin is responsible for the fire."

"I think he has a partner. We need to figure out who it is."

"Bay, I need you to be clear on what you're saying," Chief Terry interjected. "You think Kevin and a partner have magically joined together to burn out inn owners because they want the property, and that Joanie turning into a banshee has nothing to do with that. Am I following your train of thought?"

"Joanie tried to poison Alice," I argued. "If she really could control fire—and Aunt Tillie agrees that too much alder is missing to have been used in just that one fire—then why not try to burn the entire hospital down? Wouldn't that have been easier?

"On top of that, if killing Alice was the whole goal, why create a fire that did so little damage?" I continued. "Why not burn it to the ground? Obviously, whoever set that fire didn't care if anyone was hurt. If we hadn't gone inside, all of those people would've died on the second floor."

"What about the girls?" Mom asked. "They were separated from everyone else."

"They also heard whispers before the fire, warning them," I said. "They think it was ghosts. They knew to try to get outside but were trapped in the pantry."

"Why would a ghost warn them?" Thistle asked. "I mean ... can't you just call the ghosts to you and demand answers?"

"If we were really dealing with ghosts," I confirmed. "I don't think we are. We're dealing with a magical being the girls think is a ghost."

"But what?" Marnie asked.

I hadn't been able to work that out yet. "The two things are separate. Aunt Tillie is creating a spell so we can track the stolen alder. Joanie is still out there, and we need to deal with her. While we're waiting, I want to know more about the land deals."

"We can dig on them," Landon said. "We'll have to go to the county building and review records, but we can figure out who Kevin's partner is easily enough."

"We have the name of the company," I said. "Kevin told us."

"Pegasus Developments. There are no names associated with the company. It doesn't exist except for a name on some documents. The land deeds will have to have a bank account associated with it. We can track that."

That was something at least. Not much, but something. "Okay, you guys chase that. Thistle and I will tackle Mrs. Little."

"What does Margaret have to do with any of this?" Chief Terry demanded.

"She knows about the land deals," I replied. "In fact, she knows everything that happens in this town. She might know who is behind Pegasus Developments."

"What makes you think she'll tell you what you want to know?" Chief Terry asked.

"I'm not going to give her a choice. I'll make a deal with her. One week of peace with Aunt Tillie for answers."

"You can't follow through on that," Landon said with a laugh. "There's no way Aunt Tillie will agree to that."

"You let me handle Aunt Tillie."

"Ah, famous last words," Thistle said. "You're going to get the same treatment as Mrs. Little if you're not careful."

"I've got this," I assured them. "Mrs. Little is our best bet."

"Just be careful." Landon leaned forward and kissed my forehead. "Mrs. Little is getting more and more strung out because of the constant aggravation from Aunt Tillie. She's close to breaking."

THISTLE WASN'T WEARING CAMOUFLAGE OR a combat helmet when we parked in front of Hypnotic, the magic store she co-owned with Clove, but her face was all Aunt Tillie as she glared at the Unicorn Emporium.

"Let's take that witch down." Thistle went to push open the door, but I grabbed her.

"Hold on," I admonished. "We need to come up with a plan."

Thistle's stare was incredulous. "To catch Mrs. Little? She falls for our ruses all the time."

"She has to have caught on by now," I insisted.

"Oh, you're so cute." Thistle lightly patted my cheek and then hit it a little harder than necessary. "You're also naive. She's too egotistical not to want to brag about what she knows."

I cupped my cheek and glared at her. "You're mean, you know that? Really, really mean."

"It keeps me young."

"You're just like Aunt Tillie."

"Say it again, and I'll curse you to smell like Bengay too." Thistle's eyes narrowed and the threat was impossible to ignore. "If you don't smell like food, Landon really will become the cold fish that he's worried about becoming."

"Whatever."

We glanced inside Hypnotic, where Clove was working behind the counter. She didn't look up, intent on her task.

"It's inventory day," Thistle explained.

"That's why you're so eager to torture Mrs. Little," I realized.

"Hey, don't get it twisted. I like torturing Mrs. Little even when it's not inventory day. This is just a happy coincidence."

Mrs. Little and her feather duster were working on her crystal section—the Unicorn Emporium had unicorns of every shape, size, and material. She didn't immediately turn around when the bell over her door jangled.

"Nobody has time for the two of you today," she announced.

Well, that answered *that* question. She'd seen us heading her way. She spent half her day spying on the people of Hemlock Cove in an attempt to get dirt on them.

"You don't have a choice," Thistle said. "We're not leaving until you talk to us."

"Then I'll call the police." When Mrs. Little turned, there was a glint in her eyes that I didn't recognize. It felt almost triumphant, and yet there was a hint of worry too. "I have the right to refuse service to anyone." She gestured with the feather duster to the sign that said just that.

"Do you know what I hear when you speak?" Thistle challenged. "Blah, blah, blah."

My eyes went wide. Apparently, we were going to antagonize her right out of the gate today. So much for subterfuge.

Of course, subterfuge was often wasted on Mrs. Little. "I need to know what you know about the inn purchases," I said.

Mrs. Little's forehead creased. "What are you talking about?"

"Kevin Dunne," I said, refusing to let her derail me with her sudden memory problems. "You mentioned him the other day, and how he was interested in the Blue Moon Inn."

"I'm certain you're mistaken." She looked like an innocent woman utterly confused by the conversational shift. "I'm sure I would remember that."

"Are you so old you're having memory problems now?" Thistle challenged.

Mrs. Little's eyes narrowed. "Age is a state of mind. I would've thought that Tillie had taught you that."

"Aunt Tillie is middle-aged, and if we forget that, she reminds us in painful ways."

"Is this you paying me back for the Christmas decorations?" I asked. It was the only thing that made sense.

"You mean the Christmas decorations that didn't come to life and try to kill me?" Mrs. Little challenged. "The Christmas decorations that sat outside my window singing 'you're a mean one, Mrs. Little' and then made noises like they were pooping?"

I had to press my lips together to keep from laughing. "I honestly have no knowledge of that song." It was true. Apparently, Aunt Tillie's curse had taken on a life of its own in ways we weren't even aware of. "I'm here about the inns being purchased."

"If you don't want to sell The Overlook, don't sell it." She was a little too prim for my liking.

"I talked to Kevin Dunne," I said. "He said we would either sell or be run out of business. He was pretty adamant."

"Perhaps he's right. Maybe, if all the other inns are under the right management, they'll run like a streamlined company, and Hemlock Cove will be able to ascend to the next level."

A niggling thread of suspicion sparked to life in the back of my mind. "It's you," I realized out loud.

"What's me?" Mrs. Little's expression was blank.

"You're Pegasus Developments."

Thistle's mouth fell open. "We really should've seen that coming."

"We should have," I agreed. We were surrounded by magical horses. It made way too much sense.

"I have no idea what you're talking about," Mrs. Little insisted. The way she averted her gaze was telling. "Have you fallen and hit your head? Perhaps when you raced into the Blue Moon Inn and saved Grace and Hope, when you passed out, perhaps you sustained some sort of brain injury."

"How can you know that I lost consciousness?" I demanded.

"Oh, Bay, your little hero routine was the talk of the town. It's not the first time you've run headlong into danger and come out mostly unscathed. You have people thinking you're a mythological creature." She glanced at the shelf to her left. "Almost as if you're a unicorn."

Things were starting to come together in a manner I wasn't comfortable with. "You partnered with Kevin. You're trying to buy up all the inns." I took a threatening step toward her. "You're pulling the strings."

"You want to be very careful, Bay," Mrs. Little warned. There was no mirth in her voice. There was nothing about the woman that could be considered warm and fuzzy. Not even by her so-called friends. "I'll have you arrested."

"I can just see Chief Terry slapping her in cuffs on your orders," Thistle scoffed.

"Terry Davenport isn't the only game in town. There are others."

She'd been talking to Childs. What was his part in all of this?

Rather than blurt out the name and let her know I was on to her, I decided to take a different tack. "Your goal is to buy up every inn you can get your hands on and then force our mothers out of business." It wasn't a question.

"I have nothing against your mothers," Mrs. Little countered. "Tillie is another story. And, last time I checked, she owns half that land."

"You're not getting the land even if you somehow manage to run The Overlook out of business," Thistle argued.

"Oh, no?" Now Mrs. Little really did look smug. "Did you know that your mothers took out a mortgage on the property when the town rebranded? They were keen to build the inn they'd always wanted.

"They were good little savers," she continued. "They had a great start to their dreams. To get what they wanted, though, they needed more money."

I felt sick to my stomach. "Did you know they took out a mortgage?" I asked Thistle.

She shook her head. "I thought they had the money."

"That's what they told people." Mrs. Little reminded me of the Cheshire Cat as she warmed to her topic. She was nowhere near as charming, though. "They wanted people to believe that. They quietly got a mortgage through the bank. Dirk Butler likes to talk when he's drunk."

Dirk Butler, the bank manager, had loose lips.

"Again, I have nothing against your mothers," Mrs. Little said. "But Tillie owns half that land. She co-signed for the mortgage. All of the land will go to the bank if they can't pay their bills." The way she preened made me want to smack her around.

"So you joined forces with Kevin Dunne once I told you he was interested in inns," I realized. "You're Pegasus Developments, his new partner company. It's all a way for you to fly under the radar."

"It works so well for your family," Mrs. Little sneered. "The beauty of it is that we really are going to help Hemlock Cove flourish. Your family won't be part of it."

She thought she'd already won. "You only have a few inns," I argued.

"Yes, but we're going to be acquiring more in the next few months."

"You think we're going to let that happen?"

Mrs. Little made a face. "There's no way you can stop us. There are a lot of people who look happily on the idea of early retirement. That's what we're offering."

"Somehow, when we make public what you're doing, I doubt people will be willing to sell."

"You might be surprised."

"We won't let you win," I warned.

"How can you stop me?"

"You keep coming at us as if you're fighting random people," I replied. "You keep using underhanded *human* tactics. We're not limited by your rules. We play by a different set of rules."

"Magic." Mrs. Little didn't flinch when she said the M-word this time. "You're going to be dealing with other problems on that front. I'm not the only one who knows now. You have powerful enemies working against you, and they're coming from different directions."

She was definitely in cahoots with Childs. That was a problem for another time. "I need to make sure that you understand what's happening." I took a menacing step toward her. "You realize that someone in your group—and I will find out who that is and end them—has harnessed magic and is trying to burn people out and kill them."

Mrs. Little barked out a laugh. When my expression didn't crack, she sobered. "That's ridiculous."

"You weren't in that fire," I countered. "It was definitely magical.

Why do you think the building sustained so little permanent damage?"

Mrs. Little hesitated. "I thought it was just a stroke of luck."

"Not so much. There's a magical element to your plan."

"And you know what that means," Thistle said.

Now Mrs. Little was nervous. "What does it mean?"

"It means that we're going to snuff it out."

"And then we're coming for you," I said grimly. "I hope you're ready, because if you thought the farting unicorns and randy reindeer were freaky, you haven't seen anything yet. Now we're mad."

"It's not just Aunt Tillie," Thistle added. "Her games are nothing compared to what we're going to throw at you."

"You can't threaten me," Mrs. Little growled.

"We just did," I countered. "You'd better batten down the hatches, because Hurricane Winchester is coming for you, and it's going to be a Category Five storm."

"You'll be seeing us," Thistle promised as we headed to the door. "Welcome to Thunderdome."

I frowned as I followed her out of the store. "Welcome to Thunderdome?" I taunted when we were outside. "That was lame."

Thistle shrugged. "It was all I could think of. I'll do better next time."

"We need to get to Kevin Dunne."

"Why?"

"Because he has the rest of our answers."

"Well, good. I'm feeling mean. He deserves to be tortured."

On that we could wholeheartedly agree.

25
TWENTY-FIVE

I called Landon as soon as we were in Thistle's car. I was ranting.

"Take a breath, Bay," he said after I'd gone on for about fifteen minutes. "Just ... take a breath, sweetie."

"You take a breath," I fired back. "That unicorn freak is trying to buy the town and run my mom out of business."

I didn't realize Landon had the call on speakerphone until Chief Terry's voice filtered through.

"We won't let your mom lose the inn, sweetheart. I'll find out how much she owes, and we can use the money from the sale of my house to pay off the mortgage."

My breath caught in my throat. "You would do that?"

He sounded exasperated when he spoke again. "We're going to be family."

"We've always been family."

"I would've sold my house to save the inn even if your mother and I weren't getting married," he said. "I love that place as much as you do."

The aching sweetness in his voice had me doing what Landon

suggested, taking a breath. Then I remembered Mrs. Little's face. "It's war."

"It's Thunderdome," Thistle corrected. I had my phone on speaker, so she'd been able to follow the conversation.

"Stop trying to make Thunderdome work."

"Fine." Thistle pouted. "Seriously, I'm Team Aunt Tillie from here on out. We're either going to drive that old woman mad and force her out of town or..." There was no need for her to finish the intention.

We couldn't kill Mrs. Little. No matter how angry we were, we weren't those types of witches. We could torture her until she wished she was dead, though.

"We'll handle Margaret," Chief Terry said. "There are other ways to make her crazy. We can tell everyone in town what she's up to. She likes being loved. She likes being a victim. If you go after her with mean garden gnomes and farting unicorns, she gets to embrace victimhood."

"But if I were to run a front-page article on how she started Pegasus Developments, and how she partnered with Kevin Dunne to buy the inns because she wanted to take over the town, she'd be the villain," I said.

"Sounds like an interesting option," Landon said. I could hear the grin in his voice. "You'll have to be careful that everything is factual—"

"I'm not a rookie," I growled. "I know how to write a balanced news story."

"You would hurt her worse with that than with anything else," Landon insisted.

We lapsed into silence for several seconds.

"Or we could do the front-page story thing *and* curse every dog in town to hump her leg," Thistle said.

I started bobbing my head. "That's the plan. That's what we're going to do."

Landon chuckled but didn't sound opposed to the idea. "Maybe you can make her smell like three-day-old fish and chips while you're at it and make all the cats urinate on her. You know, just to make it really fun."

"Don't encourage them," Chief Terry admonished.

"I can't help it," Landon said. "I want Mrs. Little to pay as much as they do."

"Are we certain she didn't have anything to do with the fires?" Chief Terry asked. "I know she'd lie, but how certain are you that she's not responsible for the magical stuff?"

It was a fair question. Months before, Mrs. Little had sent a djinn after us without realizing the hell she was unleashing. That's how badly she wanted to win.

"That doesn't feel right," I replied. "She seemed genuinely surprised. I think this is Kevin."

"Where did he get the magic?"

"I don't know, but I'm about to find out."

"Bay, you should wait for us," Landon argued. "We can be back in town in an hour, and then we'll go see Dunne together."

"No." I was firm. "I'm not dragging you into this. Not when we're arguing about magic. I need to be the one to confront him. It has to be me because I'm the reason he decided to go this route."

Landon sounded exasperated. "Bay, you cannot blame yourself for this."

"Kevin didn't know about magic until his mistress started throwing it around and killed people."

"That's still not your fault." Landon was firm. "He cheated on his wife. He picked bad people to cheat on his wife with. You saved the girls at the school. I will not tolerate you blaming yourself."

He was right, blaming myself was a waste of time. "I'm going to talk to him," I insisted. "It has to be me."

Landon was quiet so long I thought we'd inadvertently dropped the call. Then he sighed. "Okay. Be careful."

"I don't believe he's magical," I said. "He's working with someone who is."

"That doesn't change the fact that you could be hurt."

"I'll be fine." I wasn't worried in the least. "Also, you should know that Mrs. Little alluded to having friends in law enforcement. I'm almost positive she was talking about Brad Childs."

Chief Terry viciously swore. "Why doesn't that surprise me? He's been idling toward trouble for weeks now."

"There's nothing we can do about him right now, but he's a problem we'll have to deal with eventually."

"Deal with Dunne first. I want you to let me know as soon as you leave his office. I want to make sure you're okay and heading home."

"I've got this," I promised. "He's no match for me."

DUNNE REALTY LOOKED MOSTLY EMPTY WHEN we parked in the lot. There were several vehicles, but all toward the back of the lot.

"I bet those are employees," Thistle said as she killed the engine of her car. "I don't think there are any clients here."

Three cars, I noted. One I recognized as belonging to Kevin. "Let's see if we can empty the office. If the others insist on hanging around, they're probably involved in this."

"And if they are?" Thistle asked.

"Then maybe one of them is magical."

"Yeah, that's bothering me," Thistle said. "We're missing the magical tie-in. Where would he have found someone this powerful?"

"I bet it's someone with a vagina," I replied darkly.

"He's sleeping with her."

"It makes sense. I guarantee he's gotten more tail than a donkey at a birthday party."

It took Thistle a moment to grasp the joke. "Oh, that was a Dad joke. Chief Terry would tell that joke."

"He's the best dad," I said. Then I realized how uncomfortable his next few days were going to be. "Mom is going to be angry when she realizes Mrs. Little has been spreading her personal business."

"So, so mad," Thistle agreed. "Are you ready for this?"

"Yup. It's time to put Kevin in his place and figure out exactly what we're dealing with."

There were only a handful of people in the lobby. Two men stood by the front window and high-fived and laughed as we crossed the threshold. I recognized the woman behind the counter from the first time I'd visited the office. She was Kevin's receptionist, and I had a feeling she was also one of his conquests.

"We're here to see Kevin," I announced as we breezed toward his office. "You are free to go."

The receptionist's eyes went wide. "You can't barge into his office. I need to tell him you're here."

"Yeah, we're going to skip all of that. You're going to go. Have a nice day." I waved them off before pushing into Kevin's office.

He was sitting at his desk typing on his keyboard. The sounds from his computer told me he wasn't actually working.

"Seriously?" I demanded. "Porn? You're unbelievable."

Kevin's eyes went wide. "Do you even believe in knocking?"

"Knocking is what you do when you're polite," I replied. "You don't make me feel polite."

"Well, at least we're no longer pretending to like one another." Kevin grinned. "What can I do for you? Can I hope that you're here to offer me a good deal on your family's property?"

"You'll die before that happens," I fired back.

Kevin, so jovial seconds before, swallowed hard when he took in the serious tilt of my chin. "What do you want?" He was no longer putting on an act. He wanted us gone, and dealing with us quickly was the only way to make that happen.

"I want to know who you're working with."

"I told you. I'm working with a development company. Pegasus Developments."

"Can I twist his nipples off?" Thistle asked.

"Not just yet," I replied.

Kevin shifted and rubbed his chest. "You're a very violent family."

"You have no idea," I said. "We're about to get even more violent if you don't start talking."

"If you threaten me, I'll call the police."

"Please." He was so full of himself. "The only reason you're still alive is because I saved you. I'm the reason you were moved to a safe house. I'm the only reason you're not dead."

Discomfort rode over Kevin's face. "How did you know I was in a safe house?"

"She just told you, Twiddly-Dumb," Thistle snapped.

"But ... Joanie has lost her mind and is making threats. That's what the police officers who intercepted me said. She's threatening to kill me and Katie, so we had to go into hiding. They're taking their own sweet time finding her. I just want them to arrest her so I can be done with this. As for why I'm here, I have a job to do. She wouldn't dare come after me here."

He still didn't understand.

"You'd like that, wouldn't you?" I challenged. "It would make your life so much easier if she was arrested and locked away. Then nobody would blame you when you divorced her. You would be a father protecting his daughter."

"I'm an excellent father."

"You're a terrible human being all around, and your daughter realizes it," I said. "You're not going to get what you want, because the story the cops told you is only partially true."

"I'm not sure what you mean."

"There's no way for me to explain this in a manner that you can grasp quickly, so I'm just going to blurt it out, and you're going to accept it."

"Okay?"

"Your wife is a banshee. I caught her going into Alice Milligan's room at the hospital. She tried to poison her. Then I went to your house to confront her, and she turned into a banshee."

Kevin's expression was impossible to read. After a few seconds, he looked around at the ceiling corners in his office. "Did you put cameras in here?" he asked. "Am I on a prank show?"

"You broke her." I was in no mood for his nonsense. "Your affairs made her bitter, and she believed you were having an affair with Alice because ... well, you're you. She decided she wanted to kill Alice, and her bitterness turned her into a banshee. Now all she cares about is killing the thing that destroyed her life."

He'd paled two shades. "You mean me."

"Yes."

"But ... no. I don't believe in that stuff."

I planted my hands on his desk and stared into his eyes. "Yes, you do. Stop putting on a show. Nobody is buying it. Your wife is a banshee. The only one who can save you from her is me."

"That's a bit of a stretch," Thistle hedged. "Scout and Stormy could probably take her out. And Evan. Evan definitely could."

I glared at her.

"What?" she protested. "I was just thinking out loud."

"I'm your only hope," I repeated to Kevin. "In exchange for my protection, you're going to tell me what magical being you're working with. Who started that fire?"

"I have no idea what you're talking about," Kevin snapped. "Nobody started a fire."

Did he really believe that? He was a proficient liar. "I know Margaret Little is behind Pegasus Developments," I said. When he opened his mouth to protest, I held up my hand. "I know it. Mrs. Little is going to get what's coming to her."

Kevin shrank in his chair.

"I also know you're working with someone else," I said. "That someone set the fire at the Blue Moon Inn. That someone is keeping Frank and Alice Milligan in comas. That someone stole alder from a garden and used it for the fire. That's why the building wasn't damaged as much as it should've been."

"I don't know anything about that," Kevin sputtered. "That can't be true. I'm just working with Margaret."

"You have another partner," I insisted. "There's no other explanation. We're missing a magical being. Unless ... is it you?" I looked him up and down with fresh eyes.

"Not me!"

I believed him. He was the biggest waste of space on the planet. "Then it's someone else."

"I don't know what you're talking about." Kevin's voice turned shrill. "I don't even understand what you're saying. It's just Margaret and me. I was working with another developer, but when Margaret explained how rich we could be if I cut him out, that's what I did. We're going to buy the inns he's already purchased—apparently Margaret has dirt on him and got him to agree—and then we're going after every other inn we can get our hands on."

"Because Margaret wants to run my mother and aunts out of business."

"Hey, that's all her." Kevin held up his hands. "I just want to make money."

I shifted from one foot to the other, my mind going a million miles a minute. "It has to be Mrs. Little," I said to Thistle. "She didn't tell us the whole truth. She's working with another partner."

"I haven't seen her with anyone lately."

"She wouldn't be stupid enough to be seen in public with whoever it is." I started to pace.

"Which means, now that we've confronted her, she's going to confront the partner."

I reached for my phone. I didn't get a chance to call Landon and send him after Mrs. Little, because the glass behind Kevin's desk exploded inward as a dark figure leapt through the opening and landed in the middle of his office.

Kevin fell out of his chair. The sight of his wife, who no longer looked human, was too much.

"Oh my gawd!" Kevin scrambled against the tile floor to escape.

Joanie moved to grab him.

I could let Joanie kill Kevin—it wasn't like he didn't have it coming—or I could save him and force his hand. He would owe us.

I lashed out with my magic, my hand coming out in a wide sweep, and sent Joanie flying against the wall. Thistle and I rushed forward and grabbed Kevin under his arms and hauled him to his feet.

Joanie's chest heaved as she glared at us.

"Don't," I warned, extending a finger as we backed away from her. "You can't come back from this if you kill him." I still wanted to save her. "I know you love your daughter. Remember Katie. This piece of crap is not worth losing every semblance of yourself."

"Listen to them, Joanie," Kevin said. "You don't want to kill me."

"And you're a piece of crap," Thistle said, kicking him in the calf. "Don't forget that part."

"And I'm a piece of crap," Kevin conceded. "You really don't want to kill me. Katie will have no parents. Is that what you want?"

Something akin to regret flashed in Joanie's eyes, and for a moment I thought she was going to turn into her former self. She threw back her head and screamed.

Around us, the glass doors and windows began to shake.

"Move," I ordered Thistle. She helped me drag Kevin through the door. We'd barely made it into the lobby when all of the windows in the office exploded. Glass flew everywhere and we ducked our faces. By the time we could raise our chins again to track Joanie's movements, she was gone.

"Listen, you little maggot." I grabbed the front of Kevin's shirt as he fell limply to the ground. "You're going to help us take down Margaret Little. You're going to sell the inns you've bought to people we approve of. You're going to stop sleeping with everything that moves. And maybe—just maybe—we'll somehow keep you alive and help your wife turn back into a human."

Kevin blinked several times. "I'll live?" he pleaded. "That's all I really care about."

"You really are a piece of crap," Thistle growled.

26
TWENTY-SIX

I had a feeling we were going to need Kevin, so I handed him over to Landon and Chief Terry when they arrived at the office.

"Do something with this," I ordered before starting toward the door.

Landon caught my elbow. "Do you want to share with the class what happened here?" he challenged.

"I told you. Joanie came looking for her husband."

"Yes, and I'm a little annoyed about that." Landon's eyes darted to Kevin. "Why, exactly, were you at work?"

Kevin blinked, confused. It almost looked as if Landon had asked why the sky was blue. "I work to pay bills. Keeping the lights on and the heat running takes money."

"You were supposed to stay in the safe house."

Kevin shrugged. "I was bored."

"Oh, well, you were bored." Landon shook his head before focusing on me. "I couldn't quite follow you on the phone. I need you to lay it all out for me."

"Mrs. Little is a big, fat liar," I sputtered.

"I don't know what to say to that. It's hardly new information."

I tried to set him on fire with my eyes. "Now is not the time for you to be funny."

He held up his hands in supplication. "I need to know what we're dealing with, Bay. I can't help—and I am going to help—until I know what the plan is."

I forced myself to suck in a deep breath. He was right. We had no choice but to work together to bring this one home.

"Mrs. Little essentially admitted that she was working with Kevin Dunne to run my mother and aunts out of business," I started.

"I know that, Bay." Landon looked as if he was forcing himself to remain calm. "We've already had this conversation. You were coming here to confront Dunne about the partnership."

"Kevin didn't deny working with Mrs. Little," I said. "Actually, he tried to deny quite a few things. We called him on it, and he ultimately admitted that he and Mrs. Little were buying property in an attempt to subjugate everyone in Hemlock Cove."

"I'm reasonably sure that I did not use the word 'subjugate,'" Kevin complained.

I ignored him. "He claims that he doesn't have anybody magical on his payroll," I continued.

"That is 100 percent true," Kevin interjected. "I don't know anyone magical. Except for Bay and my wife. Apparently, she's magical now." He looked troubled. "You don't think she's going to stay that pale, do you? It's going to make going to the office Christmas party more difficult than I imagined if she doesn't get her looks back."

"Yes, because that's what we should be worried about," Landon snarled. He focused on me. "Bay, get to the point. You're meandering ... which is so Aunt Tillie."

"I'm getting to the point," I growled. "We're going to fight about you calling me Aunt Tillie later. Kevin thinks they're just buying up property. He doesn't know about the magical aspect."

"Which means Margaret has to be controlling this magical being," Chief Terry surmised.

"She tricked us. Right now, she's out there warning this creature—or, worse, getting it ready to unleash Armageddon on us. She thinks she's finally outsmarted us."

"What is she going to do?" Landon asked.

"I don't know, but I think she's going to try to burn down the Blue Moon Inn. It's evidence. She knows we're going to figure out she's lying. She also knows she has limited time. I'm guessing she's already with her other partner making plans."

"But who is it?"

That was the problem. "We have dueling issues here. Joanie is definitely a banshee, and she wants to kill Kevin."

"Which seems like an extreme reaction," Kevin said.

"I don't think she wants to hurt Katie, but she's still a danger," I continued. "We need to draw her out into the open and try to heal her the way Aunt Tillie healed Donna."

"You want to turn her into a misshapen hunk of a woman?" Landon asked.

"If we're taking votes, I don't want that outcome," Kevin said. "Appearances must be kept up."

Landon slowly tracked his eyes to Kevin. "If you don't shut up, I'm going to punch you in the face. Do you understand?"

Kevin balked. "It was just a suggestion."

Landon turned back to me. "Are you sure it's best that we don't kill her?"

I held my hands palms out. "I don't know if killing her is better or not. Heck, for all I know, it might be a kindness to kill her. I only know I have to try to save her."

"Of course you do." He cupped my cheek, then sighed. "How do we do it?"

"Aunt Tillie intimated she wanted to reverse the spell she cast on Donna and try again," I said. "That suggests she's been working on something with a better outcome. She'll have a spell."

"What is she doing right now?" Chief Terry asked. "Why isn't she already here?"

"Because the fight isn't going to take place here," I replied. "Plus, she's creating the alder locator spell. Once we deal with Joanie, we have to deal with our firebug. They really are two separate issues."

Chief Terry nodded stiffly. "You want to lure Joanie into a trap, heal her with whatever Tillie has up her sleeve, and then just send her on her merry way with her family?"

"That's a bit simplistic," I argued. "Plus, we have to talk about the fact that she tried to poison Alice Milligan. She's not completely without blame."

"Fine." Chief Terry held up his hand. "We'll just magically fix the Dunne family and somehow overlook the poisoning thing. That doesn't sound out of the realm of possibility."

"Sarcasm is not your forte," Thistle said. "I can give you lessons."

Chief Terry glared at her before focusing on me. "What about the arsonist?"

"It's someone in Hemlock Cove." That was the only thing I knew for certain. "It's someone we know."

"What makes you think that?"

"Mrs. Little was worried enough to wave us off as we left town—she basically admitted her plan as a distraction—and now she's preparing to tie up loose ends while she thinks we're distracted."

Chief Terry looked pained. "What do we do?"

I could think of only one thing. "I need to talk to Hope and Grace."

Chief Terry balked. "No way. Gretchen won't allow you to question them about monsters."

"Gretchen will do whatever it takes to save her family. Somewhere out there is a creature that can control fire. It's keeping Frank and Alice in comas. It..." Something occurred to me, and I trailed off.

"What is it?" Landon asked, his hand landing on my back.

"A demon." I thought about it for several seconds. "Yeah, it's definitely a demon."

"How can you be sure?" Chief Terry asked. "You said you didn't know until right now."

"Demons can control fire. They can also appear as shadows, or 'ghosts.' They're like mercenaries. They're fine getting paid to do dastardly deeds. Most paranormals do it for bloodlust or because they can't stop themselves. This is a financial arrangement."

Chief Terry nodded. "Okay, let's say I get onboard with this. Margaret hired a demon to set a fire."

I shook my head. "I don't think she knew about the fire. I think she hired a demon to persuade the Milligans—and other inn owners—to sell. She didn't think it through. She had no idea how the demon was going to hold up its end of the bargain."

Realization dawned on Landon's face, and he nodded. "She got in over her head."

"That is what she does best," Thistle agreed.

"So how do we fix this?" Chief Terry asked.

"We don't fix the firebug. Not yet. We need Aunt Tillie's locator spell."

Chief Terry looked as if he was about to go nuclear. "I can't sit back while we do nothing."

"I have no intention of doing nothing," I assured him. "I do, however, have every intention of handling the Joanie situation first. Then we'll hit up Grace and Hope on our way to Hemlock Cove to deal with Mrs. Little and our firebug."

"I'm almost afraid to ask the next question," Chief Terry said. "How are we going to deal with Joanie?"

"We need Aunt Tillie's spell," I said.

"If she's supposed to be working on the alder locator spell, how can she heal the banshee at the same time?" Landon asked.

Something occurred to me. "Actually, we don't need Aunt Tillie to heal Joanie." I thought of Evan, what Scout had done for him. "We need to heal the banshee part of Joanie. It doesn't have to be perfect. We just need her not to be a monster."

Landon blinked. "Okay, but how?"

"Who do we know who has already healed a monster?"

Landon's eyebrows hopped with recognition. "Scout."

I nodded. "Scout can help us with Joanie. I thought we needed Aunt Tillie, but she already failed at this once."

"Where do you want to set this trap?" Chief Terry asked. "It has to be somewhere that we won't risk anyone getting hurt. If we could also avoid witnesses, that would be great."

"Well, it can't be here." I looked around the office, at the destroyed windows. "It has to be somewhere with open space and windows that we can use magic to repair if necessary."

The answer came to me in an instant. "I know where to go." I pulled my phone out of my pocket and started to text Scout. "I'll have her meet us there. We need Kevin."

The man in question balked. "Excuse me?" he squeaked. "Why do you need me?"

I sent him a saucy smirk. "That's easy. We need bait."

"Absolutely not." Kevin vehemently shook his head. "I have a daughter."

I shot back, "You're doing it. Whether you like it or not."

THE STONECREST ACADEMY WAS EMPTY. That was hardly surprising. Once they lost key members of the staff there was no way the school could remain operational. They had to shut their doors and regroup.

It was weird seeing the school so empty. We'd visited during the Christmas break, so it was hardly bustling with activity. Still, it was sad to see the school in this state.

"Do you think they'll open again?" I asked Chief Terry as we stood in front of the administration building.

"You want them to reopen a school for girls they've deemed troublesome?" Chief Terry arched an eyebrow.

"I want them to reopen for girls who need help," I clarified. "I don't think everything the school did was bad."

"I enjoyed visiting," Kevin volunteered.

"That's because you were nailing half the staff." Landon cuffed the back of Kevin's head. "You're the reason we're in this mess in the first place."

"Hey, it's not my fault." Kevin turned petulant. "I have an overactive sex drive. I was born this way. You can't hate a guy for something that's out of his control."

"Watch us." Landon flicked his gaze to the parking lot as a huge pickup truck pulled in and parked. "Scout and Gunner are here."

"And Evan." I pointed to the road, where the vampire was walking in to join us. He could move extremely fast when he wanted—faster than any vehicle—but I'd warned him we would have Kevin. He was putting on a show.

"What are we doing here?" Scout asked when she joined us. "This place looks haunted. It's creepy."

It was indeed creepy. It was also deserted. "We need to set a trap."

"And then what?" Scout asked.

"I need you to heal Joanie."

Scout's forehead creased.

I adopted my best "you love me and want to do the biggest favor known to man" smile. "I need you to heal Joanie like you did Evan."

"You want me to turn her into a day-walking vampire?"

Kevin immediately started shaking his head. "No, we don't want that."

"I hate to agree with Dinglefritz here, but we definitely don't want that," Landon said.

"Joanie's aunt is a banshee," I explained. "She hibernates most of the time and then comes out to feed during winter storms. She's punishing herself. She's a huge, misshapen monster. We don't want that to happen to Joanie."

"Evan gave me the lowdown on all that," Scout said. "I'm not sure what my part in this is. It's not as if I have a lot of pixie magic to draw on. When I healed Evan, I had a decent amount of pixie dust to help."

"Healing Evan was a bigger job. I believe that Joanie isn't really a banshee. She's only a half banshee."

"Oh, it's *Lost Boys* logic." Gunner grinned. "I'm all in."

Scout shot him a derisive look. "You're all in, but I've got to do the healing. Give me a second to figure this out. Basically, you want me to force the banshee out of her," she said.

I nodded. "Actually, if you could leave a little banshee—just enough so she can grab Kevin's nuts and squeeze them whenever he gets out of line—I would be forever appreciative."

"Sure!" Scout looked Kevin up and down. "He's obviously the bait. How are we going to trap her?"

"I figured we would go with simple runes."

"And then what?"

"Evan will swoop in and hold her while you heal her." It sounded simple, but I knew it would be more difficult than that.

"As long as you have a plan." Evan was surprisingly blasé. "What are you going to do about her trying to poison Alice Milligan?"

"I thought I would talk to her."

Evan smirked. "I don't want to tell you your business, but what if this doesn't work?"

He was assuming I was ruling out killing Joanie. "If we can't heal her, we'll have to kill her." It was our only other option. "I want to at least try to heal her. This piece of crap pushed her to the brink. If we can pull her back just a little, I think she'll want to improve her life."

"I'm not so sure about that," Scout hedged. "She put up with this guy's crap for years. It's possible she doesn't want to help herself."

"We still have to try," I pleaded. "Please."

Scout's expression softened. "We can try. In fact, I want to try. But if we fail you need to know that I won't hesitate to put Joanie down."

The knot in my stomach tightened. "I want to try first."

"Then we'll try." Scout's answer was simple. "Let's not do this in the parking lot. There's a field by the library. The buildings will give us cover."

I almost hugged her in thanks. She wasn't much of a hugger, so I just smiled. "Thank you so much for doing this."

"That's what friends are for."

"You go above and beyond."

She lifted one shoulder in a haphazard shrug. "I like to be the best at everything, including friendship."

"You have a soft heart."

"Don't ever say that again. I'm a total badass."

"Let's head to the library. The field is right there. I want to get this done, because once we deal with the banshee, I'm pretty sure there's a demon out there who needs killing."

Scout perked up. "Can I kill him?"

"Absolutely."

"This day is looking up."

27
TWENTY-SEVEN

The plan was a simple one. Thistle and I drew wards to lure in Joanie. Scout talked on the phone with Aunt Tillie to ask what she'd done with Donna all those years ago. Aunt Tillie told her what she thought she'd done wrong. Scout took it all in, nodding as she absorbed it, then smiled at me as she disconnected.

"I've got this." She shot me a thumbs-up. "We're good."

I hoped she was right.

Kevin was the whiny mess I expected when we positioned him in the center of the wards. He didn't want to stay in the open, where he was an easy target.

"I'll sleep with you if you make one of the others be the bait," he pleaded to me in a low voice.

I narrowed my eyes. "That's not a reward."

"Definitely not," Thistle agreed.

"I'll sleep with all of you," Kevin offered. "I'll make it good." He swallowed hard when Landon and Gunner took menacing steps toward him. "I wasn't talking about you guys."

"Shut up," Landon growled. "The longer you drag this out, the longer the real threat has to burn somebody's home down. We need to finish this."

"But ... I don't want to die." Kevin turned his pleading eyes to me. "I want to go back to the way things were."

"When your wife pretended not to know you were sleeping with women in three towns?" I snapped.

"Five," he corrected before he remembered who he was talking to. "Wait ... three is better. Yes, it was three."

"Can I hex his penis to shrink?" Thistle asked. "Like, you know, those big pimples that you can feel the pus moving beneath the skin? What if I turned it into one of those?"

"Don't you dare." Kevin crossed his hands in front of his crotch. "I'll sue you."

"We'll worry about his penis after we bring Joanie back," I said. "She should make the decision."

"Nothing is happening to my penis!" Kevin's eyes were wild.

"If you take off, I'll be chasing you," Gunner warned. "I will hurt you."

Gunner was a big guy—a fact not lost on Kevin—and the real estate agent nodded, a muscle working in his jaw. "Fine. I want to save my family."

I had my doubts that Kevin's family would ever be the same again. We couldn't fix everything for them. All we could do was try to save Joanie. What she did with her second chance was up to her.

"Let's do this." I snagged gazes with Scout, who nodded, and then raised my hands. "*Inretio*," I hissed as the wards flared to life. It wasn't like calling a ghost. All I had to do was wish it with ghosts to make it happen.

A banshee was different.

The wards burned hot, melting the snow, and then blinked out. They were still working, still calling to Joanie, but they weren't as bright. The spell was working as I intended.

We waited several minutes, scanning the woods surrounding the field. I was about to suggest a different tack, one that involved all of us joining together to call Joanie, when a figure appeared at the corner of the library.

Joanie's clothes were ragged. Her hair was wild and unkempt. Her skin was pale nearly to the point of transparency. Her eyes were the most haunting part of her, dark and sunken.

The transformation was almost complete. If she managed to kill Kevin, there would be no saving her.

"Oh, hey, honey," Kevin said brightly. He sounded as if he was about to lose his mind. "It's so good to see you. That's an interesting look."

"For once in your life, shut up," Evan snapped. He was moving away from our group, keeping his distance from Joanie while angling to cut off her avenue of attack. "Just this once, let something be about Joanie."

I took a step toward Joanie. She was still about three hundred feet away. She could run if she deemed us a threat. I was hoping her need to hurt Kevin was greater than her survival instincts.

"Joanie, I know things have been hard for you," I started.

Her eyes jerked to me, and it took everything I had not to cringe when our gazes locked. She looked so lost that it hurt to stare at her too long.

"Kevin is a piece of crap," I announced.

"Stop saying that," Kevin whined. "I'm misunderstood."

I ignored him. "Your life was altered because your husband was not the man you thought you married. I'm assuming he wooed you with that charm he seems to have so much of."

Kevin broke into a wide grin. "That's the nicest thing you've said about me."

"That charm was all a facade," I continued. "He's a terrible man who used you to create the perfect family, and then he used and abused you."

"That is not so nice," Kevin complained.

"I'm sure you were crushed when you found out about Kevin's dalliances," I said. "But you wanted to keep your family at all costs."

"It's not my fault," Kevin hissed. "I have a glandular issue."

Landon jabbed a finger in Kevin's direction. "I'm going to punch you when this is over. You've been warned."

I forced myself to remain focused on Joanie. "You are a victim in all of this. You have to get past it, because this is not the answer." I gestured to her new banshee look. "This will not get you a happily ever after."

"You're no longer a victim," Scout added.

I shot her a quelling look. "Of course she's a victim. Her husband cheated on her."

"She was a victim the first time he cheated," Scout countered. "She could still call herself a victim the second time. They had a child. I can see why she would try to save the marriage. By the third and fourth time, though, she was an enabler. By the tenth and eleventh time, she was just as much a villain in her daughter's story as he was."

I made a strangled sound deep in my throat. This was not the way to get Joanie to want to work with us. "Scout!"

"It's true." Scout always spoke her mind. "I'm sorry if that upsets you, Joanie, but you didn't become a banshee because you believed your husband cheated on you with Alice Milligan. You were numb to it by that point.

"Your husband's affairs made you bitter, but what made you a banshee—besides the fact that you were likely predisposed to it—is the fact that you allowed him to treat you like dirt." Scout took a deliberate step closer to Joanie. "You weren't mad at him the day that Bay and Evan came to your house. You were mad at yourself for allowing it."

My first instinct was to shut Scout up. This was going to make things worse. When I darted a look to Joanie, however, I was almost positive that her hair looked a little less gross, and her skin wasn't quite as pale.

Apparently, tough love was the way to go.

"Is that what happened?" I asked. I moved to the right a bit. Between Evan, Scout, and me, we would be able to cover any angle that Joanie utilized to rush toward her husband. "Were you mad at yourself?"

"No." Joanie shook her head, solidifying her banshee appearance again. "Alice slept with my husband."

"I would never sleep with Alice," Kevin countered. "Her kids were too old. They were too smart. If you're going to have an affair with someone who has kids, the kids have to be younger. I mean, look at Katie. You don't want that happening in reverse. Teenagers can cause damage, and they have loose lips."

"I'm totally going to punch him when this is over," Landon muttered.

"You'll have to get in line," Gunner said. "I'm going to punch him so hard he's going to forget he likes to mess around."

"That won't fix the problem," I replied. "Kevin isn't the problem. I mean, he is. He's a complete and total tool. But Joanie let the situation spiral."

"And she knows it," Scout agreed. The pixie witch folded her arms across her chest. "I don't want to tell you your business, Joanie, but you're an idiot."

My mouth fell open. Leave it to Scout to just put it out there like that.

"You let this guy use and abuse you so often that you lost yourself," Scout continued. "You became a banshee." She moved closer to Joanie again. This time, she took big steps without hesitation. "I get that you were angry because you had a kid with this guy. I mean, what a piece of dung beetle excrement he is. If you hadn't married him, you might be living a different life."

Joanie was starting to look more human again. "I shouldn't have married him," she rasped.

"Definitely not," Scout agreed. "But you did marry him. We all make mistakes. It's how you fix the mistakes that matter. Do you see this guy?" Scout jerked her thumb at Kevin. "This guy does not deserve another tear. He doesn't deserve your loyalty. He hurt you, and now it's time to hurt him back."

"I don't want to die!" Kevin screeched. "You promised you wouldn't let me die!"

"That's not the sort of hurting I mean," Scout snapped. "You are a big, freaking wimp. I want to hurt you so much. Could you be more pathetic?"

"I don't understand how he got one woman to sleep with him, let alone the multitudes there were," Joanie admitted. Her eyes were starting to look less sunken. "I'm an idiot, but how did he get the others?"

"It's that superficial charm Bay mentioned," Scout said. "He's full of it, but it doesn't last." Scout was almost in front of Joanie. "When people get to know the real him, they understand he's an empty shell. You, however, can still be a person of substance."

"How?" Joanie was suddenly leery. "I've ruined my daughter's life."

"You haven't." I stepped forward now. "Katie is a good girl. You made mistakes with her, but she wants to forgive you. She sees what Kevin did to you. As he said, teenagers are good judges of character. They're idiots sometimes, too. Katie is a good girl, and she can help you put your life together."

"But it's too late!" Joanie threw her hands in the air. "I can't go back and give her the childhood she deserves. I can't change things so she doesn't have to witness her father treating her mother like crap. What sort of message did I send her? I told her she's not worth finding someone who loves only her."

"She knows she's worth that," I insisted. "She feels bad that you don't realize that about yourself."

"You can still teach her to move forward with strength and dignity," Scout said. She raised her right hand, pink flames engulfing it and causing everybody's shoulders to jerk. "You can teach her that the now is more important than the then.

"We all make mistakes," she continued, her eyes flicking to Evan, who had managed to get behind Joanie in case she tried to run. "We all do things we wish we could take back. I lost my best friend for a time. I made a mistake that cost him the life he knew. Then I gave him a different life. We're building a new future together. You can do that with your daughter."

Joanie gripped her hands together. Her fingernails were no longer lethal claws. "I don't know how to go back."

"You don't go back." Scout held out her hand. "You move forward. You let me heal you ... or do the best that I can, because this pixie magic is still a work in progress for me. Then you pick yourself up, go back to your daughter, and take Kevin for everything he's worth."

Joanie looked interested despite the fact that she was still partially a banshee. "How?"

"I won't let her ruin me in court," Kevin announced. "I'll tell the judge about her being a banshee."

"Don't listen to him," Scout told Joanie. "He's an idiot. We have magic. We can hex him to hand over everything to you. We can also make it so his penis doesn't work."

"I'll sue you!" Kevin yelled.

Nobody was paying attention to him now.

"You have to make the choice to move forward," Scout said. "You can't wallow. You need to be the adult for your daughter." She extended her flaming pink hand again. "Be the parent she deserves."

Joanie looked almost human now, and I knew what she was going to do before she did it. That's why it didn't come as a surprise when she slipped her hand into Scout's and allowed the pink magic to wash over her.

The transformation happened fast. By the time the pink wave finished, Joanie was back to normal. She sank to her knees in the snow in front of Scout, sobs wracking her body.

"I ruined everything," she said.

Scout shook her head, her eyes moving to me. "You're at a place where you have to start over. Everybody has to start over eventually. Bay did it when she moved back to Hemlock Cove after realizing her dream wasn't to be a big city reporter. Now she has a glutton for a husband, a regular bacon addict who thinks the sun rises and sets on her. She has a dog and a crazy aunt. She has her own newspaper. A few years ago, she had none of that."

Scout hunkered down in front of Joanie. "A few years ago, I lost my best friend. I was brazen, and stupid, and ran into a house full of vampires. I thought he was ripped to shreds, and I mourned him for a very long time. Then I learned it was worse than I'd thought, and he'd been turned.

"I didn't want a happily ever after," she continued. "I didn't think I deserved it. I came here to continue flogging myself. But that didn't happen."

Joanie swiped at her tears. "Why not?"

"I took a step forward when I met Gunner." She pointed to the shifter. "Then Evan came back, and I healed him. I found my family. The parents I thought I would never see are back ... and boy are they a lot of work. But it's a new beginning. It's a different life. Different is not always better, but not always worse. You have to change your story. You have to change the story of your daughter, too."

"But how?" Joanie looked helpless. "I don't even know where to start."

"We're going to help you," I volunteered, taking a step forward. "We're going to figure it out together. You won't be alone."

"You would do that?" Joanie looked baffled. "After everything I did to you, you would really do that?"

I nodded. "I want to help." The phone in my pocket was dinged and I reached for it. "You need to want my help."

"And no more poisoning people," Chief Terry added. "Alice Milligan didn't do anything to you. She's a real victim. She's fighting for her life because some demon went after her. You don't need to compound the problem because your husband is a turd."

"Such a turd," Thistle agreed.

"I don't have to sit here and take this abuse," Kevin snapped. He turned to stomp off in a huff, but Scout threw enough magic at him that he pitched into the snow face first.

"Shut up," Scout said. "We're nowhere near done with you."

I was still smiling when I pulled out my phone and read the incoming text message. That smile disappeared in an instant. "Omigod!"

"What is it?" Landon, instantly alert, moved closer to me. "What happened?"

"It's the demon," I replied. "Aunt Tillie just texted. He's at the inn. He has my mom and aunts, and he's threatening to burn everything down unless I come."

"Does it say who the demon is?" Scout asked.

"No."

"I know who the demon is," Joanie volunteered. "I saw him when I was spying on Alice. I was there the night of the fire. I'm the one who told the girls to get out."

"You're the ghost?" I asked.

Joanie shrugged. "I was kind of shifting and then shifting back. I was watching because I was certain she was Kevin's new mistress. The children were faultless; I wanted to protect them. I was confused, and I said things to them. I was so messed up I swear I thought my aunt was there with me for a time. She was trying to talk me down. She's been missing for years."

I exchanged a quick look with Thistle. The Donna situation would have to be handled. "Who is the demon?"

"It's the fire guy. I saw him at the inn after the fire. He was there the night of the fire. He was pretending to investigate it."

"Daniel?" I couldn't believe it.

Joanie nodded. "He's a monster too."

I tracked my eyes to Chief Terry. "We have to get out there. We're going to need more help."

"Who?" Chief Terry looked perplexed.

"Stormy. We need a witch who has no trouble controlling fire."

"I'll call Hunter." Chief Terry reached for his phone.

"We'll head there now," Scout said. 'We'll stop him before he can do anything."

28
TWENTY-EIGHT

Joanie needed someone to act as a buffer. We were out of witches to spare, so Scout called Rooster to take over with her and Kevin.

"Punch him if he opens his mouth," Landon hissed as we started climbing into vehicles. Stormy and Hunter were to meet us at the guesthouse. We couldn't be caught parking in front of The Overlook, so we had to enter through the back. "Don't let him talk. Just punch him."

Rooster lifted an eyebrow. "Should I take it that this guy is a tool?" he asked Scout.

She nodded. "King of the tools. I'd punch him just for being here if I were you."

"Definitely punch him," Gunner agreed.

"What about you guys?" Concern lined Rooster's features as he glanced between faces. "I can send Marissa as backup. Your parents can come too, Scout."

Scout shook her head. "It's too late for that. Besides, it's just one itty-bitty fire demon. We'll have Stormy to counteract anything he does. We've got this."

Rooster didn't look convinced, but he nodded. "Okay. Keep me posted." His smile was kind when he fixed it on Joanie. We'd given him a brief rundown of what we were dealing with, and he had an idea what he should do. "We'll get you some food, and then I'll put a team together and we'll go to your house to remove all of Kevin's stuff. Then we'll get you settled and figure out what to do about the alert they have out on you."

"I'll cancel that on the way to The Overlook," Landon said.

EVAN HEADED TO THE INN ON FOOT, leaving the rest of us to park in front of the guesthouse. He appeared from between the trees as we gathered on the driveway.

"He has all four of them in the family quarters," Evan said. "Tillie looks as if she's ready to burst. I don't get it. Winnie is trying to talk him down, but Tillie is just sitting there."

"Maybe she's afraid he'll burn down the inn," Chief Terry suggested.

"Or maybe she knows something we don't," I added.

"Like it's a trap," Landon surmised.

I cracked my neck. "Maybe the inn is rigged to blow if we cross the wards."

"How did he get in there?" Chief Terry demanded. "I thought you had the property warded already."

"We do, but he's a demon. He could have ways around wards." I held out my glove-covered hands. "I don't know how he crossed our wards, but we know he can. He showed up for breakfast."

"Which feels like a test of sorts," Thistle noted.

I looked up when tires crunched on the snow on the driveway. Hunter and Stormy had arrived. "We need to get over there but not enter the inn."

"I can get in," Evan insisted. "I can go in through an upstairs window and make my way down to them."

"What if he sets everything on fire the second you enter?" I challenged.

"Then Stormy can stop the fire. Right?" He looked to an approaching Stormy for confirmation. "You have fire magic. You can extinguish a fire as fast as you can get one started."

"In theory," Stormy agreed. "I've never faced off with a fire demon. What if he's more powerful?"

"What if we fix things so a fire doesn't break out at all?" I asked.

"How do we do that?" Chief Terry asked.

"What won't burn?"

"Diamonds."

I chuckled. "I don't think we have enough diamonds to put that plan into action. I was thinking of water. What if we make everything in The Overlook wet?"

Gunner opened his mouth, likely to say something lewd, but Scout stopped him with a wicked glare.

"Don't turn this into something weird," she warned. Her gaze moved to me. "What did you have in mind?"

"I can control ghosts. They can make a room cold. What if we imbue the ghosts with water before sending them in?"

"They can go through the upstairs and approach Daniel downstairs," Scout said. "Then, when he's surrounded by water, we can converge and end him."

"It's the only plan I've got," I admitted.

"It's a good one."

"What about me?" Stormy asked nervously. "What do you want me to do?"

"Put out any fires he manages to start," I replied. "You're our insurance policy."

She looked worried. "What if he's stronger than all of us put together?"

"If he was stronger, he would've flexed by now," I replied. "He's working for money. Mrs. Little promised him a payout. She likely didn't know how he was going to force the sale of the inns, but she knew he was up to something. I want to know how they got together in the first place, but we'll deal with that later."

"Mrs. Little is going to wish she'd come up with a different plan by the time Tillie is done with her," Chief Terry said. "She's not my primary concern. Daniel is. Just out of curiosity, how did he become a demon?"

It was a question I'd been considering since we left the school. "He was likely born a demon."

"Shouldn't we have known that?" Thistle asked.

"It's possible he didn't come into his powers until he was an adult. He went to school to become a firefighter."

"He trained somewhere in the Upper Peninsula," Chief Terry confirmed. "He returned here and joined the department a few years ago."

"Investigating fires," I said. "He was investigating fires he set. We'll send the ghosts in. He'll be watching for us, but when the ghosts take over, he'll focus on them. That will allow us to get inside and end this."

WE HID in the trees at the corner of the inn's main lot, and I called the ghosts. I didn't recognize any of them but Viola, who was irritated about me interrupting her bingeing until I told her she would be saving Aunt Tillie, and thus lording her heroics over Aunt Tillie for the foreseeable future.

"I can do that," Viola said, a wicked gleam in her eyes.

I focused on my magic, changing the cold the ghosts normally carried to water. It was an elemental spell I threw together on the fly.

"Are you ready?" I asked when the spell was as close to perfect as I could manage.

"I'm ready." Viola's expression was fierce. "I'm going to save Tillie, and she's going to hate it."

"Go in through the attic," I instructed. "Douse everything as you go. Then corner the demon. We'll take it from there."

Viola saluted. "Aye, aye, Captain."

Landon took my hand. "We need to improve the wards at the inn," I said when the silence started stretching too long. "This is the second time in the past year people have made it past our wards."

Landon pressed his lips to my forehead and the warmth sent a shiver down my back. "Be careful. I'll be there. But this is your show. Don't sacrifice yourself to save your mother and aunts."

"I have no intention of sacrificing myself. I have the feeling that as soon as Aunt Tillie realizes we've fireproofed the inn, she'll take him out."

"Viola is waving in the window," Thistle hissed. "It's time to go in."

We probably looked like a ragtag team as we trudged through the snow to the back door. It didn't matter. We were a unit.

I snagged gazes with Daniel through the window. He looked excited. His smile dimmed when I opened the door, stepped over the threshold, and nothing happened.

He recovered quickly. "How nice of you to join us." He gestured to the floor. "If you would be so kind as to sit, we have some things to discuss."

"We're not getting on the floor," I replied. The ghosts I'd called were behind Daniel. He wasn't looking in their direction, which indicated he couldn't see them. I flicked my eyes to Aunt Tillie, who looked as if she was trying to figure out the plan. She sat on her hands—likely so she wouldn't start throwing hexes—but she didn't look nearly as downtrodden as Evan described. "Are you okay?" I asked.

"We're fine," Mom assured me. "How did you know to come here?"

Was she kidding? "Aunt Tillie..." I trailed off. I didn't mention that Aunt Tillie had managed to text us. "Did you do that without being able to see the screen?" I asked.

Aunt Tillie shrugged. "What can I say? I'm gifted."

"What is she talking about?" Daniel demanded of Aunt Tillie.

"Suck a lemon," Aunt Tillie shot back. "In fact, maybe I'll make you suck a grenade before the day is out."

Daniel looked more annoyed than frightened. "We talked about this. As amusing as I find your threats—that one about locking me in a room with a bunch of clowns was inventive—you're not allowed to talk to me as if you have any control over what happens here. I'm in control."

"You've got that wrong," I interjected. "I'm in control."

Daniel's smile was back. "How do you figure that?"

"Did the inn burst into flames you could control when we walked in?"

It was only then that Daniel realized why his trap hadn't sprung correctly.

"Yeah, there it is." I nodded. "You don't have any power here, Daniel."

He opened his mouth, shut it, and then adjusted. "I'm a powerful warlock."

I frowned. "You're a demon. Or do you not realize that?" I glanced at Aunt Tillie.

She shook her head. "The boy is confused. It seems that he discovered his aptitude for fire when he set the dorms at Lake Superior State University on fire after a sexual encounter his freshman year. He had no idea what he was, but he thought it explained his fascination with fire, so he decided he was a warlock when he came back to Hemlock Cove and realized magic was real."

"I've been watching you." Daniel wagged his finger at me. "Your family is ... quite impressive. But you can't wield fire." His eyes moved to Stormy. "You can. I've seen all of you working together."

"That's why you're interested in her," I realized. "You think that her being a fire witch is important to what you are."

"She's my destiny. We'll be lovers for the ages."

"I have to kill him," Hunter announced. "I can't listen to that."

Landon made a slashing motion across his throat. "Let the witches handle this. If you drag things out, we'll miss lunch."

Something occurred to me. "Where are Peg and the puppy?"

"They're in the basement," Mom replied. "Daniel locked them down there. Apparently, that's where he put the alder."

I flicked my eyes to Landon, who was heading toward the hallway. "Don't." I shook my head. "Not yet."

"I'm getting my dog," Landon growled. "Peg, too. What kind of monster threatens a helpless puppy and pig?"

"I don't want to hurt them," Daniel countered. "That's not my intent. I need you to come to a meeting of the minds with me."

"Because Mrs. Little tipped you off that we were coming for you," I surmised. "I'm going to make that woman pay."

"She has it coming," Daniel agreed. "I had no interest in seeing your family lose the inn, but I needed money."

"How did you come to partner with Margaret?" Chief Terry demanded.

"I heard her talking about wanting to make Tillie pay a few weeks ago," Daniel replied. "I found the farting unicorns delightful. Margaret does not. She wanted to take over the inns. She was willing to pay when I offered my assistance. She didn't know what sort of help I had in mind, but that doesn't matter. We struck a bargain, but she wanted to sever our partnership a few hours ago because you're on to her. She said it would only be a matter of hours before you figured out she was working with me. She suggested I get out of town."

"That probably would've been smart," I said. "Nobody ever accused you of being smart, though."

Daniel's eyes narrowed. "Be careful, Bay," he warned. "Don't push me too hard. I can do terrible things."

"So can I," I fired back. "I can control ghosts. I can order them to bypass your trap. Normally, they exude cold. For this endeavor, they've been exuding water."

Reality was a cold slap across a naked cheek for Daniel. "That's why the inn didn't go up." He looked around. "You magically made everything wet."

I nodded. "The inn is out of your reach. And with only one trick up your sleeve, you have no way to escape. It's done."

"It's not." Daniel took a menacing step toward me but pulled up short when I didn't retreat. "I'm a god."

"No. You've got some demon in your blood," I countered. "I think you were born with it. You're not a full demon. You're no threat to us."

"How do you figure?" Daniel still looked haughty. "All I have to do is walk outside and set the trees on fire. You can't make the whole world wet."

Gunner opened his mouth again.

"I'm going to ban you from ever watching porn again if you're not careful," Scout warned.

Gunner turned sheepish. "The jokes are sitting right there."

"You're done, Daniel. But I have a question: what did you use to keep the Milligans unconscious? We need to reverse that. They have daughters waiting for them."

"I didn't want to hurt them," Daniel said. "That's the last thing I wanted. I was just keeping them under until one of their relatives sold the inn."

"You haven't answered the question," I persisted.

"Catnip," he replied, his lips curving. "It provides protection while sleeping. I read about a potion in a group online and saw that there was catnip in Tillie's infamous field. That's a nifty setup you have, by the way. It took me forever to figure out how to get in. I had to burn a hole in the magic."

He was dangerous. Because he'd been raised away from his kind, he had no idea how dangerous. "Well, thanks for that. We'll reverse the spell before the day is out."

"Not if you're dead," Daniel sang out. "I can see that's the only way I'm going to survive this. I have to kill all of you." He had the gall to look apologetic. "I'm sorry for what's about to happen. I really am. But I have no choice."

He raised his hands, and then grunted when Evan used his speed to appear in front of him and punch him so hard in the stomach that Daniel fell and almost slammed his head against the floor.

"We're done with this," Evan said as he moved behind Daniel and grabbed his hands. "We need to get him out of here. I'll deal with him on the bluff."

I opened my mouth to ask what he was going to do with him. Then I realized there was only one thing he could do. Daniel was too dangerous to let live.

"Won't people look for him?" Mom asked.

"You heard him," I replied. "Mrs. Little warned him that we were coming. She'll assume he took her advice and left town. Landon and Chief Terry can announce that he's an arsonist on the run. It won't matter that we never find him."

"Sounds good to me." Gunner moved in with Evan and grabbed Daniel's other arm. "You guys will have lunch ready by the time we're done with him?"

I flicked my eyes to a returning Landon. Would he allow them to take Daniel to the bluff and kill him, or would that be a step too far?

"We're totally having lunch," Landon said. "Right after I take my best girl and boy out for a little tinkle in the snow."

I opted to ignore the "best girl" bit. "And I'll reverse the ghost spell with the water," I added.

"That's on you, babe." Landon winked. "I'll handle the tinkling."

"I'm so glad Gunner is outside and didn't hear that," Scout said.

Mom dusted off her hands. "Water leads to mold, and I don't want that in my inn." She beamed at Terry. "How do you feel about grilled cheese sandwiches and tomato soup?"

"One of my favorites," Terry enthused.

It was one of mine too. I remembered long winter afternoons of eating soup with Chief Terry and my cousins. "It seems like we all know what we're doing." I glanced at the back door, to where Daniel was struggling against Evan and Gunner. He didn't have a chance of escape. "After lunch, we need to reverse the catnip spell," I said to Aunt Tillie.

She nodded. "It will be easy now that we know."

"And then we need to talk about Donna," I added.

Aunt Tillie scowled. "That's none of your business."

"We healed Joanie before coming here today. I have an idea for Donna."

Interest gleamed in Aunt Tillie's eyes. "Am I going to like this idea?"

"I think so."

29
TWENTY-NINE
ONE WEEK LATER

It was picnic day in the pot garden. We'd decided to take advantage of our magical haven before another storm blew through. This one threatened a foot of snow in less than eight hours. We still had time to enjoy ourselves before hunkering down for the night.

I sat on a blanket next to the alder and watched my family and friends cavort. When Mom explained she was setting up a pot roast buffet in the garden, there was no keeping Gunner away. That meant Scout was along for the ride.

Hunter and Stormy were just looking for something to do. They were engaged and happy, sharing space with Easton until they could claim ownership of their house in the spring. They seemed happy to pretend it was a summer day, even if Hunter did occasionally look at the pot with a dubious eye.

Next to me, Landon shoveled in pot roast while watching the dog—who still didn't have a name—chase Peg around the stalks. He couldn't stop smiling.

"What about Winchester?" he said.

"Winchester?" I was confused. "For what?"

"For his name," Landon replied. He used a napkin to wipe the corners of his mouth. "I thought maybe we could name him after his Mom, the bravest woman in the world."

I was dumbfounded. "You want to name the dog after me?"

"I want him to have a name," Landon replied. "And when I tried to think of a good name, something that reflected what a good boy he is, Winchester was the first thing that came to mind."

I was touched. And suspicious. "Are you doing this so I'll let you eat as much bacon as you want tomorrow?"

"No. I mean it. But if you lay off about the bacon complaints tomorrow, I'll be a happy man."

All I could do was roll my eyes. "Winchester is interesting. I kind of like it."

"Then Winchester it is." He planted a kiss on my cheek before focusing on the blanket in front of us. "They look happy," he said, inclining his head toward Joanie, who had Katie with her—explaining about the field hadn't been easy—and was talking to her aunt Donna, who was back in human form.

Scout had pulled it off. Well, Scout and Aunt Tillie working in tandem had pulled it off. They'd reversed Aunt Tillie's first spell, and even though Donna hadn't reverted to her banshee form immediately, Scout put a little effort into the spell and managed to contain the banshee inside Donna. It would never take over again. Then they'd changed Donna's face a bit, so she wasn't recognizable.

The story was that Donna was a different aunt. She was still wanted for murder. We claimed she'd moved to the area to help her niece, who was filing for divorce from her deadbeat husband. Joanie had someone to lean on. Donna no longer had to live in the dark. And Kevin? Yeah, he was going to take a beating in the divorce.

So it was happy endings all around.

For everyone except Daniel. I hadn't asked what happened on the bluff. I didn't want to know. The Michigan State Police were still searching for the fire investigator because he was a suspect in a string of arsons. After he was blamed for the Blue Moon Inn fire, people started digging on the strange fires that had occurred when he'd been in college. There were a few Hemlock Cove fires people were wondering about too. He would ultimately be blamed for all of them.

As for the Milligans, we'd snuck into the hospital under the cover of darkness and reversed Daniel's spell. They woke right after we'd made our escape. Nobody could explain why they'd been under for so long, but they'd been reunited with Grace and Hope and were already working on inn renovations. The Blue Moon Inn would be back up and running by spring.

Saying no harm had been done was incorrect, but the harm was already being erased.

Mostly.

"What are you thinking?" Landon asked after we'd fallen into silence for a full minute.

"We're really lucky," I replied. "We have a healthy family. My mom and Chief Terry have agreed to have a small family ceremony after all. We're going to build our dream house one day. We have a dog."

"And we have love," Landon added.

I smiled at the sentiment. "And we have love."

"And Aunt Tillie."

That was enough to erase my smile. "She's still in trouble for hiding a banshee on family land."

"What about the mortgage on the inn?" Landon asked.

"Chief Terry has assured me that as soon as he gets the payout for his house, he'll take care of the mortgage." My mother had been embarrassed when informed that everyone knew about the mortgage. She was promising to pay Chief Terry back, a notion he was vehemently fighting.

I figured that was their business.

"You know we're going to have to do something about Mrs. Little?" Landon prodded as he put down his empty plate. "She's getting more aggressive. She's a danger to the family."

"I hope you're not suggesting killing her." I tried to keep my tone light.

"That's not the plan," he said, "but we have to do something."

"You're right. She's no longer just a funny nuisance."

"I never found her funny. I knew she was dangerous when she was part of the plan to keep you from getting The Whistler. The more this keeps happening, the more desperate she's going to become."

"The more what keeps happening?"

"You guys keep winning. It's not even you guys. It's Aunt Tillie she wants to beat. She's close to losing it, Bay. We need to figure out a way to stop whatever she has planned next."

"We don't have to do it today," I said. "She'll be licking her wounds for a few weeks."

I snuggled in at his side.

"I'm not giving up the attic," Aunt Tillie growled from my right. "It's not going to happen. My clowns live in the attic."

"Those clowns are going," Mom insisted. "I don't care what you do with them, but they're going. Terry needs an office. After what he did for us, you are going to willingly hand over that space."

Aunt Tillie looked as if she was going to argue. Then, a familiar gleam appeared in her eyes. "I can do whatever I want with them?"

"That's what I said." Mom bobbed her head.

"Awesome." Aunt Tillie was suddenly sunshine and light as she stood. "I know exactly what I'm going to do with them."

"This is going to be bad," Landon said when I smiled.

"Being stalked by Christmas decorations was bad for Mrs. Little," I said. "Something tells me being stalked by clown dolls will be worse."

"It's going to be glorious," Aunt Tillie countered. "And, guess what? It's going to blizzard tonight. Who wants to take a walk with me and the clowns?"

Nobody volunteered.

"Let me rephrase that," Aunt Tillie gritted out. "Who doesn't want to smell like rancid beans tonight?"

Clove's hand shot in the air. To my astonishment, so did Landon's.

"I'll help with the clowns, but only because I want them gone," Landon said. "And I expect to be rewarded for my efforts if I'm going to be carrying those things through a storm."

Aunt Tillie's eyes narrowed to suspicious slits. Then she straightened and grinned. "One bacon curse coming right up."

Landon's smile was big enough to take over his entire face. "That's exactly what I wanted to hear."

Laughter erupted around us. All was right in the Winchester world.

Tomorrow was a new day, but I was going to enjoy today.

Printed in Great Britain
by Amazon